The Kitty Genovese Murders

A Lily Faye Novel

by C.M. Lowe

Copyright © 2018 by C. M. Lowe
All rights reserved.

This is a work of fiction. Names, characters, businesses, places, events, locales, and incidents are either the products of the author's imagination or used in a fictitious manner. Any resemblance to actual persons, living or dead, or actual events is purely coincidental.

SECOND PRINTING, 2019
ISBN: 978-0-57-842253-4

https://www.facebook.com/cmlowe3
https://www.amazon.com/author/cmlowe

Twisted Paradise Publishing, LLC

Cover design by Laura Boyle.

To the ex who said this book would never see the light of day.

More importantly, this book is dedicated to my grandfather.
Thank you fostering my love of reading and for always being my #1 supporter.
I love you.

1.

AT LARGE

A murder outdoors in the middle of March was bad enough without the current conditions. A light but persistent mist slunk down upturned collars of CSI jackets and pelted miniature daggers into the hands and faces of investigators. The earlier rainstorm refused to relinquish its hold on the situation, and as such was already putting the scene at risk. The potential for DNA evidence was long gone by the time Head Detective Lily Faye arrived on the scene at half past three a.m.

"What's the situation, Stilinski?" she asked as she approached the first responder, an officer from the 6th precinct of the NYPD.

The young rookie stood several yards away from the body. His jacket betrayed his trembling with small swishes as the waterproof fabric rubbed against itself. Whether the shivering was from the weather or the presence of Stilinski's first corpse, Lily didn't bother to determine. They had to focus on gathering the facts of the case while CSI and forensics gathered evidence behind them.

"Female. Mid to late twenties," he reported. As he looked back to the detective, flecks of water swung free from his short, mussed, brown hair. "Multiple lacerations to the throat, stomach, and breasts. There's evidence of sexual assault, but that's unconfirmed until we send DNA samples to the lab." He paused as he crossed his arms and hunched over to contain what little body warmth remained. "There's not a lot of blood left because of the rain but it's bad, Detective."

Lily wasn't surprised by the last comment, although some investigators might consider it unprofessional. On the contrary, she was impressed with his objective assessment of his first homicide. Detailing the mutilation of a body was never easy. She'd even seen the Chief fumble with it before.

"Any ID?" she asked as she flipped her own collar up.

She had never felt such immediate regret before. A spattering of small drops had steadily collected on the back of her jacket, although nothing but a light mist lingered in the air. When she pulled her collar up, the drops converged into a single stream of water that slid straight down her spine and soaked into her shirt. Her teeth clenched and her fingers curled into fists in an effort to suppress a shiver of her own.

"Negative," Stilinski answered without taking notice of her silent struggle with the elements. "We've got guys from Evidence looking around to see if she dropped a purse in the attack, but there's nothing on the victim."

Lily nodded and looked down the street. Attacking a pedestrian in the middle of a block of businesses and a large apartment complex was brazen, even if it was late enough that the businesses were closed and most of the residents asleep. The reflection of the lights off the rain-soaked pavement would have made the crime more visible, and the probability of witnesses was high enough to begin with. Anyone could have seen the two struggling or heard the woman screaming for help. Someone must have.

The realization pressed hard on the detective's shoulders until she felt as small and helpless as a mouse. Why didn't anybody call? Lily couldn't fathom such a severe lack of action from so many people, even in such a large, calloused city.

"There are other ways to ID the victim, Stilinski," she reminded as she looked to the cop. "I want the Evidence team scraping up whatever DNA we can still find on her. How quickly did CSI set the tent up?"

"Half an hour after I got here?"

The uptick at the end of his sentence spread misgiving through Lily as if it were the air she was breathing, a frosty force causing her lungs to crystallize.

"Hopefully that was quick enough to preserve something, then," she said. "Call the Chief and see if we can get some floaters from other precincts to help canvas these apartments. Someone had to hear something."

"On it," Stilinski nodded and race-walked to his car to carry out her orders.

Lily watched him slip into the car, using those few moments to prepare to approach the body. Although she had seen numerous corpses over her last six and a half years on the force, no two scenes looked the same. Stilinski's description gave her a general idea of what to expect but he hadn't told her the things that had the highest potential to surprise her: the amount of blood, whether or not the victim's eyes were still open, or if the victim was missing any clothing. There were so many gruesome potential details to steel against.

When Lily ducked under the police line, her questions resolved themselves in reverse order. The victim's clothing was accounted for, although her shirt and jacket were torn to pieces. Lily could see the woman's skin didn't look much different. Her jeans sat firmly around her hips, still buttoned but gaping open at the ripped zipper. Her eyes had been closed for some time, based on the way two pools of raindrops collected over her lids and dripped down the sides of her face like tears. The shreds of her shirt were stained a dark red, but the earlier rain had washed most of the blood away.

A cursory glance told Lily the victim had been stabbed upwards of a dozen times. The largest slashes across her torso lay over her heart and clear across her throat. As the detective crouched down, she noted these were surface wounds only; they weren't deep enough to be the cause of death. Those along the stomach penetrated further but didn't appear close to any vital organs. Lily noticed one slice across the throat that may have punctured the trachea, but she couldn't see well enough to know for sure.

There were two marks that caught Lily's attention, both resting between the victim's ribs. These were positioned over each lung, which meant there was a high possibility the victim had suffered bilateral pneumothorax. The thought made Lily shudder; suffocating as a result of air leaking out of the lungs had officially made her list of ways she didn't want to die.

The fact that so many of the wounds were superficial and wouldn't have been an immediate cause of death was concerning. As she studied the placement of the marks, Lily realized she had seen this pattern before. It almost exactly matched the pictures she studied back in the Academy, of a young woman who was murdered decades ago in the middle of a block of apartment complexes. In fact, most of the crime scene mirrored that murder too perfectly to be a coincidence. The only real difference between the two cases lay in where the women died: one in the stairwell of an apartment building, the more recent on the sidewalk.

As Lily straightened up and walked toward the cars to document her findings, she felt the chill Stilinski had been guarding against creep up her neck. She paused only to rap on the window of his car and leaned in to speak to him when he rolled the window down. A wave of heat smacked her in the face as she did, a welcome reprieve.

"I want her moved to post-mortem as soon as possible. I'm going to take a few notes and start canvassing, but we need to get her off the street."

The cop nodded. "Nobody's come up with her purse yet, huh?"

"Not that I've been told."

"So, you think it was a robbery?"

"I'd be willing to entertain the suggestion but it's too early to look into that exclusively," she said. "Anyway, they'll take fingerprints at the lab and we can hopefully get identification that way. I think I have the cause of death, too, but I want an autopsy report to make sure."

"The coroner's on his way in now. We'll get her moved in the next few minutes."

"Good. Thank you," she said, and then walked to her own car.

She slipped inside and turned the key in the ignition. Her nearly white fingers shook as she fumbled to crank the heat up. She flexed her hands a few times to eliminate the stiffness settling into them before picking up her notebook and pen.

Jane Doe. Late twenties. Multiple lacerations to stomach. 2 puncture wounds in lungs. Surface wounds to chest, stomach, and throat. Sexual assault possible.

Then, on another page, Lily wrote the shortest profile of a killer she'd ever noted in her career.

Possible copycat. At large.

2.

AMONG US

"Faye!"

At the interruption, the arm Lily had been using to prop herself up at her desk fell onto her keyboard with a loud clatter. Her head snapped to the side and tilted upward to see the Chief of Police standing beside her, his arms crossed. She didn't remember drifting off after she sat down, but her boss's amused smirk and raised eyebrows suggested she'd done exactly that.

"Didn't realize I'd started paying you to sleep on the job, Detective."

Francisco Alcarez was tall and sturdy with wild, scraggly eyebrows that stood in startling opposition to his short, gelled hair. Despite his current stance and his glare, he had a kind mannerism that far exceeded that of the rest of his staff. This combination of compassion and his ability to command authority made him Lily's first and longest running role model in the States. If she had learned anything from him during her time on the force, it was how to run a team with that unique balance between grace and justice.

That wasn't all she'd learned from Alcarez, though. He wasn't her first introduction to sarcasm, but he was the most consistently sassy man she'd ever met. So she matched his statement with a snail's pace examination of her damp, crumpled crime scene jacket, which still held flecks of the earlier rain in its deeper wrinkles. She concluded her examination with a pointed stare at the sopping heap of socks and shoes lying limp near the Chief's feet, and then tilted her head toward him. She drew a slow breath, like the hammer of a gun clicking back in preparation to fire.

"I thought that's why I got promoted in the first place," she retorted in a thickening accent. "I mean... I have absolutely no idea what you mean, sir. I finished canvassing at seven-thirty and it's—" She glanced to the digital time displayed in the corner of her computer monitor. "—eight now. So in the half an hour I had to get from there to here, I definitely went off route and out of my way to stop at home, change, and get a full eight hours of sleep. Which, as you can imagine, is why I'm still wearing wet clothes and appearing to doze off at my desk. Not that I was actually dozing, mind you. That would be unprofessional."

"Well, get yourself a cup of coffee and wake up, smartass. We've got work to do," he rolled his eyes and dropped a thick case file on her desk. He glanced down at the floor and added, "And put your shoes back on. This is an office."

"You got it, Chief," she replied through a yawn, which made the sentence sound more like, "Oo ahht eh, eef."

Alcarez walked away without indicating whether he understood her.

That was fine with her. Prolonged conversations were a pet peeve they shared, especially when there was more work to do. Gratitude for their no-nonsense ways swelled in her gut, but the feeling lost its power the second she stuffed her feet back into her damp shoes.

For a fleeting moment in which cold seized every muscle in her body in its unflinching grasp, she questioned how badly she really needed coffee. If the cost of pouring herself a fresh cup was leaving these shoes on, did she actually want it? Or could she survive without it if it meant forgoing the ice blocks encasing her feet? She only needed to put up with it for a few minutes, long enough to walk to the break room and back. If she could stand it for that long, she could reward herself by not wearing shoes the rest of the day. That was the only upside to desk work.

"Hey, boss? Got a second?"

She looked up to see one of her direct reports, Russell Jordan, standing a few feet away as though he were afraid to invade her personal space. Although he was older and had been on the force longer than she had, he always stood a little too far away from her and regarded her like she might take a swing if he got too close. When she looked closely enough at him, she swore she could see his upper lip trembling at even an initial attempt to speak to her.

"Yeah," she agreed and forced her brain to acknowledge him instead of how cold she was as she stood up. Still, the next thing she blurted out was, "Sorry. I'm freezing." Stupid brain. "Here, walk to the break room with me. I need coffee."

She wasn't willing to stand still long enough to address whatever he needed, and then go get coffee. Not in these shoes. There was no reason to drag out the torment of wearing them for longer than necessary.

The detective followed, always a step or two behind her rather than walking at her side. He stood a foot taller than she, was at least twenty years her elder based on his mostly gray hair, and knew more details about the station and its protocols than she ever would. He had a tendency to catch the smallest of details, which allowed the state to pursue the maximum sentence against a perpetrator in court. Lily couldn't understand why a man with a mind like that seemed afraid of her.

"What's up?" she asked once they arrived in the break room and she realized he wasn't going to speak until prompted to do so.

"I was hoping I could trade someone to get Saturday off," he said, hanging back while she continued to the coffee machine. His stature blocked the entire doorway. "I'm trying to get some work done on my dissertation. I've made good progress on it but I'm still behind schedule and I'd like to catch up. For some reason, I'm a lot more productive during the day with that kind of stuff."

Lily heard the request and the word "dissertation," but little more of his elongated explanation. She had no confidence in her fine motor skills, and as such focused far too hard on pouring her coffee without spilling it. Only once she'd accomplished the task did she answer him.

"I don't mind you and Harris switching, but we need round the clock coverage now that we've got this homicide to deal with."

"Well, Harris hasn't been in yet to ask, but I checked around a little. Stilinski said he could switch if nobody else would."

Lily turned to frown at him. "Stilinski?" she repeated. "What? No. You need to switch with someone on our team. Stilinski isn't going to be any help if I need a detective on duty."

A beat passed between the two before his mouth twisted from its grimace into an "oh" of understanding. He'd adhered to these protocols enough times to know he needed another detective covering his shifts. An officer wouldn't do, even if that officer had been the first responder.

"Are you getting enough sleep, Jordan?" she asked. She couldn't tell if the fluorescent lights were casting shadows or if the bags under his eyes were deeper and darker than usual, but he looked about as awake as she felt.

"Not really," he admitted rubbed a calloused hand along the back of his neck. "It's been kind of hard to get more than four hours between the kids and work and finishing up school."

That was one of the many reasons Lily was glad she had never gone for a doctorate and was fine with being single. The demands of any one of those things were bad enough on their own, but all three combined? It was unthinkable.

"Well, this shouldn't be one of the places stressing you out, especially once you walk out of the station," she said as she turned back to add sugar and a little creamer to her coffee. She would never understand how people drank this stuff black. "Leave your work here. And I'll approve the trade-off with Stilinski if the Chief does just so we can have a body here to lend a hand, but I'd rather have Harris on your shift if the two of you can manage. We're going to need someone with homicide experience on this one."

"Yeah, no problem," Jordan agreed. "Thanks, boss."

"Sure," she said and stepped back out into the main office with him. The moisture in her shoes created an unpleasant squelching noise as she walked, but she tried to make conversation to ignore it. "So. How's your dissertation coming? Hate your topic yet?"

"Not yet," he assured, and then chuckled. "My thesis is pretty morbid, so it's at least interesting."

"Sounds like perfect subject matter for a detective."

"That's what I thought."

Lily smiled and hunched over her cup. She inhaled until her lungs swelled to full capacity, the nutty scent of her creamer swirling through her nostrils. This was her happy place, her moment of peace in the middle of chaos. If she wanted to make any headway in the middle of a fresh homicide investigation, this moment was crucial.

Thankfully, a moment was all she truly needed to help her refocus. After four deep breaths, she set her coffee down, kicked off her shoes and socks, and stood to peel off her wet jacket. She hung it on the coat rack near her desk and then began to shuffle through the stack of papers waiting in the "Incoming" mailbox sitting on the right hand corner of her desk.

She flicked past a couple of overtime requests, department memos, and handwritten notices from the secretary before she found the stack she was looking for. She lifted it out of the box and dropped the rest of the papers on the top of the remaining pile, wishing more than ever that she had the space to set up a system based on level of urgency.

For now, she was stuck with the current system so she made the best of it and turned her attention back to the top sheet in the stack to make sure it was properly labelled as Case# 30033 - Montview Apartments - Canvassing Report. She thumbed through the rest of the pile verify that each sheet contained a similar heading at the top and an officer's signature at the bottom. Then, she flipped back to the first piece of paper and began to read.

"Oh, and Faye?"

She glanced up to see that Jordan had returned once more, this time with the daily newspaper in one hand and a pair of socks in the other.

"Crumple some of the pages up and stuff them in your shoes," he said and brandished it toward her. "It soaks up the moisture and dries them out faster."

"Thanks, Jordan." She took the paper from him with her free hand, which was far more slender than his. "How did you think to do that?"

"Just one of those things dads know, I guess," he shrugged his massive shoulders. "Ah, I brought some socks from my locker, too," he added as he brandished them. "In case you need something dry to warm you up. Don't worry; they're clean."

Lily could have guessed as much without him specifying. The suffocating scent of the floral detergent assaulted her nostrils as soon as he held the socks toward her. Considering she didn't want to smell like a bowl of potpourri, she waved his offer away with thanks. She valued her ability to breathe too much to accept.

"No problem. Oh, and I called Harris. He said he would cover for me Saturday, if that's okay. He's taking my day shift and I'll take his night shift on Sunday."

"That's fine. You have a shift change form for me?"

He held that out as well and waited while she reviewed the details of the arrangement. Once her eyes scanned to the bottom, she signed off on it and handed it back.

"Take that to the Chief so he can approve it before the end of the day. You know how chuffed he gets if he doesn't have 48 hours' notice."

"Got it. I'll go right now," he assured and nodded to the newspaper. "Don't forget to put that in your shoes. And thanks, boss."

"Sure thing. Thank you."

She turned back to the news to unfold it and started to crumple the first page before a block of chunky black letters caught her eyes. She paused to scan the large color photo of the drizzly crime scene and haggard witnesses, accompanied by a half page story of the murder that morning. The details were shoddy, but that wasn't a surprise. She considered it nothing short of a miracle if a reporter managed to sniff out and publish more than the basics.

As expected, this article wasn't going to win a Pulitzer anytime soon.

The article stated that the victim was a Jane Doe, the investigation was active, and the crime had taken place in front of the Montview apartment complex on West Fourth Street. Citizens were warned to be on high alert throughout the city. There was no mention of sexual assault, the timeline, or even the fact that the evening's inclement weather had likely washed away any usable DNA samples. Everything looked to be above board an in accordance with police procedure until Lily reached the last paragraph.

"Anyone with information concerning the crime, suspect, or victim should contact the police as soon as possible. Let us be reminded that while we may feel safe walking the streets in the daylight hours, great precaution must be taken after darkness falls. Tragedy such as this morning's events serve as a grim reminder that we have few we can trust and that, as long as this investigation remains open, a killer walks among us."

3.

NEWSROOM

On a normal day, the command center of the New York Post was packed to capacity with reporters, photographers, and interns, all scrambling to meet the next deadline. Stacks of the newspapers stood as high as the desks the reporters used on a rotating basis. There were few designated workspaces here; the seats went to the lucky or the ruthless.

Alyssa Spencer, a tall woman with a threateningly thin frame, fell into the latter category. That was why her name plaque rested on one of the only desks near a window. Although the reporter wasn't planted in her seat at the moment, she was in no danger of losing her prime piece of real estate; she wasn't the only one missing from the room today.

For now, the entire press room stood empty and silent. The paper's editor relocated command central to Conference Room A on days when a massive story broke, and it was to this conference room that every available employee flocked in hopes of winning the day's top assignment. By now, every news outlet in the state had printed or aired some coverage on the homicide of Jane Doe, but the New York Post was the only one to lay claim to publishing the story first.

"And a big thanks to our hard-hitting Alyssa Spencer for turning the story over so quickly," the Editor-in-Chief, a burly man with hair such a deep shade of black that it only could have come from a bottle, stated from the head of the cherry colored table. "What a shark, huh? But there's still a lot of work to be done before we start handing out congratulations. The Times and the Daily

News are already offering big incentives for witness statements and police information. We gotta stay on top of 'em at every turn! Understood?"

A general murmuring of agreement rose from the group, a half-hearted reminder that the seasoned reporters in the room didn't need this pep talk. This was accompanied by the dozens of pairs of eyes flitting toward the door in regular intervals as the boss spoke. Fidgeting ran as rampant through the room as fleas on a dog or cat, and every reporter was fighting the urge to run back to their desks and scratch their collective itch.

"So we need a game plan," the man continued despite the restless air in the stuffy, packed space. "Spencer, you've got point on this case. I want a new angle nobody else is going for. Forget the details of the case. Dozens of outlets are already reporting on that! I want you to go in for the money shot. Talk about the officers working the case. Get their backgrounds, statements, what they ate for breakfast after the crime took place! I want every detail. The people need to know if they can trust our public safety officers, right?"

"Yes sir," Spencer nodded.

"Exactly," her boss returned the nod with a stiff one of his own, although it resembled a flopping fish more than it did a person in control of his bodily motions. "And as we know, they can't. Expose that nerve and drill into it," he flashed rows of luminescent white teeth and drove his clenched fist against the palm of his hand, grinding them into one another.

"I'll get right on it," Alyssa said and picked the black pen out of a neatly arranged assortment of ink colors to write on the yellow pad of legal paper sitting in front of her.

When the Editor-in-Chief adjourned the meeting, Alyssa joined the chaos as it whirled out of the conference room and back into the press room. Within seconds, the entire room was a swirling vortex of chatter, ringing phones, and rustling papers. The steady hum that filled the room might have been soothing were it not so loud.

"Excuse me!" Alyssa barked as one unfortunate intern, a young male with his head thrown back in a cocky laugh, chose the wrong time to step backwards without looking out for oncoming foot traffic and almost hit her.

The boy shot forward, body swaying from the opposing movement it hadn't been prepared to make. His mouth dropped open as he turned to watch her pass, though he didn't speak.

She made it to her desk without further incident and picked up her phone. She flipped through her short list of recent calls and dialed the non-emergency line for the 6th Precinct of the NYPD. It only took two rings before she got an answer.

"NYPD non-emergency line. How can we help you today?" a light and friendly female voice inquired.

"Yes, my name is Alyssa Spencer. I'm a reporter for the New York Post. I was wondering if I could get in contact with the lead detective on the Jane Doe homicide case?"

"Let me see if she's available. Would her voicemail be okay if she's not?"

Alyssa wasn't fond of that answer since it put the cards in the detective's hand instead of her own, but she had no other choice during the first contact. "That would be fine," she conceded.

"Okay, let's see… it looks like she's on another call right now. I'll transfer you over and let her know you're waiting if you'd like?"

"Sure. Thank you."

"No problem," the secretary said in a cheery tone Alyssa suspected she wouldn't maintain once the call ended, and then the line went silent.

While Alyssa waited on hold, Lily spoke to the coroner and tapped out a report compiling the information gathered through canvassing.

"I'm sending the fingerprints to the lab now. We should have an official ID in a couple days," the man informed in such a boisterous voice that the volume on Lily's phone was set as low as possible without muting it. "I did my report on the official cause and time of death, if you want to come down and talk it through."

"Yes. Have you got time in an hour?" she asked and glanced up to see the red light blinking on her phone. She would have to see if she needed to take that call, find a good stopping point for her report, and collect Stilinski before she could head out.

"I do! For all the rigor mortis, dead people are pretty flexible," the coroner chuckled.

Lily grimaced as she stopped typing to let the impact of the joke roll over her. She suppressed a sigh, saved the report, and logged off her computer. Then, she pushed her chair back a foot, phone cord stretching as she leaned over to pull her socks on.

"Okay. Stilinski and I will see you then. Thanks Charlie."

"You got it, Detective," Charlie replied without sounding at all disappointed that she didn't acknowledge the joke.

Lily set the phone back on the receiver without transferring to the next call.

"Faye?" she heard the secretary shout from the front desk. "You've got a reporter on hold on line two."

"Send it to my voicemail. I'm on my way out," Lily replied as she yanked damp newspapers out of her shoes and stepped into the footwear. "I'll get to it later," she said and walked across the station in search of Stilinski.

When she found him in the break room, she prompted, "Charlie's got the autopsy results. I'm stopping for coffee on the way, so we need to head out soon."

Stilinski glanced down at the coffee pot and Styrofoam cup he was holding. He stared for a second before he looked back up.

"But there's coffee here."

"Running through a machine that I haven't seen cleaned once since I started working here. Seven years ago," she pointed out. "We're going to Starbucks. When will you be ready?"

"I'm ready now," he said as he set the cup down on the table and the coffee pot back on the burner. "Are you?"

"Just need to grab my coat," she said and headed back to her desk to do so.

When she pulled on her jacket, her gaze flickered to her phone. The blinking hold light was gone, but a new one flashed to signal she had a voicemail. She ignored it while she collected her notepad, pen, and tape recorder. A smug satisfaction cropped up in her stomach when she turned her back on the phone. She had no intention of speaking to a reporter before she had a better handle on the case, and she had little inclination to break her silence even then.

Alyssa Spencer had other plans.

4.

ANONYMITY

Lily dragged Stilinski to three different Starbucks locations on the way to the coroner's. In her opinion, one of the good things about living in New York City was the number of coffee shops, because three stops didn't cause them to travel more than the same number of blocks. The bad thing about living in the city was the guarantee of waiting in a queue for the coffee. On the third store, Lily surrendered to its inevitability.

"This works," she grumbled as she led the way to the line crammed inside the glass walls of the shop.

"Are you sure?" Stilinski half-grinned as he pulled the door open and stood aside to let her in first. "If you want, we can try yet another one. We still have time."

"No, it's fine," she said as she slipped inside past another patron, who was attempting to block the door. "And I don't appreciate the sarcasm, thank you."

"I'm just saying, we could have placed a mobile order and had our drinks twenty minutes ago," Stilinski snorted.

"Would you shut the fucking door?" the man snapped at her and made a show of hunching over and shivering. "I'm freezing my nuts off here."

"Woe is you," Lily commented dryly and made her way to the end of the line, which snaked around the cash register and stopped in the middle of two round tables.

"Gotta love the city," Stilinski grimaced as he joined her. "I don't know how you deal with people like that guy."

"You get used to it," she said as she stuffed her paper white hands into her coat pockets. "It's not so bad once you realize they're only trying to make you miserable because they're miserable."

"How is that not as bad?"

"Because it's not really directed at you. You can't make them happy, regardless of what you do. Knowing that makes it easier to deal with."

Stilinski cast his gaze toward the menu. "Still seems like a rotten way to live."

"Maybe it is for them," she shrugged. "But I'm perfectly content. I like my life. That's all that matters at the end of the day."

"Yeah but what about everyone else?"

"I'm not in charge of them. You can't afford to let people like that," she jutted her chin toward the man in front of them, "push you around in our line of work."

"Yeah, but who does it hurt if you ignore comments like that?"

"It hurts everybody," she asserted as the line shifted forward. "People treat you the way you teach them to treat you. If they get away with it once, they'll never stop. It's not about one guy whining about the cold. It's about maintaining your position of authority, especially while we're on duty."

He grunted and hooked his hands in his belt loop. "Seems like we're losing authority a lot these days, doesn't it?"

"Unfortunately," she sighed. "Which is why we can't afford to compromise. This is the way New York City is. We try to make it a safe place to live but we can't force people to be pleasant."

"Guess not," he agreed.

She encouraged, "You'll get used to it. You should try to get out and see more of the city during your off hours. It'll help you adjust."

"I shouldn't need time to adjust anymore. I've been here almost a year," he chuckled. "But you're right. I don't get out much. That might be the problem."

"It is."

The pair split to order and pay. Once Stilinski stepped over to the pick-up counter to join Lily again, she gave him an incredulous look.

"Decaf?" she asked, stressing the first syllable. "Aren't you exhausted?"

"Yeah, but caffeine and I don't get along," he grimaced as he tucked his wallet into the pocket of his pleated slacks. "Too much of it makes my ADHD freak out, and I kinda want to be sharp today. For the case. So you're welcome."

"Ah," she chuckled. "In that case, I appreciate your caution."

"Lily?" the barista called and slid a large cup across the pick-up order counter. She scooped up the next drink and frowned at the name written before hesitantly calling, "Stil— Stilinkey?"

"I think that's me," he grinned as he reached for it. "Decaf drip coffee?"

"Yep," the barista gave a curt nod and went back to her other drinks.

The cops squeezed out of the store and hit the sidewalk, where Stilinski tugged his phone from his breast pocket. He released a throaty, quiet chuckle as he snapped a photo of his cup. He put his phone away again and looked up to find Lily staring.

"What?"

"Why do you do that?" she chuckled. "Your first name is a lot easier. Why don't you just give them that?"

"Oh, come on. This is way more fun," he grinned and set off toward the morgue. "You missed the cashier trying to figure out how to spell it, but look. It's not even close."

He brandished the cup so she could see a couple of crossed out attempts and a scribbled, "Stillsinkey." She leaned forward to examine it and sounded out what had been written.

"Call it a social experiment," he added. "I want to see how frustrated they get before they ask me how to spell it. So far, nobody has. They just make horrible guesses, which always make it onto my Instagram."

Lily laughed. "I take back what I said before. You fit in with the locals just fine, you jerk."

"I'm just turning a negative into a positive. You can't tell me you've never shared a picture of your name spelled wrong on Instagram."

"I can, actually. I don't have an Instagram," she said, wrapping both hands around her cup as they turned toward the morgue.

"What? How do you not have an Instagram?"

"I just don't see the point. I take pictures for me, not other people."

"Wow. Keeping them all to yourself. How selfish," he teased. "I bet you don't even have Snapchat, do you?"

She held her silence and blew into the mouth of her cup to cool her drink.

"I knew it! Wow. What about Facebook? Or do you still have MySpace?"

"Ah, MySpace," she snorted. "The good old days. No, I do not have MySpace. I have Facebook, if we're being technical, but nobody can find it unless I add them first. I keep the highest security settings and don't even use my real name."

"Someone's paranoid."

"I am not. I'm cautious. It's for the safety of my friends as much as it is myself, considering how many people probably want to find a way to blackmail or threaten me. I've put a lot of people in jail over the past few years, and they would probably love to find something they could use against me when they get out."

"Yeah, it's not hard to make enemies doing what we do. Speaking of, what are your thoughts on this case?"

She glanced around the busy streets and shook her head. "I don't know yet. I'm mostly concerned with the number of people who heard something and didn't call us. Have you submitted your report to me yet, by the way?"

"Yeah, I think I was one of the first. Wrote it up as soon as I got in this morning."

"Oh, okay. It's probably at the bottom of the pile I've been trying to go through, then. Who told you about the crime scene?"

He took a sip of his coffee before explaining, "Dispatch got a call a little before three from a drunk woman who was walking back to her apartment from a club."

Lily switched her coffee to her right hand so she could dig out her phone with the left. She opened her tape recorder app and spoke into it, "Interview the witness who found the victim. See if the interview can be conducted at the witness's home or in public."

"Why?" Stilinski asked when she stopped the tape and saved the recording.

"It sets them at ease, especially if anything illegal was happening in that club. They don't tend to give good information or have much recall ability if they're preoccupied with their own actions incriminating them. That fear gets worse sitting in an interrogation room, especially if they've never been in one. So I try to keep them as comfortable as I can, to make sure they remember as much as possible."

"Smart."

"Isn't it just? That's why I'm the detective," she smirked.

When they arrived at the morgue, she made a show of opening the door and standing aside to let him pass through this time.

"Why, thank you. How chivalrous of you," he joked and gave a stiff half-bow before he stepped inside.

"It's the least I could do after your gallantry earlier," she mused.

She paused at the front desk to set her coffee down behind the counter and advised Stilinski to do the same. She didn't bother to check in, though. There was little need considering how often she was here. The secretary knew when to expect her.

Lily led the way to the examination room, a small and macabre gray box. Stacks of squares with handles decorated one wall, from which waves of air conditioning seeped into the rest of the space. A large metal table stood at the center, and on it rested the body of their victim covered to the shoulders by a heavy white sheet. The fluorescent lamp hanging overhead accented every area of discoloration on the woman's otherwise translucent skin.

A tall, middle-aged man stood with his back to the cops as they walked in, leaning over a smaller table filled with sharp instruments. He had jet black hair and a lean, almost frail looking frame that resembled a candy cane in his current posture. He straightened to his full height as he turned to face his guests. He towered over Lily but didn't quite meet Stilinski's eye level. As he spotted the cops, his dark brown eyes lit up and his pointed chin wrinkled in a smile.

"Detective! Officer. Good to see you!"

"Charlie," Lily returned the smile with a charming one of her own. "I only wish the circumstances were better. What can you tell us about the victim?"

"Well, she's no longer a Jane Doe, if that tickles your fancy," the coroner informed. He peeled off his latex gloves and passed the detective a folder. "That's yours to keep, by the way. I made a copy to file away already. Her name's Jessica Anderson."

"That's really good to know," Lily agreed as she flipped open the folder and surveyed the usual facts: victim's name, height, weight, hair and eye color, and last known address. "How did you find that out? I thought the prints were gonna take a few days."

"They are, but they recovered her wallet. Thought you would have been told already."

"It's probably in a report," Lily waved it off. That ruled out a huge motive, so that was excellent. "Let's talk about cause of death, though. You said you got that, right?"

"Surely do," Charlie nodded and tugged on a fresh set of purple latex gloves before he stepped over to the body. He glanced over Lily's shoulder and asked, "Are you sure you can handle this, son?"

Stilinski's skin held a green tint and his eyes were stuck on the victim's face. He had gone so still, neither the detective nor coroner could tell if he was still breathing.

Lily frowned. "You don't have to be here for this part if you don't want to," she told him. "You can wait in the hall. I'll debrief you after."

He shook his head. "I've worked with cadavers before," he said. "I'll be fine as long as there's not much blood."

"Then boy, do I have good news for you. She's been drained," Charlie assured and peeled the sheet back to reveal the multiple stab wounds and frayed flesh along the woman's torso.

Stilinski emitted a small noise of distress but held firm.

"So! The obvious, short answer for cause of death is blood loss," the coroner explained.

Lily held a hand up to stop him from continuing. "Are you sure it was blood loss and not asphyxiation? There are no puncture wounds in the lungs?"

"Nope. The lungs are completely intact. There are wounds directly below them, but nothing that pierced the lungs themselves. What makes you ask?"

Lily saw too many similarities between this case and the Kitty Genovese case that she hadn't considered anything but bilateral pneumothorax. If she had been too stuck on that to deduce the correct cause of death, what else was she overlooking in her attempts to fit the crime into the narrative of her theory? Was her theory about a copycat completely off base or had the killer made an unintentional error that led to a vast, key difference between the two crimes?

"It just reminded me of a case I read about once," she said. "I was looking into a potential link. But you're positive the COD was blood loss?"

"One hundred percent. It's unsurprising, because she has no fewer than twelve stab wounds to the abdominal region, one across the right breast, and what I believe are three distinct cuts across the throat."

Lily raised an eyebrow and leaned closer to the victim's neck. "Are they all deep enough to cause significant blood loss?"

"Two of them are deep enough to cause some damage, but the only significant one is the gash that opened her trachea," Charlie explained and pointed a finger at the woman's neck. "That one is what finally killed her. The more interesting cut is the first one I believe was made, based on the lack of blood around the area." He pointed to a cut surrounded by a bruise, just below the jawline.

Lily had to squint to see the cut but when she confirmed it, she frowned.

"There shouldn't be a bruise on top of it," she said. "Unless one of the parties involved tried to stop the bleeding." She looked to Stilinski and asked, "Would you mind putting in a call for a forensic photographer? I want some pictures of this on file. It's a long shot but maybe we can get a partial now that the bruising is so pronounced."

"Yep. I'll go do that now," Stilinski said and stepped out of the room, leaving its doors swinging in his wake.

"Is he going to be okay?" Charlie asked as he stared after the cop.

Lily chuckled. "Yeah, he'll be fine. This is his first homicide," she explained.

"Gotcha. Well, he's going to get used to them around here."

"I really hope you're wrong about that, Charlie," she said, although she knew full well he wasn't.

5.

STRIKE ONE

"I told you we'd need to stop somewhere after," Lily said as she settled into a chair across the table from Stilinski. "Eat up. We've got a lot to do this afternoon."

She set a tray between them, loaded with four large slices of pizza with various toppings. Instead of taking a slice for herself, she turned her attention to the autopsy report and began to examine its contents. After scanning over the model drawing to get a better idea of the placement and extent of the victim's wounds, she noticed a lack of movement from Stilinski and glanced up.

He had his elbows up on the table and hands clasped together in front of his mouth. The green tint on his skin vanished during the walk from the morgue to the pizzeria, but now he was staring down at the pizza as if its mere existence made him want to throw up. Most concerning about his behavior was his silence, though. Lily couldn't remember him being silent since they'd met on his first day.

"Are you sure you're okay?" she asked. "We can box this up and take it back to the station if it's making you nauseous."

"It's not that," he said from behind his hands and continued to avoid her gaze. "I'm a good officer."

Her eyebrows popped up. "I know you are."

"I'm not squeamish."

"I never thought you were."

"Why not?" Now, he looked at her and lowered his hands to the table next to their tray. "You kept asking if I was okay back there."

"Sorry—are you upset that I noticed you looked a little pale?" she frowned. "You know I'm not judging you or your ability to do the job, right?"

"I walked out because I couldn't handle it."

"That's not why you left the room, Stilinski. You left because I asked you to call the photographer."

"Oh, come on, Faye. You know better—."

"Look," she cut him off with a sharp, authoritative tone. "If you want to fight me on this, that's fine. But I'm throwing you a bone here because I know what the first homicide case can be like. It doesn't matter how prepared you think you are. There's a huge difference between a cadaver in the academy and a victim you know died brutally, alone, on the street."

"Really?" He reached forward to pick at one of the plates on the tray, but still didn't touch the food. "So… you're not gonna tell any of the guys in my unit that the rookie couldn't handle being in the same room as a corpse?"

"I've watched a few of those guys faint in that exact same morgue," she confessed and flipped the folder closed so she could free her hands for pizza. "You didn't even get close to that. I'm not going to tell them a thing." She scooped up a slice and took a bite before adding, "We give each other a hard time at work, but we don't joke about stuff like that. We're dealing with human lives. Cases like these… they're not about our reactions. They're about whether we can get justice for the victim's families. At the end of the day, that's all the guys in your unit care about. That's all any of us care about."

His gaze connected with hers again and the corner of his lips twitched. "Thanks, Faye," he said as he peered up at her through his eyelashes, radiating a bashful air. "You're kinda okay for a detective."

She chuckled. "Yeah, you're not so bad for a rookie, either."

He grinned and reached for a slice of pizza.

By the time they returned to the station, half the afternoon was gone and Lily had officially fallen behind on her desired timeline. She hadn't finished wading through the canvassing reports yet, nor had she started compiling a list of suspects or finished studying the autopsy results collected from Charlie. As soon as she sat at her desk, she withdrew Stilinski's report from her box and set the others aside.

"Hey, Jordan?" she called across the small cluster of desks which housed her detectives. "You working on anything with a hard deadline right now?"

"Yeah, but I'm finishing it now," the man answered and he looked up at her. "Need me to work on something else?"

"If you would," Lily said with a nod toward the remaining reports. "Can you go through these and compile a witness list? Names and addresses, if you can find them in the reports. I have a feeling we're going to be doing a lot of follow up on this case."

Jordan nodded as he took the stack of papers.

"No problem. I'll have them done by…" he paused to flip through and calculate before finishing: "the end of my shift. You want me to combine the rest of the report into a summary so you don't have to go through them all for details later?"

"If you've got the time after getting the witness list, that would be phenomenal," she agreed. "Actually, let me know when you finish the list and then I'll see if I can spare you for the summary. That's going to take a hell of a lot longer than copying names and addresses will."

"Okay, I'll keep you updated," he said and began sorting the papers.

"Brilliant. Thanks."

With Jordan chipping away at his task, Lily turned her attention to Stilinski's initial report of the homicide. It would need to be updated now that they knew more about Jessica Anderson, but it still contained what she needed for now. Her stomach knotted as she scanned through the scant evidence checklist. It served as the confirmation she'd dreaded: the rain had washed away most of the viable DNA evidence. The provided information was helpful, though. It established the presence of tool markings on the body, the submission of a rape kit, the possibility of semen on the body, and the presence of blood. Finally, it indicated forensic photographs were taken at the scene. Most of the information seemed normal enough, but a couple of them made her squint. After a few seconds, she stood and walked through the station to find Stilinski.

"Stilinski? You got a second?"

"Yep, I do! What's up?" he asked without removing his gaze from his computer screen to acknowledge her.

"I need clarification on the evidence you checked off," she said. "The tool markings refers to the stab wounds, right?"

"Yeah, but the guy who took the rape kit said there was a lot of, uh…well… there was some…" After a struggle, he coughed and trailed off.

Lily shot him a piercing gaze, her mouth fixed into a firm frown. "This isn't middle school, Stilinski. I've been doing this a long time. You can say it."

He glanced over at her, grimaced, and looked away again.

"Genital mutilation."

"With the knife?" she clarified in a higher octave than usual. "Oh, come on! You've got to be kidding me!"

Her vehement reaction finally elicited some movement from him, and he swung his chair around to face her.

"Wish I was, detective," he muttered. "You seem upset about that… any reason why, aside from the obvious?"

"Remember that case I was referencing earlier? This was a very specific part of it," she explained as she grabbed a pen and added what the tool markings were to the evidence checklist.

"Coincidence?"

"I don't know. I sure hope so but I'm not optimistic enough to think coincidence exists in this line of work."

"Well, what was the case you're so worried about? Might help me to have a little context here. Maybe I can find something useful to connect everything?"

"Well, if you can do that, you'll be moving up to detective pretty soon," she joked. "Ever heard of Kitty Genovese?"

His eyebrows knitted into a deep furrow that gave her an answer, although he replied: "In criminal psych back in college."

"Yes, that would have been the place. Her murder spurred a whole movement of study on the Bystander Effect," she explained as a wave of her dominant hand emphasized her words. "Thirty eight witnesses saw or heard the initial attack. Some guy shouted out the window for the attacker to leave her alone, and the attacker fled. Long story short, nobody called for help, she tried to make it to safety with severe injuries, the attacker came back, stabbed and sexually assaulted her, and left her barely alive. Her neighbor found her in the stairwell of their apartment square and called for help, but she died before the ambulance arrived.

"The horror of the fact that thirty eight people knew of a crime in progress and didn't stop it completely overshadowed the coverage of her actual death, and the press gave zero attention to the fact that she'd lived a good life. She was well liked by most of the people she interacted with growing up. Never made enemies. Just got caught in the wrong place at the wrong time and suffered horribly because of it."

Stilinski held his silence throughout his body, which held stock still and tense for a few seconds.

"Holy shit."

"Yep," Lily nodded. "And the way she was killed almost exactly matches the wounds on our victim. If we have a copycat, that means he might do this again."

He groaned and rubbed his eyes. "Don't say that right now," he complained. "I can't pull many more shifts like this. It's been hell."

"You're one to talk. I've been walking around in wet shoes all day," she grumbled. "At least we know we've got information to work with now. Can you run a background check on the victim, fill in the rest of the face sheet, and get me a copy?"

"Yeah, I'll update it. You've got the autopsy report, right? That's got her basic info in it to hold you over until I finish this."

"I do now," she concurred. "Speaking of, though, one last thing and I'll stop bugging you. You marked off blood here. I think you just meant the victim's, but I wanted to check."

"Yeah. At least, we didn't find anything that looked like it belonged to the killer. The rain really screwed us over on that evidence."

"There may be hope yet if we get that rape kit processed soon," she noted. "Semen is pretty damning evidence."

"And I don't even want to know how you go about matching that up," he grimaced.

"You'd have to ask forensics, anyway. Thankfully, that is not my division," she said and dropped his pen back into its designated cup beside his monitor. "Thanks, Stilinski. Let me know when you update that face sheet."

"You got it, Faye."

Lily returned to her desk and opened the autopsy report again to review the information about the victim. Her name was Jessica Anderson, approximately age 26. Dark brown hair, green eyes. 5' 7", average build. Appendectomy scar dated early 2000s.

The words began to blur on the page, and Lily paused to squeeze her eyes shut. She rubbed the lids with her fingers until she was seeing white spots against the darkness. When she opened her eyes again, her vision was even worse than before. It was slow to clear, but she went straight back to work as soon as it did.

"Okay. Focus, Faye," she murmured. "You can do this." She squinted at the paper for a few more seconds before she conceded,   "Nope. Can't."

She reached into one of her desk drawers and grabbed an unprotected pair of glasses. She shoved the thick rectangular frames onto her face and tried again. Able to distinguish the letters this time, she skipped down to the family history.

Father: Michael Newton Anderson.

Lives in: Phoenix, AZ.

Status: Alive

"Great."

She scratched down a reminder to call the father later, and read on.

Mother: Tanya Alexandra Anderson.

Lives in: New York City, NY.

Status: Deceased.

"Seriously?!"

"You okay, boss?"

She looked up to see Jordan giving her a concerned half-smile from his desk.

"Yeah," she sighed. "Sorry. Can't catch a break with these leads. I'll figure it out."

But she didn't. Although they had the name of the victim to go on, Lily hit dead ends at every turn. There were hundreds of Jessica Andersons in New York City with Facebook pages, so digging that way would take more time than she had. She was still waiting on Stilinski's new report, so she couldn't make progress there. The witness report Jordan compiled and left on her In tray was her only option.

"Hey, boss? I'm going to head out for the night," Jordan interrupted, at some point after time started to blur for Lily and become nothing more than a fuzzy concept. "You look like you could use some sleep, too."

Lily squinted up at him through her glasses and sat back.

"Yeah, you're probably right. It's been a long day."

"Yeah," he agreed with a sympathetic smile. "If I can help anymore, leave a list on my desk, okay? I'll start on it when I get back in."

She nodded and smiled the best she could within her currently wobbling world of sleep deprivation.

"I know. I appreciate it. Thanks, Jordan."

"No problem. Have a good night, boss," he said before heading out.

"You too," she yawned and looked back to the papers strewn across the desk.

Jordan was right; she needed to go home. Maybe sleep would clear her mind and help her find a useful lead when she came back in the morning.

She shuffled and sorted her papers into as neat a pile as possible before checking her email. It was meant to be the last thing she did to catch up on whatever she'd missed throughout the day and that was all it was, for the first few seconds. She scanned the previews and found Stilinski's report a quarter of the way down her screen. That would have to wait until tomorrow.

She was about to close the program when her computer dinged with the arrival of a new email. The sender line was blank. She didn't know that was possible. Every email came from someone, after all.

The bigger concern was the subject line, which served as the first line of text for this particular message. It consisted of two simple words.

You're Dead.

A slow chill dripped down her spine and left her skin spotted with goosebumps. She wrenched her hand away from her mouse as if it were searing her palm. She turned in her chair, her eyes wide as she fought the haze of exhaustion to search the dark shadows in the room. The sound of her accelerating heartbeat echoed through her ears.

Someone was after her now, and that made ordinary occurrences like staying late and having inadequate lighting feel electric. A metallic, acrid taste filled the back of her mouth as if lightning had struck inches away from her. This bolt was a warning shot, and Lily was convinced in that moment that there would someday be a fatal blow, a reckoning.

Her reckoning.

Lily reached back to the mouse, took a slow breath, and clicked on the email.

Solve this case and you're dead. Quit now and save yourself.

6.

POOLS OF RED

Despite her initial reaction to the email, Lily slept well. In fact, she hadn't slept so well in months. The foreboding warning calmed her rather than riled her up, and for good reason. After a long day of hitting walls wherever she searched, it was good to have a lead. Who would think to threaten her into abandoning a homicide except the killer, or at least someone close to him? Civilians didn't tend to prank cops with death threats, even those stupid enough to send anonymous communication for the sake of adding to the hysteria surrounding a murder investigation. The killer had to be growing desperate.

And desperation led to mistakes. The email might have been more concerning if it didn't give Lily so much hope that she would be able to hunt down her suspect before he eluded her or fled the state. A single piece of DNA was all it would take. Hopefully, the rape kit would give them that much. That would provide Lily with enough evidence to place the killer within a close enough proximity with the victim to transfer biological material to her body.

Now that she had managed a good night's sleep and changed into a clean, dry outfit for the day, she was ready to get back to work. As she drove into the city from her townhouse, she detailed the day's plan of attack. The witness list Jordan submitted would have to wait. Reviewing the victim's background check and scheduling interviews would be top priority.

Setting up an interview with Jessica's father would be tricky. She needed to ensure he had been informed of her death before she asked to speak with him. Even then, she would need to find a tactful way of posing difficult questions to a grieving father. Lily didn't deal well with grief in her own life or with others, but she knew how important speaking to him would be.

Speaking with the woman who reported the crime would be even harder than facing a man who had now lost his entire family. Not only had the woman experienced the trauma of finding a dying woman mauled beyond saving, but Stilinski's report indicated she had been intoxicated at the time. Her memories of the event would hardly be reliable with that level of impairment. Aside from those hindrances, Lily had to take into account that an intoxicated woman stumbling around the city at three in the morning probably wouldn't be keen to speak to the police at all.

Still, she had a couple of tasks to start with. As soon as she made it to the station, she navigated to her email and scrolled past the threat at the top of her inbox. Instead, she selected Stilinski's updated report and the victim's background check, then sent both to the printer.

She was halfway to the machine when Stilinski walked up with two Dunkin Donuts cups in hand. He brandished both toward her.

"Morning. Thought I'd bring you some superior coffee today so you can see the difference for yourself," he grinned. "I didn't know if you liked cream and sugar, so I brought one black just in case."

"Superior coffee," she repeated through a half laugh. "We'll see about that. Is one decaf, though? I don't want to steal yours." Besides, she didn't want either one if they were both decaf, which she found useless.

"Yeah, they're both regular. I didn't get much sleep last night," he explained. "So take your pick."

"I'll take this one, then." Lily reached for the cup with cream and sugar, taking it when his grip loosened. "Thank you. That was really thoughtful. Actually, I'm glad you showed up when you did," she added and nodded for him to follow her to the printer. "I'm just about to look over the background check and report you sent yesterday."

"Oh, good," he said as he trailed behind her. "Didn't get a chance yesterday?"

"I didn't have the brain capacity to deal with it yesterday," she said as she set her cup on top of the printer and logged into the system. "And I prefer paper copies, so I automatically assume that's the way everyone else functions… even though I'm probably in the minority. I didn't even think to check my email until I was getting ready to leave for the night."

"I don't blame you. Yesterday was kind of insane. I didn't have half your focus by the time my shift was supposed to end."

"I'm glad I looked focused because I didn't feel it," she mused as she printed her documents and collected them from the printer tray. She turned to look at him and asked, "How late did you end up staying? I thought you had a seven to seven."

"Nah. Midnight to noon," he answered. "I probably left at five, right after I emailed you the report."

"You stayed five hours after your shift?" she frowned. "You must be mental."

"Well, I had information you were waiting on," he shrugged. "I didn't want to leave before I sent it to you. I might have if I had known you weren't going to see it until now, though," he joked.

"You worked a seventeen hour shift, Stilinski. How are you standing right now?" she asked as she turned to lean against the printer and crossed her arms. "If I had known you were only staying to help me out—."

"I'm not doing you a favor. I'm working for Jessica and her family. The sooner we get this guy, the better."

"Right." She gave a curt nod and took a moment in silence to hide her surprise at his initiative. Most officers didn't provide that kind of help, let alone rookies. "Well, thank you, in any case. But I am sorry you were here so late on my account."

"Don't be. You did a lot for me yesterday, too," he assured. "Let me know if you have any more questions about that report."
"I will."

Her curious stare followed his retreating form as he walked to his desk. Maybe there was more to the rookie than she'd expected.

She returned to her desk with the documents in one hand and coffee in the other, scanning through the updated face sheet. The report now indicated more background information on the victim, including her address and her roommate, Derek's contact number. She set her coffee down to free her left hand, and then added the roommate to her list of calls to make.

The narrative portion of the report identified Jessica Anderson as a bartender at a small Irish pub in the village. Her shift had ended at 2:30 a.m. but Jessica didn't leave until shortly before three to make what should have been a twenty minute walk back to her apartment. The most obvious route she could have taken home was well lit, and it typically contained enough passersby to make it seem safe. Her boss, an Italian named Bob, noted this wasn't the first time Jessica had walked home after a late night.

Lily added Bob to her list and continued browsing the report. What really struck her about Stilinski's account was his initial conversation with the woman who reported the crime, a hysterical Kayla Simmons. After placing the initial 911 call, Simmons remained at Anderson's side while the woman clung to life. Twenty minutes passed before she called 911 again. In the time it took dispatchers to send an ambulance, Anderson died in Simmons's arms.

Why had it taken twenty minutes and a second call to send the ambulance to the scene? The average response time hardly ever dipped below ten minutes, so why had it taken twice as long to deploy help to a fatally injured woman? If they had responded in even the median amount of time, would Anderson be alive now? Could she have been saved?

With the questions burning in her mind, Lily looked up Kayla Simmons's number and called. The phone rang four times before Lily heard the rustling of someone picking up and adjusting the receiver on the other end. A meek, ragged voice greeted the detective, drawing a shudder from deep in her gut.

"H-hullo?"

"Hello. My name is Lily Faye. I'm the Head Detective with the NYPD." Her own voice sounded robotic in its factual, straightforward delivery. "Could I please speak to Kayla Simmons?"

The response sounded empty and dull: "You got her."

Lily waited for a follow-up question that didn't come before she answered it anyway. "Hello, Ms. Simmons. I'm sure you know we're investigating the Jessica Anderson case," she said, being extremely cautious not to mention the words homicide or murder. "If you'd be able, I'd really like to sit down and hear your take on the events of that evening. Any information you can provide will aid my investigation and could help catch the individual responsible."

Silence. Lily waited. A sniffle. More silence.

"Ms. Simmons?"

"M'here. Not really with it, y'know? Kinda shocked."

"Of course," Lily agreed, keeping her tone as soothing as she could make it. "We don't have to talk right this second. Would tomorrow or Friday maybe work for you?"

"Gotta be forty-eight hours from now."

Ah. The key witness had drugs in her system, and probably also harbored a fundamental misunderstanding of how long it would take for them to clear out. If it would make her more comfortable to have time to "get clean", so be it. Lily would need Kayla to have at least a little focus on the day of the interview, anyway. The biggest problem would be using the interview in court and somehow making the argument that the witness was reliable enough to convey the true events and timeline of the crime. The defendant's attorney was going to love the drug angle.

"That would be fine. Would Friday at eleven o'clock work for you?"

More silence, presumably while Simmons tried to calculate.

"Later's better."

"I can do two," Lily said. "Would that be okay?"

"Yep. Can't come with a search warrant, though."

Subtle. "I won't, Ms. Simmons. I'll only be there to ask questions about Ms. Anderson, not to look around. You don't even have to let me inside the premises if you don't want to."

"Good. Y'can come in, though. Got my address?"

"I have one in the system but it hasn't been updated in a while. Can you confirm that what I have is correct?"

Kayla confirmed and Lily ended the conversation there. She hung up and penciled the interview into her pocket-sized planner. Friday at two. Now they were getting somewhere.

Simmons turned out to be tame in comparison with Mr. Anderson. As soon as Lily introduced herself to the man, she regretted calling. He launched into a five-minute tirade against the police and New York City. Lily spent the majority of his rant trying to figure out why he thought the latter was relevant to his daughter's case.

"Sir, I understand how you're feeling right now," she cut in when he took a breath, "but we can't help catch the man who did this to your daughter unless I have a chance to sit down and talk to you." She pushed the words out so quickly they almost slurred together.

The man fell silent at the request aside from his heavy breathing hitting the receiver. "You want to help?" he asked, his voice trembling like that of a scared child more than the previous steady and loud tone of an angry father.

"Yes, sir," Lily said, reservation calcifying into a rock in her throat that tried to prevent her next words. "I want to help you."

More silence followed before he spoke again, his voice cracking. "Then tell me my daughter's still alive."

The resulting sobs from his end of the connection sent Lily diving to mute her microphone. "Jordan!" she barked after she had. "Come here!"

Jordan jumped out of his chair as if it had been electrified and scrambled to loom on the other side of her desk.

"I have the victim's father on the phone sobbing," she whispered and clasped her hand over the mouthpiece, even though her end of the conversation couldn't be heard. "I don't do well with tears. Help me."

"Oh. Well...what would you want someone to say to comfort you if you lost a family member?" he asked after a few seconds. "When everyone was giving condolences about your parents, what did you wish they had said?"

Lily stared down at the phone while she thought it over. Losing her parents several years back remained the most painful experience of her life, but the hardest part wasn't the loss. It was facing the people around her after. She wasn't an empathetic person, so the fact that others were crying over losses that should have belonged only to Lily and her older sister was infuriating. The circumstances surrounding the loss of their parents left Lily without any time to mourn, so why did anyone else get to?

She had a different style of grieving than most people, anyway. She chose anger over tears, but she'd had a lot of reason to be angry after her loss. Sympathy from strangers only made it worse.

With that in mind, she hit the mute on the microphone and said the only thing she could think of.

"Mr. Anderson, we both know answering my questions won't bring her back. But your information might be able to spare another father from having to deal with this kind of pain in the future. What you're going through right now isn't something you want anyone else to experience, is it?"

Jordan gave an encouraging smile and nodded at her. She mouthed a thank you and let him return to his desk. There was a lot to be said about working with parents; Jordan had more wisdom in this area than she thought she ever would.

She wished she hadn't let him set back to work so quickly, though. Mr. Anderson continued to hiccup and whimper on the other end of the phone, rather than give her an answer. What was she supposed to do now that her appeal hadn't elicited a response?

"Can I give you until tomorrow?" So far, Thursday was her only completely free day. "We can talk about this then, if you're available."

"Y-yeah, that would be good," Mr. Anderson agreed. "I'm in town until the f-funeral. Can we m-meet somewhere?"

"Absolutely. Where are you staying?"

"I'm at Hotel Pennsylvania," he said. "There's a Starbucks right down the street."

"Sure. I know the place," she assured. "How does two o'clock sound? Right after lunch?"

"That's fine."

"Great, thank you. Let me give you my information so you can call me if you need to talk before then."

She did so and had him repeat it back to her to make sure he'd recorded it correctly. Once she knew he would be able to contact her if he needed to, she hung up and expelled a heavy sigh.

"Thanks, Jordan," she said as she glanced over at him. "That was rough."

"Sounded like it," he grimaced. "You did great, though."

She didn't know about that, but it had yielded the desired results.

"Thank you. Nice to have you in my corner."

"No problem," he said to conclude, although he didn't return to his own work.

She stared back at him for several seconds and finally asked, "Something on your mind?"

"Oh, no. I just wanted to run the shift change by you again. You're okay with Harris taking Saturday?"

"Yep. Chief signed off on it already?"

"Yeah, he did."

"Perfect. You should be all set, then. The shift is officially Harris's responsibility now."

Jordan nodded and turned back to his work, while Lily returned to hers.

She feared she would need to use his advice with the victim's roommate, a twenty-six-year-old writer named Derek Williams. While she listened to the drone of ringing and waited for the call to connect, her computer pinged with an incoming email. She didn't look up, preoccupied with preparing for another weeping mess of a man. That wasn't what greeted her.

"This is Derek." The voice that answered was deep and rumbling, but lacked the overwhelming grief Lily anticipated.

"Oh." It took her a second to calibrate to the utter lack of emotion. "Mr. Williams? This is Detective Faye with the NYPD. I'm looking into the investigation regarding the circumstances of your roommate's death?"

She thought it might prompt some kind of response, but his tone didn't change as he answered, "Oh, yeah. Need me to come answer some questions? I have an alibi, just so you know."

Lily's eyebrows rose. "Really?" she asked.

His brand of nonchalance was new to her in terms of homicide investigations. He spoke too clearly to be drunk or high, but people close to the victim didn't tend to be so relaxed.

"Yeah. That's what you need, right? For me to come answer some questions about her life and what she was usually up to on nights like that one?"

"That is what I need," she agreed, her words stilted with misgivings. "Sorry. I don't think I've ever had anyone offer to come down here."

"Yeah, well I'm heading into work right now, so I thought I'd cut to the chase before I have to clock in."

He was working the day after his roommate's death? That seemed like a strange way to deal with grief, if he was even grieving. He didn't sound like he had taken this too hard.

Finally, someone Lily could understand. She was no expert on dealing with grief, but she could relate to this form of it far better than Mr. Anderson's style.

"Oh, sure. Well, would anytime this week work for you? I've got tomorrow morning open."

"That'll be perfect. I work at noon tomorrow," he said. "Just come down to the station, then?"

"Yeah, and when you get here, just let our secretary know you have a meeting with Detective Faye. If you have any questions before then, you can call the non-emergency line and they'll patch you through to me."

"Sounds good. Thanks, Detective. I'll be in around 9:30."

"Great. See you then. Thank you, Derek."

Lily frowned as she returned her phone to its cradle and jotted a note next to Derek's name. His lack of emotion alone wasn't enough to make him a suspect but it was out of line with the typical behavior of someone who suffering a deep loss. His mannerisms during the interview would help determine whether he was a prime suspect or simply in denial. Of course, making the appointment and following through were very different. She hoped he would show up.

There was no use worrying about it at the moment. Although she had crossed three major items off her to do list in the first hour of her shift, she had a lot left to work on. She read through the rest of Stilinski's report as she sipped her coffee. It wasn't as strong as she preferred but it helped lift her spirits.

The new details gave her enough direction to frame the three upcoming interviews. A puff of pride expanded in her chest at the realization that she had gone from having no leads yesterday to three today, all of which were accomplished without studying the witness list. She was eager to get to the list now, but another ping from her computer pulled her from her optimistic train of thought.

The threat she saw this time wasn't as juvenile as the first. There was no subject line. The preview of the body stated: *"I told you to stop inve…"* Lily could fill in the blanks, but there was a larger cause for consternation: a small paperclip icon in the upper right hand corner of the preview. She held her breath as she clicked into the email and scanned past the threat, which warned her to end the investigation or else end up like the subject of the photos. Lily opened the attachment, heart pounding in her throat, choking her.

The first photo opened on her second monitor. At first, all Lily could see were pools of red. Then, a thin strip of pale beige pulled the picture into focus. Lily's stomach rolled as she recognized the beige strip to be a corpse's arm.

This time, the killer had attached pictures of Jessica's mutilated body.

7.

WITNESSED

"Maaaaatt! How's my favorite forensic tech?"

The sandy haired man Lily strode toward swiveled around in his chair and slumped his broad shoulders at the sight of her.

"Why do you only come around when you want something?"

"Why do you think I want something?" she asked, undeterred by his grumpy greeting; it was par for the course as far as Matt went. "Maybe I'm just here to say hi."

His eyebrows popped as he crossed his arms. He was a man of few words, and silence worked well for him. It was difficult to maintain a ruse around him for long, even for someone as well-versed in interrogation techniques as Lily was.

"Okay, fine. I need a favor," she broke their stalemate after only a few seconds and tugged her phone from her pocket. "If I forward you an email, can you trace where it came from?"

"Generally, yes," the tech agreed, although hesitation clung to his deep voice. "What kind of email are we talking about?"

"The strictly confidential kind. As in, pretend I was never here, confidential," she said as she tapped away at the screen of her phone.

"Why the secrecy?"

"Because it's probably a non-issue but I can't make it common knowledge until I know for sure," she said. "Okay… aaaand, sent."

Matt leaned closer to his computer and opened the email when it popped into his inbox. He stared at the screen for at least three times as long as it should have taken to read the first short threat Lily had received. The rest of his face scrunched and his jaw clenched. Yet again, he elected not to speak when he finished processing the contents, but looked up at Lily with piercing, dark slits for eyes.

"So… that means you can trace it?" she asked, but he didn't respond. "Matt, come on. It barely even qualifies as a threat."

"You are not a good judge of what does and doesn't constitute a genuine threat. By the way, this does."

"If I agree that it looks genuine, can you at least focus your concern on tracing it? Because you're being an unproductive kind of worried right now, and I need the other kind."

"Lily…"

"Matt," she retorted. "I've had death threats before, okay? Yes, I am concerned with this particular one because of the circumstances of the case I'm working right now. That's why I'm here in the first place. But I'm not going to let it derail me by sitting around, biting my nails because someone figured out how to send an anonymous email. I need you to agree to total secrecy and help me, or I'm just going to leave and do nothing about it. Got it?"

Deep green eyes locked on his hard brown ones. Neither detective nor technologist blinked for several seconds. Then, an itching sensation began at the outer corners of Lily's eyes and crawled inward. Just when she worried she might have to relent, she leaned in and blew in his face.

"Ow! Dammit, Faye," he groaned as he jerked backwards and rubbed his eyes. "I'll help you, but you owe me."

"Whoa, Deja vu. It's like you've said that to me before or something," she smirked and set her hands on her hips. "Yes, I owe you, okay? Just help me out."

"It would take you the rest of your life to pay off that list of IOUs," he huffed and looked back to the computer. "Okay, let me see… It follows the typical patterns of anonymous messages."

"What does that mean?"

"See the little copyright mark in the corner here? Not really typical of an Outlook email, right?"

"Right…"

"That means it came from some kind of website that uses an anonymizer to scramble the IP and email addresses," Matt explained.

"So can we trace it back if we know what site it came from?"

"Probably not. Every anonymizing site uses virtually the same kind of software, so knowing the name of the site this person used to send the threat isn't helpful."

"Well that should maximize our chances, yeah? If they all use the same software, you should be able to apply any tracing counter paths back to them all, right?" Lily frowned as she stood behind him to watch his work, her arms crossed over her stomach.

"I can probably ping a location, but not the exact computer unless I can decode the scrambled IP address," he said as he opened a coding program on his second monitor and began typing values Lily couldn't decipher. "If it's coming from a computer lab or an office space with a bunch of desktops, I won't be able to lock in on the exact person. If it came from a laptop…"

"You can ping the location it was in at the time, but it could have moved anywhere since then," she finished with a sigh. "Damn portable technology."

"Most people see that kind of tech as a good thing."

"Well, it's inconveniencing me right now."

"Potentially. We don't know that for sure," he pointed out and hit enter.

As the code generated on screen, he warned her that it wouldn't be a quick process. Results could take hours, maybe even days depending on how advanced the encryptions were.

"Dammit. Seriously? All right. Give me a call when you find something, then," she said as her phone buzzed to remind her of an interview. She withdrew it from her pocket and snoozed the alarm before adding, "I'm serious, though. Can you please do me a favor and keep this under the radar for now? It wouldn't make any sense to worry the Chief with it until we know it's credible."

Matt's sharp jaw tightened as he regarded her.

"You're not even telling your boss?"

"Usually, I would," she granted. "I just don't want word about this getting out yet. You know how citizens get; once the hype starts, they'll all be sending threats they have no intention of acting on, and that'll only muddle the investigation. Most of the warnings never amount to anything, anyway."

"And what if this is one that does?"

Lily's phone began to vibrate again. This time, she silenced the alarm.

"Then we'll deal with it when it comes," she decided. "That's why we're bothering to look into it, right? To discredit it. I have to go. Call me the second you get those results, okay?"

"You got it," he muttered and swung back toward his computer as she left.

She heard him make another comment under his breath, but she didn't have time to make him repeat it just so she could argue. She had too much to do without worrying about these threats, even if the language and intensity in the more recent email had escalated. She couldn't be sidetracked worrying about herself when she had to focus on the criminal investigation at hand. If she lost focus now, the killer would get away and that wasn't going to happen as long as she could prevent it.

Determined to find out exactly how to prevent that fate, Lily returned to the scene of the crime and entered the apartment building where most of the witnesses resided. After she received the second threatening email, she had thrown herself into cold calling everyone on the witness list to set up interviews. Out of a pool of roughly thirty witnesses, only two answered Lily's call and scheduled short interviews for the same afternoon. The only others she managed to contact when she cold called turned down her request for an interview.

To further complicate an already hectic schedule, the two individuals had inadvertently scheduled their interviews back-to-back, so Lily wouldn't have as much time to spend on them as she would have liked. Even still, she would take what she could get. Although the time crunch wasn't ideal, the fact that they were taking place less than 48 hours after the murder meant the event would be fresh in their minds, but not as clouded by emotion as it may have been during the initial canvassing.

She scaled the stairs to the third floor and walked down the hall, knocking on the door to apartment 302. While she waited, she flipped open her case file and glanced over the witness's information one more time. The interviewee's name was Mrs. Hamilton. She was an elderly woman who had reported hearing a couple in a heated argument on the street on the night in question.

Lily heard the *shh shh* of the woman's shuffling footsteps grow louder on the other side of the door well before she heard a creaking voice ask, "Who is it?"

She closed her case file and looked up, smiling into the peep hole. "Detective Faye," she said, trying to match the woman's increased volume and slower cadence. "We spoke earlier on the phone?"

"Ooooh." A heavy lock disengaged with a hearty click, and the door swung open to reveal a tall but frail looking woman with a cloud of white hair wisping around her head. "Come in, dear," she said as she opened the door and stepped to the side.

"Thank you so much. I'm sorry this is such short notice, but I appreciate you accommodating me," she smiled as she stepped in and took a cursory glance around the entryway. "Oh, it smells wonderful in here."

The entrance, living room, and kitchen were sparse, but each held enough decor to prevent the apartment from suffering an impersonal, clinical atmosphere. The shelves lining the short hall held a small collection of porcelain knick-knacks that gleamed under the fluorescent lighting. The scarce amount of furniture in the living room consisted of a matching set of beige chairs and a couch, all splashed with a bright pink flower pattern. The kitchen contained an aqua colored round table and two matching hard-backed chairs. Everything carried the crisp but hefty scent of lemon disinfectant.

"Oh, thank you, dear," Mrs. Hamilton smiled. "That nice young man down the hall helped me clean this morning. He's raising money for a car. Would you like some tea? I just put the kettle on."

"I would love some. Thank you. Can I help with anything?" she offered.

Mrs. Hamilton was quick to pass the task of making tea to Lily while she took a seat at the polished table. Lily suppressed a chuckle as she picked up where the woman left off. Putting a guest to work in her own home was exactly the sort of thing Lily's grandmother used to do, and the familiarity made her grin.

"So you mentioned the young man down the hall?" she asked as she set the table with matching aqua cups and saucers. "Did he say if he was around last night?"

"Oh, yes. We talked quite a lot about the inconvenience the police caused by knocking so early in the morning," Mrs. Hamilton said in an increasing volume as the kettle began to whistle over their conversation.

Lily removed it from the stove and turned the appliance off. She bit her tongue in order to keep her silence as she poured water into the waiting mugs.

"Thank you, sweetheart. You're much more helpful than your coworkers," Mrs. Hamilton said as she added generous portions of cream and sugar to her tea.

Lily cupped her hands around the mug as she sat in the vacant seat at the table. "I'm sorry if our officers gave you any trouble," she began after a long moment of contemplation. "I'm sure you can understand that it was a long night for all of us."

"Oh, certainly," Mrs. Hamilton nodded. "But it was still terribly timed, you know."

"I know," the detective confirmed, barely restraining a retort that murder didn't often occur at a convenient time. "I'll keep this interview short, though. Could you tell me what you heard or saw that night?"

"Yes, well, I haven't been sleeping well for some time now. I woke very early in the morning and I made myself tea. I do like to sit by the window while I drink it, see what's going on outside. So that night, I saw a man run up to a woman walking by herself. It looked like he hugged her. I didn't think much of it at the time."

"You said their exchange was interesting, though? What made you think that?" she asked as she slid her hands around the warm mug, as if protecting herself from the chill of that rainy evening again.

"Well, she did push him away. But you know how the mind can justify things it sees to mask the truth in tragic situations. I suppose I thought they were a bickering couple. It was dark, you see. It didn't look like anything more than a spat."

"And you didn't hear them exchange any words, by chance? She didn't shout anything?"

"I wouldn't be able to hear if she had, dear," Mrs. Hamilton frowned as she swirled together a second concoction of sugar and cream into her tea. "I had the hearing aid for my right ear out. The only time I put the left one in when I get up is to hear the kettle whistling."

"I see. And it's your living room window that overlooks the street, right?"

"Yes, it is."

"Would you mind if I take a look?"

"Go on, then."

Heavy, velvet curtains framed either side of the window, but there was enough space between them for Lily to peer outside with ease. What struck her was how direct the view to the crime scene would have been. At only three stories up, the chances of Mrs. Hamilton seeing the murderer well enough to describe him should have been high.

"Mrs. Hamilton? Do you happen to remember what the man looked like? Race? Build?"

"I'm afraid I didn't get a good look at him. It was dark and my eyes aren't the best. He seemed tall compared to the woman, at least by a head. Certainly over six feet. He was stocky, too, though. Not fat, mind you, but he didn't look spry."

"Would you say he had an average build? Did he seem muscular or just larger?"

"Oh, I couldn't possibly tell that in the dark and through all the rain," Mrs. Hamilton shook her head. "He seemed to be wearing a bulky jacket, though. I only noticed that because the street lights shined off it. That's part of why I couldn't see what color he was. I would guess black."

"That's actually not the statistical probability," Lily replied in as gentle a tone as she could manage in the face of the casual racism. "Most murderers are middle-aged white men, even in a city this diverse. The rest of it is great information, though," she encouraged as she pulled out her notebook and jotted down that the jacket was reflective. "That'll help us narrow it down a bit. Is there anything else you can recall?"

The woman squinted and scrunched her lips together. "I never saw him leave, but I did see him run up to her," she explained. "It looked like he had a limp."

"A limp?" Lily's eyebrows rose as she looked up at the woman again.

"He wasn't walking straight, at any rate. Maybe he was intoxicated."

"That could be." Lily wrote it down. "That's excellent to know," she smiled. "Thank you for your help, Mrs. Hamilton. This is all really good information to have."

"You're quite welcome, dear," Mrs. Hamilton smiled and ushered her back toward the exit.

It wasn't until Lily stepped out into the hallway and checked her phone that she realized how much time had passed inside the vortex that seemed to be Mrs. Hamilton's apartment. She swore under her breath and lunged down the hallway to the next apartment. By the time she knocked on the door to apartment 307, she was running seven minutes late.

"Mrs. Mallory? This is Detective Faye with the NYPD."

The door opened to reveal a towering woman dressed in a gray pantsuit who bore a striking resemblance to a raven. She had twisted her matte black hair into a tight bun at the nape of her neck. Beady brown eyes glared at Lily over the top of rectangular glasses, which rested halfway down the bridge of the woman's squash-shaped nose.

"You're late and I have other business to attend to," Mrs. Mallory said in an unyielding tone and shut the door with a resounding snap.

Lily blinked at the slab of wood a few times, her lips parted in surprise. After the initial surprise faded, she withdrew her phone and watched the time change to five thirty-eight. Then, she put her phone away, counted to ten, and knocked again.

"Mrs. Mallory? I am so sorry. Trust me: I'm usually the only punctual person in my department. I just came from another interview that ran later than I'd hoped. I'll only take a few minutes of your time and be out of your hair before you know it."

"She's not coming in now," the woman snapped from the other side, sounding further away from the door.

"Mom, she's just trying to help. And you already told her you'd do the interview," a male voice chimed from the other side. "Just let her ask questions like we planned and we'll have her out in no time."

The pair argued in hushed but forceful whispers after that. It continued for so long that Lily turned and almost stepped away when she heard footsteps thudding closer on the other side. She turned back and stared at the door as it opened, a slow and hopefully calming breath filtering in through her nose. Along with it wafted a startling scent of bleach and a floral laundry detergent, which poured out of the apartment without the thick wooden barrier standing in its way.

"I'm so sorry about that," a smooth-skinned, brown-haired, teenage boy said with a grimace of a smile as he stepped aside to let her in. "She thinks if people aren't on time, they shouldn't bother showing up. It's not personal."

"A philosophy I completely agree with," Lily said. "This was out of my control, unfortunately." The smell almost gagged her as she stepped fully into it. "Can I ask why the apartment smells like the washing machine threw up?"

"Yeah, sorry about that," he said and rubbed the back of his neck. "Mom goes kind of crazy on cleaning days. I've been trying to air it out but it's too cold to keep the windows open. It's a little better in the kitchen, though," he assured and indicated there, his eyes not quite meeting hers. "She's ready to talk to you in there."

Here, the stinging scent of lemon only muddled the air more. A low throbbing took residence in Lily's sinuses and made her determined to keep this interview as short as possible.

"Thank you for seeing me, Mrs. Mallory. I do apologize for the tardiness. I'm sure you can understand how hectic the workday can become."

"I do," the woman said in a tone chillier than the city's air in the midst of winter. She took a seat at the small, round kitchen table and chastised, "That is why I create buffers if I think appointments may run longer than expected."

"Yes, and I usually do that," Lily said in an unflinching tone of her own. "Now, I have some questions to ask and I'd like to do so quickly, so I don't waste anymore of your time."

Mrs. Mallory's eyes widened, although her eyebrows remained frozen in place and no wrinkles appeared on her forehead. Her lips plumped as if being pressed together, although no lines appeared around the corners of her mouth. Her expression might have betrayed shock and indignation if what Lily suspected to be ample doses of Botox hadn't frozen the woman's features in place.

"Please recount in as much detail as possible what you saw the night of the homicide," Lily said as walked in to stand in front of Mrs. Mallory.

"I was still awake finishing work. Some of us aren't asleep while important things happen."

"I'm aware. I wasn't asleep at the time, either," Lily stated and crossed her arms over her chest.

Mrs. Mallory stared but said nothing more.

The teenager shifted away from the doorframe, which creaked in relief. "Uh, can I get you a drink?" he asked as he stepped further into the room and reached toward the refrigerator.

"No thank you," Lily said without breaking Mrs. Mallory's power-tripping gaze.

Without warning, a pair of hands clamped onto Lily's shoulders and wrenched her toward the floor. Pain split across her skull as she slammed against the sharp edge of the counter on the way down, and a warm, thick liquid began to drip down her forehead as she crumpled on the floor. Her vision flickered gray for a few seconds as her stomach roiled and bile filled her throat.

Mrs. Mallory jumped to her feet, the image of her drenched in red through Lily's eyes; it took the detective a moment to realize she was looking at the entire scene through a curtain of her own blood.

"What the hell was that?!" the mother shrieked as she leapt to her feet and grabbed hold of her son's shirt in two large fistfuls. "You were supposed to knock her out!"

That was all Lily needed as far as cause went. She stayed where she was but drew her gun and trained it between the pair. She had to squint at them through one eye, the other closed to protect it from the blood sliding off her brow and splattering into miniature starbursts on the white tile.

"Sit down! Both of you!" she barked, then paused long enough to swallow away the threat of throwing up. "I am fully within my rights to shoot given that you just assaulted a police officer, and I will not hesitate. SIT!"

Aiden scuttled back to the table and sat straight-backed in the chair, hands half raised. His face turned ashen as he looked to his mother with wide eyes. On the other hand, his mother stayed where she was.

"As a respected member of this community, I have to ask you to leave!" Mrs. Mallory said, her face purpling. "You can't come in here with your gun and—!"

"Ma'am, with all due respect, shut the bloody hell up," Lily snapped.

She kept her weapon raised in her left hand while she fumbled for her cell phone with the right. She hit the last number she'd called and put it on speaker.

"Officer Stilinski."

"It's Faye. I need backup at the Montview Apartments, unit 3-0-7," Lily snapped. "Dispatch an ambulance, too."

"Shit. What happened? Who's hurt?"

Lily didn't want to stay on the phone for too long and detract attention from her assailants, so she gave a clipped response before she hung up.

"I am."

.8.

BOOKED

"Faye, what the hell did you get yourself into?" Stilinski asked as he approached the back of the ambulance, where Lily had taken up residence sitting on the bumper.

The detective held her head still but let her gaze sweep sideways to land on him. She snorted, then grimaced as the paramedic swabbed a pad of peroxide-soaked gauze across the wet, shining red line across her forehead. Her jaw clenched tight, muscles visibly straining until the paramedic removed the irritant.

"Trust me, I've been asking myself that since that prat in the back of my car snuck up on me," she grumbled and relaxed her stiff posture as her attendant prepped a needle and suture thread. "Witness's damn son has a record and an apparent grudge against the police. When he heard I was coming back to interview his mum, he evidently decided knocking me out would be a bloody genius move. I've no clue what he intended to do after, but I don't think he thought that far ahead. Anyway, the idiot pushed me into the counter and this happened," she waved in the general direction of her head. "Answer something for me: if you're going to try to knock somebody out, don't you think you would try a more foolproof method than pretending to trip and then shove them into the counter?"

"Sure. You want me to draw him a diagram or something?" he joked and crossed his arms.

She shot him the closest expression she could manage to a glare, which only meant pursing her lips. She couldn't furrow her eyebrows as she normally would, too aware of the fragility of her open wound.

"Ha ha. Do me a favor and take his mum's statement?"

"You got it, Detective," he nodded. "Which one is she?" He glanced around and spotted the woman hysterically promising her son that his father would bail him out "Okay. Never mind. Is she...crying? Her face isn't moving."

"Yeah, I suspect ample amounts of Botox are the culprit there. Good luck with that nutcase," she grumbled before the paramedic warned her to hold still and started stitching the wound up.

Lily remained as silent and statuesque as she could while the needle and thread darted through her skin. The prickling of its movement seemed dull compared to the pulsing headache she now had, but she still looked around to seek a distraction from the pain. A white hot searing flared behind her eyes when she tried to scan the scene. She closed them instead and turned her mind toward the next steps she and Stilinski needed to take.

First, Aiden would be processed at the station. Lily needed to take ample amounts of ibuprofen before she would be able or willing to conduct the inevitable interview after that. She personally saw no trace of the nice young man Mrs. Hamilton described in this kid and she wanted to find out which of the women's impressions of him were correct. Then, there was the obvious concern: he fit one of the many physical descriptions of their murder suspect that the officers collected. That fact paired with the assault of the police officer assigned to the homicide case gave her nothing but reason for further suspicion. For the time being, this made him suspect number one.

She doubted this homicide was that simple. The adage about the first forty-eight hours being the most important had always held true in past investigations, but she had never encountered such a strong suspect in the first twenty-four. She expected the killer to begin making mistakes after he proved how spooked he was with the first threat, but not to the extent that he got himself arrested. As much as she wanted to believe the killer was in custody, she had a much more logical awareness that her interactions with Jessica Anderson's murderer had barely begun.

Stilinski walked back over after as the paramedic tied off the stitches. His entire face had taken on a strange shade of purple and his nostrils flared as he growled, "How much does it take until I can arrest her, too?"

"Take her in."

A nagging thought reminded her that this would double her paperwork, but she didn't care. It could wait until tomorrow, anyway. All she wanted to do was give her statement regarding the attack and go home.

"Do we have cause enough to book her?" he asked. "I guess I could get her on disorderly conduct alone, huh?"

"Just add it to the list of the charges. I've had cause for a while," she said. "That attack was premeditated. They were discussing it before I even came in, but it was vague enough that I thought they meant something much less sinister. They knew what they were doing when I walked in. Just be quick with it, yeah? I want this wrapped up so I can go home."

She stood and extended her hands to either side of her in anticipation of the blood rushing back out of her brain. Everything around her wobbled for several seconds before the dizziness abated and allowed her to see straight again. After a deep breath, she walked with Stilinski to her car.

"Let's book them at the station and then you can take them to the jail, if you don't mind?" she requested.

"Yeah, that's fine. I'll be right behind you," he said and removed his cuffs from his utility belt.

Lily walked around to the left side of the car and watched Stilinski read Mrs. Mallory her Miranda rights from the small card all officers carried. He handcuffed and guided her back to his car, despite her booming threats to get a lawyer involved. As with the first incident that occurred outside this apartment complex, a number of faces pressed against open windows in the building to watch the scene.

Given the apparent curiosity for an incident which occurred in broad daylight instead of under the disguise of darkness, Lily wanted to find out if anyone in Montview thought to call the police this time. Were more people willing to report incidents involving the police than they were to report cold-blooded murders committed by civilians? When she and Stilinski arrived at the station, she stepped out of her car and looked over at him.

"Hey, do you know if dispatch got any calls about the Mallorys before I asked you to alert an ambulance?"

"Not before I had them send it out," Stilinski answered through a grimace. "But we got two other calls over the radio while I was on my way."

"What were the other two calls?" she asked.

She suspected she knew, but couldn't have prepared herself for the idiocy of the answer.

"They were noise complaints from the neighbors," Stilinski scowled.

"Noise complaints?" she exploded, her eyes bulging in disbelief. "Bloody noise complaints? Literally nobody in the damn apartment complex called while a woman was being butchered in the street, but they're happy to complain about noise? Are you bloody kidding me?"

As always, Stilinski took a calmer approach.

"Faye, we don't know what made them decide to call. Maybe they're trying to be cautious after the homicide," he pointed out. "Or maybe they just learned their lessons after we canvassed for four hours in the middle of the night."

"They damn well better have! Because there is no bloody excuse for their behavior, then or now!"

Stilinski stared at her for a few seconds while she panted out her righteous anger.

"You sound like you could use a break."

"You have no idea," she muttered and glanced to her phone. "I have a couple more hours, though."

"Come with me to the jail, then. We can stop at Starbucks on the way back for decaf coffee," he offered and grinned. "Maybe we can find more people for you to yell at so we can let off some steam."

The anger melted off her like butter in a hot cast iron skillet. Its dissipation caused her lips to flick upward before she said, "Fine. You're lucky you know the magic word. Let's get these two processed and transferred. Then Starbucks. Think they'll let me in covered in blood?"

"It's not that bad," he assured as he walked to the back doors of the car to gather Mrs. Mallory. "Just a little on your shirt. Keep your jacket on and you should be fine."

Lily nodded and went back to her task as well. Processing the mother and son took longer than she wanted, and putting the duo in the back of the same car to move them was an absolute nightmare. Mrs. Mallory's legal threats only ceased to give Aiden sharp warnings not to say anything until they could call his father. By the time Lily and Stilinski dropped the two off and got back in the car, Lily felt like her head had split open all over again.

The officer and detective sank into their seats in the car and sat, unmoving.

"Holy shit," Stilinski said at last.

"I've never hated two people more," Lily uttered, her numbed gaze fixed on a scratch on the dashboard.

"Yeah… that was rough."

"I need coffee."

"Decaf," Stilinski reminded. "I don't know much about head wounds but I don't think you're supposed to have caffeine this soon after an injury."

"Yeah," she grimaced and closed her eyes. "That's fine. It's more a comfort thing at this point."

Stilinski took the cue and started the car again. He drove to the nearest Starbucks in silence while Lily closed her eyes and tried to ride out her headache. He let her sit in the car while he ducked into the shop, purchased their drinks, and slid back into the car. With coffee in hand, she started to fill him in on the incident while he drove back to the station. By the time she finished discussing her theories, they were once again situated at her desk with their chairs pointed toward one another.

"So? What do you think?" she asked at last, and then punctuated the end of her turn speaking by taking a sip of her now lukewarm drink.

Stilinski sat back, his eyes widened as he drew in a slow breath and rolled his shoulders. He licked his bottom lip before saying, "I think… you need a nice, calm day for once."

"No kidding," she muttered. "This wasn't even supposed to be a busy day. That's tomorrow."

"What the hell are you doing tomorrow?"

"I have character interviews with Anderson's roommate and her father," she grimaced. "Her roommate didn't seem concerned at all and her father is a grieving mess."

"They both sound like they're going to suck. Which one's harder for you?"

"The latter, which is unfortunate since I come across it a lot," she said. "I have plenty of experience with death, but getting straight answers out of people consumed by grief? It's so hard to be sympathetic and straightforward. I'm good at one or the other, not both."

"Yeah, it's rough. It's almost like you know more of what you don't want to say than what you think you can say, right?"

"Exactly."

"Well, I'm sure you'll figure something out. You're better at a lot of things than you think you are," he smiled. "But as far as today goes, I'll back your theory up with the Chief if you want to press charges against those whackos. It makes a lot of sense."

"It does, doesn't it? I just wish I knew the motivation.

9.

SELF-DEFENSE

The station door barely closed behind Lily on Thursday before three different voices called for her. A wobbly groan slipped from her lips as she peered around and tried to associate faces with the voices. Maggie. Harris. The Chief. Her head throbbed with every name or title that popped into her head.

"Bloody h—okay. One at a time. Preferably whoever has coffee for me," she grumbled.

"No coffee, but mine's quick," Maggie, the receptionist, piped up. "Alyssa Spencer keeps calling for you."

Lily squinted at the woman. "Do I know an Alyssa Spencer?"

"That reporter? She called before you and Officer Stilinski went to see Charlie on Tuesday."

"Oh," Lily bristled and shuddered the feeling away. "Send her straight to my voicemail if she calls again. I'll get to it when I get to it. Harris," she glanced to her right at the detective. "What've you got?"

"Case report summary from Jordan. He's off until Sunday, so he wanted to make sure it got to you," Harris said as he handed the folder to his supervisor.

Lily flipped it open to verify it contained all the necessary portions of the report. Harris had a proclivity for fulfilling a task only in its technical requirements. There were few times he adhered to the law of common sense, and she was unsurprised to find this was another one of those instances. The folder he'd provided contained only the two-page report summary from Jordan.

"Hang on. Harris, where are the rest of the reports?" she asked. "The ones Jordan used to compile this summary?"

Harris pivoted on the heel of his foot to face her again. His sharp eyes darted to the file, then to her, then back to the file. His shoulders jerked up in a half shrug, and the motion caused his entire ferret-like frame to sway.

"Not sure, boss."

Lily pursed her lips and said nothing.

The silence rooted Harris to the spot, although he held his own silence as long as he could. He began to fidget with the handcuffs on his belt three seconds in, and he broke the silence five seconds after that.

"Well, I mean, I have some idea, maybe. I just don't know if I can get to them since Jordan isn't here," he started to justify.

"I'm sure what you really mean is that you've placed every last one of the reports back in the box on my desk, and that I'll find them the second I walk over there," she said in a stern tone that brokered no alternative. "Because the only other conclusion I can draw is that you've stolen official police records and tried to lie to me about it, which would be stupid enough to do even if I was fully awake and had already ingested several cups of coffee. You're a smart bloke, though, aren't you? Which is why I know the files are on my desk. Is that correct, Detective Harris?"

He dropped the handcuffs and his head snapped up to meet her gaze. He looked from her to the Chief and raised his hands to waist level, his palms facing upward as if physically holding a silent question: aren't you going to do something about her? When Alcarez only crossed his arms and shook his head, Harris's lips tightened into a guilty grimace. He faced his direct supervisor again but stared at the floor while he nodded.

"They're on your desk, just like you said. All of them," he said in a sour, waning tone before he scurried back toward their shared workspace.

Lily rolled her eyes and turned toward the Chief.

"He's a moron."

"He's your moron," Alcarez pointed out and turned away from her. "You picked him."

"I inherited him. Do not make me responsible for that," she said as she followed him back to his office. "What's up?"

"Just wanted to confirm what happened last night," he said as he walked behind his desk and took a seat. "Stilinski gave me his report, but he only knows what happened after the noise complaints were called in."

"Don't remind me about those damn noise complaints. What is wrong with the residents in that building?"

"Beats me. You know them better than I do, especially the Mallorys."

"Yeah, them," Lily said, the muscles in her jaw flexing. "They're bloody brilliant to work with."

"They sound like stand-up citizens, planning an attack on a police officer. Walk me through it."

"I was running late because I booked two interviews back to back," she explained as she took a seat and touched a ginger hand to the stitching on her head. "I inevitably got held up during the first one, but I was only seven minutes late when I showed up at the Mallory residence. I knocked. Mrs. Mallory answered. She made an incredibly snide comment about how valuable her time was and slammed the door in my face."

"She sounds nice."

"Right? A real gem from the get go," Lily agreed and dropped her hand to rest on her lap. "That was when I heard her son on the other side of the door, convincing her to let me in. I wrote the exact words in my own report—I'll get you a copy of that soon—but he said something to the effect of, "let's answer her questions and get her out." Of course, I took that to mean he wanted to cooperate so they could get the interview over with sooner. But I clearly misread that. I was inside the apartment all of sixty seconds before he cracked my head open."

"And you have no idea why he attacked you like that?"

"Can't find a motive yet, but I haven't really had time to look into it. I'll run background checks on both of them today."

"Pass it off to Stilinski and tell him to take their statements, too. We'll let him deal with their lawyer. I don't want you to pull your focus off this homicide," the Chief waved it off before asking, "So what happened after Ms. Mallory let you inside?"

"Aiden, her son, was the one who let me in," she said. "Mrs. Mallory was pouting in the kitchen by then. I walked in and told her flat out that I didn't have time for it and I was there to get answers she had previously agreed to give me."

"Good for you."

"Thanks. So I started to question her about what she saw on the night of the homicide. She wouldn't answer me, so her son broke the awkward silence by asking me if I wanted anything to drink. He started walking toward the fridge, I thought. I said I didn't need anything. I was focused on Mrs. Mallory so I dismissed that he was still walking. I thought he was getting himself something to drink now that he'd made the offer to me. But he wasn't going to the fridge at all. He grabbed my shoulders, stuck his foot in front of mine, and shoved me. I fell forward and hit my head on the counter on my way to the floor. The idiot thought I would be knocked out by then, so he wasn't expecting me to make a countermove."

"And is that when you pulled the gun?"

"Yes, sir. I only did it after I'd been attacked," she assured. Lily turned pink and picked at her cuticles to avoid looking at him. "It was warranted and completely defensible. If I didn't think Aiden would try something again, I wouldn't have pulled it. But I didn't know if he was about to grab a knife and come at me after that, you know? Not to mention I was compromised. I couldn't see out of one eye because of all the blood. I just didn't want to take a chance that either one of them were going to continue the attack."

"You're not in trouble here, Faye. I just want to make damn sure that every time we're so much as touching our weapons, we have a reason for it that'll hold up in court. "

Lily nodded. She could understand the caution, given society's hostility toward the police. She had seen many an officer's reputation and career ruined in recent years because of the frenzy caused by media releasing partial information on an incident. Aiming a fully loaded Glock at a kid's head was grounds for immediate dismissal if she couldn't prove that they was a legitimate threat to her own life. Even then, the right reporter could take her down, so the Chief's caution was well justified.

"Like I said, they premeditated the attack. I don't know what else I could have done while I was trying to see through the wave of blood running down my face, especially if I wanted to detain the kid."

"Good point," he exhaled. He grated his sandpaper-rough hands against his face before adding, "You know I'll stand behind you no matter how this plays out. So far, we're okay but if that reporter who's been bugging you hears about what you've been up to and puts the wrong spin on it…"

"I know," Lily cut him off. "Trust me, sir, I don't want that happening any more than you do. Actually, I probably want it less than you do."

"I'm not going to start an argument about that," he said, "but I do want you to remember to be careful if you decide to talk to that reporter at all. Your PR work isn't the best."

"Okay, that's not fair. I snapped at one guy two years ago and that's the memory that stuck. I've had good interviews since then!"

"You've had better interviews since then. Not good enough ones to let you off the hook for that comment," the Chief warned. "Just be careful. Especially with the spotlight this investigation's been getting."

"I'll do my best," she agreed. "I wanted to talk about that, while I'm here. I think this is going to happen again."

"Another murder?"

Lily bobbed her head up and down twice before a fresh stinging poked around her wound. "I can't say why I think it. I don't have any evidence. But this was too calculated to only happen once. The killer's MO goes so far beyond excessive. He didn't want her dead; he wanted to play with her. I don't think that kind of killer usually stops after one."

A black cloud seemed to shade Alcarez's eyes as he looked to the open door. He leaned forward and lowered his voice, the gruff rumble of it carrying just far enough so she could hear.

"I want that intel on the down low. Need to know basis until this happens again. We don't need to be concerning anyone with the idea of a serial killer right now, got it?"

"Yes sir," she said and matched his volume. "It's just a theory anyway, and I hope I'm wrong."

He nodded and sat back to flip her case file shut. "For once, I hope you are, too, Faye. Nobody else knows about this?"

"I haven't told anyone." She'd shared the Kitty Genovese connection with Stilinski but they hadn't done more than mention the possibility of another murder happening in the same manner. She hoped it would be nothing to worry about.

"Good. Keep it that way for now. We don't need to start a firestorm before there's reason to."

"Got it. Let's hope it doesn't get any bigger than this."

"Agreed. You're dismissed, Faye. Let me know what happens with those interviews."

"You got it," she said and walked out.

The Chief was right. If there was a serial killer on the loose, telling people would only spark a frenzy. News traveled at the speed of light around here, and the last thing she needed to do was start a riot in a city that never seemed to stop rioting.

10.

ADVANCES

By the time Derek's interview slot rolled around, Lily had stopped answering her phone. It was standard procedure for Maggie to call the officers to let them know when their appointments arrived, but she had already tried connecting Lily with the Spencer woman so many times in the past hour that Lily started ignoring all her calls. The detective had nothing to tell the press about the homicide, anyway. So when the phone rang again and she saw Maggie's name pop up, she sent it straight to voicemail.

The hope that her simple action would resolve the matter lasted a maximum of two and a half minutes, at which point the secretary walked back to the detectives' area herself. She stood beside Lily's desk with her hand on her hips and tapped her foot until Lily acknowledged her.

"You might be the only person in the world who actually taps their foot. Please stop."

"Fine. I just thought you might like to know your nine-thirty is here," Maggie snubbed.

Lily's gaze rocketed over to the woman. "Seriously? You couldn't just say that instead of tapping your foot?"

"I tried calling you and you didn't seem to be interested in that, either. Forgive me for thinking you had ten seconds to speak to the lowly little servant at the front desk," the girl huffed and spun on her heel before walking away.

Lily took a deep breath to temper a retort. It was never a good idea to piss off the secretary, especially when she had just been doing her job.

"I'm sorry I didn't answer your calls, Maggie. I'll try to watch out for them."

She followed Maggie to the front of the station and ignored the woman's pointed silence. She knew she would have to answer for that later with another apology, but for the time being, Lily turned her attention to the dark-skinned male sitting in the row of chairs to the left of the entrance.

"Mr. Williams? I'm Detective Faye," she introduced and held out her hand to shake. "Thank you so much for coming down on such short notice."

"Yeah, no problem," Derek said as he stood up and shook her hand. "I hope I can help."

"Any information you can provide will be greatly appreciated," she said. "Let me show you to one of our interview rooms. Can I get you a cup of coffee or anything?"

"No, thanks. I'm good," he assured. "I'm not a big coffee guy unless I need the caffeine while I'm at work or something."

"Ah, understood. It's just as well. The coffee sucks here," she smiled as she led him back to their block of interview rooms and opened one. "Where do you work?"

"Down at the Malibu Diner in Chelsea," he said. "It's a temporary gig until I can get something published."

"You're a writer?" she asked and indicated for him to take a seat at the table.

Of course he was an aspiring writer who worked at a diner for the time being. Aspiring artists waiting tables seemed to make up most of New York City's citizens.

"Yeah, but probably not the kind you're thinking about," he said as he took a seat. "I write academic papers and attend conferences to present my research."

"Oh, wow. Definitely not the kind I was thinking of," she admitted. "Is that a lucrative enough career so you could eventually stop working at the diner?"

"Not necessarily. Not on its own, anyway. But if your papers are accepted at conferences, you can get either schools or the conference organizers to pay for your trip," he explained. "It probably won't pay my rent, but it's a great way to get some free travel."

"I suppose it would be if you're willing to put in the work to get the papers accepted," she said. "That's impressive. You must be a highly logical thinker, then."

"I am," he nodded.

"That works out well for me. I think we'll understand each other better, since we think on the same track." She sat and withdrew her phone from her pocket. "Do you mind if I record this?"

Derek shook his head. "Not at all."

"Thanks. Makes it a little easier to go over your notes later when you're dealing with a high volume of interviews," she said as she navigated to the necessary app and hit record. "Which I anticipate, given the amount of attention the case is getting."

"Yeah, those reporters are being a real pain in the ass," he agreed. "A couple of them came into work yesterday trying to get a statement. I didn't want to say anything until I spoke to you."

Lily glanced up at him with a soft smile. "I really appreciate that caution. Of course, you're as free to speak with them as you'd like, but I'm sure you know how difficult their interferences can be to work around."

"Oh, yeah. I'd be fine not talking to any of them," he said. "That's not the kind of publicity I want."

"Understood," she said. "Well, let's get down to work, hmm?"

"That sounds great," he agreed.

"Excellent. So what can you tell me about Jessica? How did you two end up as roommates?"

"I put up a wanted ad on the bulletin board in the diner," he explained. "You know what the city is like. When you first move here, you barely have any money saved up and you have all these dreams of hittin' it big on one try, because all you hear about New York City are the success stories. The idealist stuff. That's what I was going off when I moved here. I was good with my studio apartment for a couple of months and then realized that all of a sudden, I could only afford to eat or pay rent, not both. So I had to start looking for a roommate."

"I'm sure," Lily said, grateful she had found a townhouse far enough outside the city that she didn't have to deal with the insane rent prices. "So Jessica answered your ad?"

"Yeah. The diner's a pretty popular place with other college kids, so I had a lot of applicants."

"Really? What made you decide on Jessica, then? How did you go about narrowing that down?"

"Well, the applicants may have been desperate for a place, but I had a little more wiggle room to be picky. I had a deadline but I could see as many people as I wanted. And I ended up interviewing way too many because of that. I got so sick of meeting people who wanted to walk through my place that I said fuck it and accepted the next person I got a call from. That was Jessica."

"As luck would have it."

"I doubt it was luck," he mused. "But whatever it was, I was glad for. Jessica was a great roommate."

"Really? In what ways?"

"We got along pretty well right off the bat, but we worked pretty much opposite shifts," he said as he sat back and crossed his arms over his chest.

"She's a night owl—or was, I guess. I'm a morning person. Our work shifts reflected that. If she wasn't working, she was at school, anyway. So we didn't see each other much but at least when we did, we didn't have any problems. She cleaned up her messes and I cleaned up mine."

"And how long were the two of you roommates?"

"Almost two years. When my lease ran out, we didn't really talk about renewing it. We both sort of decided we liked the arrangement and didn't want to leave it." His chin dipped toward as he licked his chapped lips. "We were going to have to renew it again at the end of May. And now I've got to find someone else."

Lily noted an acidic undertone in his last statement. A sympathetic half-smile formed on her lips as she studied him, although he didn't look up at her during in the silence. Did he realize how callous he sounded, considering the brutal way his roommate of nearly two years had been killed? Maybe that was due to his linear mindset, but, much like their phone call, she found his lack of response disconcerting. The closest thing to an emotion she could deduce from him was irritation.

"Only a month or so early," she said. "Surely you've been thinking about it?"

"Not really. Like I said, we had an unspoken agreement to continue living together until something prevented it. I didn't anticipate that something being murder."

"I don't think most people would be able to predict this."

"No. I guess I just thought we'd only stop living together once I got a girlfriend and had her move in or something."

"And if that had happened while you and Jessica were living together, would you have moved out or asked Jessica to?"

"No, I think we would have asked Jessica to move out. It was my place to start with, you know?"

"Of course. I suspect the outcome would have been the same had Jessica been the one to marry first?"

"Yeah, but I don't know how likely that was," he shrugged. "I've had a couple girlfriends over the years but she never brought anyone home. Don't think she had much time with the way she was working."

"How do you mean?"

"It's like I said earlier. She was either at school or work. I didn't really know her to do much else. She never mentioned a guy. Usually when we talked, she was venting about work or about whatever one of her classmates was annoying her with at school. I told her she should cut back or she was going to burn herself out, but she was always so stubborn, you know? Liked having the extra money from picking up overtime shifts, even if it meant she was falling asleep in class the next day. She just liked to work."

If another officer had stepped onto the other side of the viewing glass and started listening at this point in the conversation, they might have believed Derek was speaking about Lily instead of his deceased roommate. She knew she was the definition of a workaholic; most of the time, she didn't consider herself truly on a case until the Chief had to threaten to terminate her if she didn't go home and get some rest. She preferred to be awake and busy over sleeping and idle. She was always running.

She still refused to admit to anyone, even herself, what she was running from.

"Besides, I think she was asexual."

Lily's eyebrows flicked high onto her forehead.

"What brought you to that conclusion? Did she ever speak to you about it?"

"Nah. That's not the kind of thing you tell someone you don't know that well, even if you are living with them. But she would say things sometimes, just small comments, that made it seem like she wasn't interested in the idea of sex."

"Well, that's certainly not the only facet of asexuality, but you're right; it could be an indicator," she nodded.

She didn't know enough about it to say much more, but that was good information to have. If the murderer tried to make a move on Jessica and she had spurned the advance due to her sexuality, that might have served as motive.

"She never complained about anyone hitting on her, did she? Maybe at school or work?"

"She worked in a bar. Every time I saw her, she complained about some drunk idiot staring at her chest and asking her out. Most of it just sounded like drunk talk, though. The kind of stuff you can't remember saying the next day."

"Are you describing drunk talk from personal experience or observations of others?"

"Both, I guess. I studied hard in undergrad but it was college in one of the most populated areas in the U.S. You couldn't get out of there without going to a few parties and doing some stupid stuff."

"The typical university experience," she said with a small smile.

It hadn't been hers, though; she was still living at home with her parents at the time and worked whenever she wasn't in school.

"Basically. The party scene. Anyway, I guess she always seemed kind of agitated but never worried someone was going to act on it. It didn't sound like she ever took them seriously."

Lily tapped her finger on the desk, the noise filling the room like the steady ticking of a metronome. Perhaps Jessica had never expected her customers to be serious about it, but it was easy for alcohol-fueled ideas to become drunken actions. This was a good trail to start on, at least while she had few other trails to lead her to suspects.

"Did she mention any of her regulars? I expect there are plenty to go around in a bar."

"I bet there are, but I'm not sure. I can't remember her mentioning anyone by name," he confessed. "I can give you the number of her manager, though. He's the one who worked with her most, so he would probably know about that stuff a lot more than I would."

"That would be brilliant. Thank you," she said. "Go ahead and tell me what it is when you're ready. I'll review it on the tape when I need it."

He provided her with the contact information, checked his watch, and asked if she needed to know anything else. They had a brief conversation in which Derek revealed that Jessica wasn't a party-goer but that didn't hinder her ability to be well-liked on campus. Once that concluded, Lily pushed her seat away from the table and stood.

"I think that's all I have for you for now, Derek. Thank you again for coming in. I'll give you a call if we need anything else."

"Yeah, please do. If you need to take a look around the apartment or anything, let me know, too. I think her dad's coming by to pack her stuff up tomorrow, but I'll work something out if you want to come by."

"Thank you. I'll let you know if we end up needing to take a look." She didn't anticipate it but if she had no other options or needed solid evidence against a suspect, she would know where to begin looking for hints first.

She walked him back to the front desk so he could sign out. While he was doing so, he glanced over at her. He looked back down, finished signing out, and thanked her again for the interview.

"And if you need anything else… information on Jessica, or even someone to hang out with… feel free to call," he said, fixing her with an unyielding gaze so intense, it almost made her squirm. "Like I said, I'm willing to help however I can. And hey, if you're ever looking for an apartment—."

"I own a place," she cut in before he could take that train of thought any further down the track. "If we need any further assistance, I'll have Maggie schedule another interview."

Derek nodded and let his gaze linger. "Right," he said after a few long seconds of painful silence. "Thanks again, Detective," he said with a ghoulish grin before he walked out of the station.

Lily stayed rooted at the front desk until he disappeared down the street. Only then did she return to her desk, hoping she hadn't just spurned the advances of a cold-blooded killer.

11.

CHALLENGE

The rest of the morning flew by. The interview had only taken an hour, which left Lily more than enough time to prepare another cup of coffee, call the manager of the bar Jessica worked at to set up an interview, and begin reviewing the facts from Derek's interview. She also workshopped several theories before lunch, although none were as obvious as the same old trope that emerged from a myriad of past cases: Jessica may have been killed by a bar patron she'd rejected earlier in the evening while working her last night shift.

The problem with this theory would be tracking down a specific set of patrons. There were sure to be a large number of drunk men in the bar at the time of Jessica's last shift. The only thing Lily could hope for was the manager's consent to look at the security tapes. That way, she could see when Jessica left for the evening and could watch anyone who may have followed her out. There was no guarantee she could track the patron's identity from there, but maybe she could get a better visual on the suspect than the witnesses at Montview had.

The case summary Harris delivered hadn't narrowed down a singular description of the suspect, either. Depending on the angle from which the crime was viewed, witnesses reported that the suspect was either an African American or Caucasian male. Possible heights ranged from five-foot-seven to six-foot-five, and the build fluctuated from athletic to mildly obese. This was why having more than a handful of witnesses per homicide complicated the investigation. With a smaller pool of witnesses, it was generally correct to infer the suspect's physical characteristics fell within the median of the provided descriptions. That rule couldn't be applied in this case, given the extreme range of what the witnesses thought they saw on a dimly lit street in the middle of a rainy night.

"Harris? Can you get me a breakdown of the different suspect descriptions? I need to know how many witnesses reported seeing a white male and how many saw African American."

"If you need me to, Faye. You want me to break down the ratios for height, weight, and hair color, too?"

"Please. Wait—did any of them mention hair color?" she asked with a frown. "That's not in the summary report."

"I didn't get a chance to look all of them over before you asked me to return them," he sneered without looking over at her. "But the first couple described hair color."

Lily frowned. "Yeah, include that and any other identifiers, please. I need the summary and the original reports back by three p.m."

She paused for a response and didn't get confirmation that he actually heard her, so she added, "Got it?" in a sharp tone.

He didn't bother restraining a frustrated huff. "Yes, ma'am," he muttered and stretched his arm toward her for the reports.

Lily pulled it out of reach and waited for him to look at her.

"Harris, I don't know why you've chosen today of all days to let your intolerable attitude problems flare up, but I need it to stop right now. I don't care what kind of issues you may have with me or my leadership. I am here to do my job, which is to solve this homicide as quickly as possible and get a murderer off the streets. Are you here to do that, too, or do we need to reevaluate your role in this station?"

The corner of his lip pulled back over his teeth and his nose wrinkled on one side, as if he were an animal preparing to bare his fangs in a show of dominance. He stared her down for a few seconds, but let the expression melt away once he saw she wasn't relenting. Finally, he straightened up, relaxed his shoulders, and nodded.

"I'm here to do that, too," he grunted.

"Good. Then from now on, you'll address me as your supervisor. Maybe if you can remember you're not in charge, you'll stop walking around like everyone else is inferior to you. We can't function under whatever the hell kind of anarchy you're trying to create, especially right now." She handed over the folder and once again warned, "Three p.m. And don't make copies for your own records later. This is my investigation."

He audibly ground his teeth together as he took the file. "Yes, ma'am," he said again, although his tone lacked the same sarcasm it held previously. "Three p.m.," he added and leaned back toward his computer to get started on the task.

Lily drew herself up straighter in her chair as she set back to her own work as well. She understood Harris's irritation, considering she beat him out for the Head Detective promotion despite being younger and a more junior employee than he was. Adding to the insult of losing out on a promotion, Harris also lost it to someone who had never even served as a detective. When Alcarez had offered here the promotion, he'd warned her that Harris would be difficult to work with in the same breath. Harris lived up to that expectation in a grandiose way. She hated to pull rank so often, but her detective didn't tend to leave her a choice.

Thankfully, with that out of the way, she could get back to work. Now that she didn't have to worry about the breakdown of the suspect's profile by witness, she could focus on the clean-up from the Mallorys' scheme. She pushed herself out of her chair and walked across the station to Stilinski's desk.

"Hey," she said as she leaned back against it and crossed her arms. "Are you doing any follow-up on the Mallorys today?"

"Yeah. I want to head back down to the DOC and get their statements today. Their lawyer should be there, so we can move forward with the charges pretty quickly after that if you want to."

"Great. I have to go to an interview with Anderson's father in a few minutes, but I should be back in time to charge them before that 24 hours is up and they can walk out. I'll call you if I'm not and we can run through the charges so you can take care of that yourself."

"Sounds good. So you are going to press charges, then?"

"Of course I am. Shouldn't I?"

"Yeah, I think so. I was just thinking about which ones. It's assault and battery according to the law, right? It would be one thing if they were just planning to injure you and failed, but they actually managed to." He indicated toward her cut. "That's five to twenty-five just because there's physical damage."

"Five to twenty-five is the best case scenario for us," she agreed with a shadow of hesitation in her voice. "I don't think we'd get much more than the minimum for Aiden, and they'd probably let him out on parole."

"So what's more important?" he asked. "Actually getting him in jail or sending the message that people can't push officers around and expect to get away with it?"

"Ideally, we'd do both," she said. "But if we can only manage one over the other, I suppose I'd rather send the message."

"Exactly. Especially right now. So this looks like the best way to go, no matter what the result is."

"Yeah, that's a good route with Aiden. I'm not sure we can pin Amy Mallory with anything, though."

"I'll worry about her. I'm planning to charge her for criminal threats and resisting arrest," he said. "It might not be much and I doubt she'll get more than a couple months, if that, but I'm not going to sit back and let her think she can get away with this. There's a reason battery escalates to a felony if it's committed against an officer."

"Sends a message to her," Lily nodded. "That's the least she should get. I've been walking around with a migraine all day, thanks to her harebrained son."

Speaking of sending messages reminded her to fire one off to Matt. She wanted to know about the status of his side project, but it wasn't great that she hadn't heard from him yet. Hopefully, he'd just been busy, and not harboring bad news.

"Well, take it easy if you need to," Stilinski warned. "We're not going to resolve anything if you work yourself to death."

"Maybe, but that's only because you don't give yourself any other choice."

"I know," she agreed, but her phone rang and saved her from explaining that taking a break wasn't going to progress anything either. "There's no time for that."

"Whatever you say."

Lily grunted as her phone rang. She excused herself from Stilinski, but only walked a few feet away as she answered it.

"Tell me you have good news for me, Matt."

"Maybe I shouldn't talk, then," the forensic tech answered.

"Nothing yet?" she frowned as she crossed her arms and drummed her fingers against her bicep.

As much as she'd protested that the threats didn't concern her, they did. Someone was trying to mess with her investigation, and there was little to suggest the threats would stop at two. She just hoped they could track the sender down before the killer's behaviors escalated to another murder.

"Looks like this is taking closer to days than hours," he replied. "I'm sorry, Lil. I am working on it."

"I know. That's all I can ask, as long as we get our guy in the end."

"Right. We will," Matt agreed, although he sounded as convincing as an amateur poker player bluffing during the World Series of Poker. "You haven't gotten any more of them, have you?"

"Two in all," she confessed and ran an unsteady hand through her hair. "But nothing new."

"Wait, when did you get the second one?" he demanded.

"I...erm...sort of had it before I brought you the first one," Lily winced. She probably should have told him that sooner. "Trust me, it'll be okay. I'll let you know if more come in."

"Please do. I'll let you know when I find something."

"Thanks. Talk to you then," she said and hung up before stepping back to Stilinski's desk.

Stilinski glanced to her, brows furrowed but eyes wide with curiosity. To his credit, he didn't pry. He did keep looking back to his computer and then peering at her, though. The looks only increased as the silence did.

"Just a separate thing," she said at last to put him at ease.

"I didn't ask."

"Subtext."

"Still didn't ask."

"Good. There's nothing to tell."

"Right. So we're agreed about pressing charges?"

"Yep," she nodded. "No need to wait until I get back from my interview, then."

"Will do."

"Great." She checked the time on her phone and said, "All right. I should probably head to the interview. I've got to make it to Penn Station in the lunch rush."

"Yikes. You might already be late," he said as he stood up to collect his jacket. "Let me know how it goes."

"Will do," she echoed and then walked out to her car.

She arrived at the Starbucks near Penn Station with only a few minutes to spare and strode in, taking a look around. Michael Anderson wasn't difficult to locate. He had managed to stake claim to two chairs in the corner along the front window by hunching over them. He had a salt and pepper five o'clock shadow and matching eyebrows that stuck out every which way along his forehead. His hair was as disheveled as the rest of his clothing, and he gave off the same general vibe as that of a homeless man. Something about his posture, his wrinkled and casual clothes, and his bedraggled appearance made him look like he would be more comfortable huddled around a trash can fire than sitting in the middle of a coffee shop crowded with business people and college students.

Lily set her gaze on him and took a deep breath. She cleared her throat and sidled over to him.

"Mr. Anderson? I'm Detective Faye."

The sooner she initiated the conversation, the sooner she could get it over with.

12.

THE WHOLE TRUTH

"She was a good kid, you know," Mr. Anderson hiccupped fifteen minutes later over a steaming venti green tea. "Not a straight A student or anything, but just as good as. Smart as a whip. She was going to school to be a professor."

Lily didn't understand why parents always mentioned their kids' grades in direct correlation to how morally upstanding they were. Perhaps they thought it demonstrated the existence of some kind of value system in their children, but Lily had seen too many intelligent criminals to believe grades had anything to do with being a "good" person. Still, the school aspect of Jessica's life introduced a new pool of potential suspects to the case. Now that the detective had an opening, she pursued the line of thought.

"She's been in school for quite a while, hasn't she?" she asked as she warmed her hands on her venti macchiato. "I imagine she's been away from home for a while?"

"Not really. Just away from me," he explained in a low, moping whine as he picked at the corner of a napkin sitting between the two. "Her mother and I divorced when she was in high school. I moved across the country to be closer to my parents. Jessica and her mother stayed here."

"I'm sorry to hear that," Lily frowned. "When was the last time you saw either of them?"

"I don't think I came back until my ex-wife's funeral," he answered and released the brown shreds of the napkin. He traced the lip of his cup with his index finger and sucked in a wet sniffle before adding, "I should have come back sooner."

"Mr. Anderson, if I can be so bold…" she bit her lip and let out a breath. "You have two ways you can respond to this. Grief is going to be part of the process either way. You can't avoid that. But you can decide if you're going to let regret cripple you or if you're going to find a way to move on, into a life Jessica would have wanted you to have. Nobody else can decide for you, but if I could? I'd suggest the latter."

Silence followed for so long, Lily wondered if he'd fallen asleep. The way he had been squinting out the window ever since they settled in with their drinks made him look like he was unconscious anyway, so it was even harder to tell now. Either way, Lily sat by and waited. She didn't want to interrupt if he was trying to process her advice.

"You're right," he spoke so abruptly and with such conviction that it made Lily jump. "Sorry," he uttered when he noticed her flinch. "Just thinking about it all, you know? Feels like that's all I've been doing lately."

"I'm sure you've had plenty on your mind," she agreed as she steadied herself.

"No kidding," he snorted and lifted a hand to scrape it along his unkempt facial hair. "I meant it. She was a good kid."

"I don't doubt it, sir."

"I was never too happy about her working in that bar, but I knew why she had to do it. We were never a rich family and she was a kid trying to go to college for eight years in New York City. She was going to be a professor, you know. Said one of the noblest things a person can do is be a teacher, especially at that age. 'Cause college kids are so cynical, you know? It makes them apathetic about the world and she didn't want to see that happen anymore."

"I've seen that first hand around here more times than I can count," Lily empathized. "They've moved away from trying to change issues to just complaining about them instead of doing anything. It makes me worry for them hitting the workforce."

"Can't imagine someone in your position acting like that. Nothing would ever get done."

"And with the stakes this high, nobody on this case can afford to act like that. I want justice, Mr. Anderson. I want to find out who did this to your daughter and make sure it never happens again. But I can't do that unless I have a few answers from you. Would you mind helping me out a little? The sooner we find a connection—anything in Jessica's past that may have led to this—the sooner we get one more dangerous person off the streets."

He bobbed his head up and down for a few seconds. The motion stopped long enough for him to gulp his tea, and then resumed when he set it back on the table.

"Yeah. I'll help anyway I can. I want that son of a bitch to rot."

"Then we have something in common. So, what can you tell me about Jessica's classmates? Did you know any of them?"

"Not personally, but she mentioned a few of them when we would speak on the phone. We did that about once a week."

She smiled at him and began to tap her thumb against the cup without registering the movement. "That sounds like a nice tradition."

"It was. Highlight of my week," he said. "She didn't seem to have any lasting problems with any of her classmates, but I could tell you stories all day about who stole whose seat in English last week."

"I'm sure it was abounding every week. Can you recall any individuals she mentioned more than others?"

"As far as classmates? I think she had a few classes with some girl named Jordan that was bothering her. I never got her last name but Jessie was always complaining about her."

"Do you remember the nature of any of these complaints?"

"Nothing too bad. Mostly that she was always hanging around after class or trying to invite herself to visit Jessie at work. I guess she showed up a couple of times, too. Clingy stuff like that. It didn't sound like this girl had many friends."

"Maybe not," she agreed. "I'm sure it's difficult to make friends in a doctorate level class, especially if Jessica already had an established group to hang out with. I don't suppose you remember your daughter mentioning any altercations with male students, though?"

"No. Most of the time, the only guy she talked about was Derek. I think maybe he liked her or something."

Lily perked up at that and searched the man's vacant expression. "What makes you think that?"

"Just the way he was talking to her some days, I guess," he shrugged and continued staring down at a singular spot on his cup with laser focus. "Seemed kind of protective, you know? Which didn't make a whole lotta sense to me. Yeah, they were living together but it wasn't like the place was Jessie's first choice. And he always sorta acted like he was her saving grace or something, like he'd pulled her in off the streets or a shelter, or something. You talk to him already?"

"I did, this morning," she said. Normally, she wouldn't disclose information like that, but telling him might help her determine whether or not she needed to take a closer look at the waiter. "He seemed incredibly blunt. Have you ever spoken to him directly?"

"Nah. I just heard him on the other end of the phone sometimes when he and Jessie were hanging out. They had this running movie night thing, I guess. Jessie would always call me right before it."

Lily straightened up to pull her notebook and pen from her inner jacket pocket. "Movie nights, huh? Do you remember if this was happening every time she called you?"

"Mostly, I think. She told me they did it every week to unwind. Said Derek complained about not seeing his own roommate enough. That's why I thought he liked her. He was always the one saying they didn't spend enough time together."

This side of the story almost fit Derek's narrative, but there were a few red flags. Why did Derek insist he didn't see Jessica enough if they had weekly movie nights? Why hadn't he told the police about this routine? More than that, why had he insisted he and Jessica worked opposite schedules and were never home at the same time? Why insist that he didn't know much about her? If he hung out with her on a regular basis and overheard most of her conversations with her father, he would have known everything about her current life that Mr. Anderson did. Obviously, that wasn't the entire truth.

She would have to have another chat with Derek.

"Thank you, Mr. Anderson. That was really helpful information," she encouraged as she wrote a reminder to speak to Derek again. "Can you think of any other incidents Jessica and Derek may have had?"

"Not really," the man shrugged. "I mean, she was getting ready to move out but I don't think they had any disagreements about that."

"She was?" Lily was under the impression that the living arrangement would have been renewed at the end of May. "Do you know why she was planning to move out? Did she maybe have a partner she was thinking of moving in with instead?"

"Never mentioned seeing anyone when she talked to me, but I guess she could have been. I think she was just getting sick of Derek, and she had a little extra cash from her inheritance from her mother. She always wanted her own place, anyway."

"All right. That's good to know," she nodded and made note of that as well. She'd need to look back into her interview with Derek when she returned to the station. "Can you think of any other instances which could be helpful to the investigation?"

Yet again, the man fell silent for longer than Lily was comfortable with. He finally shook his head.

"Can't think of anything else."

Lily thanked him for his time and let him go on his way. While she made her way back to the station, a single, worrisome thought poked out of the crevices of her mind and began to buzz, louder and louder until she couldn't ignore it.

Muddled as the case was now, it would only get more convoluted from here.

13.

VENGEANCE

The caffeine from Lily's macchiato wore off before she stepped back into the station. She dragged herself inside, kneading at the base of her skull to stop what she hoped was merely a tension headache, and not due to the gash on her forehead or the disproportionate amount of coffee she'd been ingesting in order to stay awake over the past few shifts. Either way, the pain was enough to convince her to avoid interacting with anyone else this afternoon.

If only she had that luxury.

"Faye! Stilinski! My office!"

Lily grimaced and pressed her left hand against her temple. She ambled into the Chief's office and sat down without pausing to remove her coat. Stilinski came in nipping at her heels and followed suit.

"May I just point out that the station is not that big, sir," Lily said, the desperate throes of exhaustion eking into her voice. "The yelling is not necessary."

"My station, Faye. Suck it up," Alcarez warned. "What are you, hungover? Too much wine at lunch?"

"Caffeine headache. Or possibly the remnants of having my head bashed against a kitchen counter. Not sure which."

"Well, get through this next hour and you can take off a little early if you need to," he offered and reached for his phone. He set his hand on it and looked at the two. "Now, I understand you're pressing charges against the Mallorys? Both of you?"

"Yes, sir," Lily nodded.

"I'm charging the mother, sir," Stilinski explained. "Detective Faye is dealing with the son."

"Okay. Then I'm going to call our attorney and get that process started. He'll need you to detail the charges before he can process any paperwork. How much longer until we can't hold the Mallorys anymore?"

Stilinski glanced at his watch and reported, "Another hour, sir."

The Chief nodded and made the call. The conversation with the prosecutor, Mr. Jefferson, was mercifully short. Lily wasn't one to mince words, and Stilinski followed her lead easily enough. Within ten minutes, they provided the lawyer with the charges and set up interviews with the man for the following week. They would discuss the strategy for the court hearing in detail then, but they had plenty of time until their presence would be requested in front of a judge. That was good enough for Lily, who was more than content to let the high-powered Mallorys sit in a small cement cell while she worked on her real case.

"Not a bad day, huh?" Stilinski asked as he stepped out of the Chief's office with Lily.

"Aside from the constant, throbbing reminder that I was temporarily bested by a punk teenager, yeah," she pondered. "It hasn't been a bad day. I got a lot done."

"Good. Anymore leads?"

"Yeah, I need to follow up on a few of them. I got a lot of information from my interviews today. I'm going to review the recordings from those and see if I can find anything good. I'll let you know if I do."

"Sounds good, Faye. Thanks."

Lily returned the sentiment and went back to her desk. A brief search of its drawers produced a small bottle of ibuprofen. She popped two of the coveted pills and chased them down with the freezing, half empty cup of coffee she had left on her desk before lunch. A hair-raising shudder raked down her spine before she set herself back on track. She pulled open the top left drawer and rifled through a stack of crumpled papers and receipts until her hand closed around a thin cord. She tugged until she freed the headphones from the nest they were trapped under and then plugged them into the jack on her phone.

Her recap began with the review of her conversation with Derek. As she listened, she weighed his words against the knowledge gained from Jessica's father. She pulled her notepad and pen out again, meticulously writing out direct quotes that seemed innocent at the time, but now held subtle, darker undertones. As much as she hated to admit it, there were a great deal of them.

Then, there was always the issue of leading the witness. Lily took care to review the questions she asked and the specific wording she used to ensure she hadn't given Derek an opportunity to shed a better light on himself than he deserved. She liked to think she had honed her interview skills well enough to avoid this issue by now, but it was too early in the investigation to place blind faith her skillset. Everything needed to be double-checked.

By the time she made it halfway through the interview, she found her sweet spot. Her determined focus nearly allowed her to forget her headache completely. That was when Harris slid over to her desk with a summary of the file in hand. She paused the recording and pulled one earbud out, but didn't look up at him as she continued to write.

"I thought I told you I wanted those back by three," she stated. "It's four-fifteen."

"Yeah, and there were almost thirty of them to go through. Do you know how long it takes to read thirty case reports?"

"You've had them for eight hours, Harris. Surely, it doesn't take that long."

"It took as long as it took. I've got the summary report written up and the suspect's possible features broken down according to how many witnesses described which features. That's what you wanted, right?"

"I wanted you to do it on the deadline I gave you."

"You're kiddin', right? You were sitting in Chief's office at three, anyway. I couldn't barge in and give 'em to you then!"

"You could have left them on my desk. In the future, that's what I expect you to do. Are we clear?"

Harris dropped the thick folder on top of her mailbox from chest level without aiming. Instead of landing neatly in the box, the folder hit the side and flung it off her desk, taking the rest of her mail with it. He released what sounded like an attempt at a muffled curse before he stooped over to sweep everything up.

Lily finally set her pen down and stood up. She stared down the bridge of her nose at him while he pushed the files and a few loose envelopes back into her box. He set it back on the edge of her desk, smart enough not to comment on the fact that she made no move to help him clean.

"Detective, you are in a professional work environment. If you can't behave like an adult, feel free to clean out your desk and start enrolling in preschools instead of applying for jobs."

Harris stared back at her, eyes wide with a newfound fear born of his own wrongdoing.

"I didn't mean to do that," he admitted as he averted his gaze and clapped his hands together behind his back. His tone was no less defiant than usual as he added, "But I'm sick of these assignments. It's rookie work! I've been here longer than you!"

"And I'm grateful you stayed on when you failed to get the promotion over me," she told him in an even voice that didn't falter when his mouth fell open.

It was the first time she'd openly addressed his performance, but it was long overdue. With a killer like this on the loose, she needed everyone in the department operating at full capacity. There was no time to waste on petty arguments when every second she spent lecturing him was another opportunity the killer had to either escape their grasp or strike again.

Harris didn't feel the same, based on the way he stuttered for several seconds after her accusation. "I-I didn't…b-but…that's… i-it's not what this is about!" he spat at last. His ears colored red and his voice began to rise with his desperate explanation: "I just know I can handle more than grunt work! I'm a detective, for f—."

"And I'm the Head Detective," she cut in. "I assign the work. You do it. If you have a problem with that, take it up with me. Don't pout and throw tantrums like a child."

"I got a lot of problems with you, lady!" he snarled, letting his embarrassment dig him into a deeper hole. "Number one being I should've had your job!"

"But you don't."

"Yeah, probably because I'm not enough of a whore to have slept with the boss to get it!"

His face drained of color so quickly, it looked like someone had thrown him into a black and white television show. He raised a hand in front of him and clamored for a way to take the words back while her expression twisted into an ugly snarl of pure fury. He tried to back away as she stepped around her desk and rounded on him, but he collided with the next desk over and lost balance, careening to the floor.

"That's n-not what I meant!" he sniveled and lifted his arms to cover his head as she raised a hand.

Although she wanted nothing more than to slap him, she settled for pointing. This was her workplace, after all, and he was her subordinate. She'd never been so reassured of the latter fact as in this moment while he cowered away from her, but she was too furious to care. Her eyes blazed with hatred and her lips curled into an inhuman sneer as she leaned over him.

"If I ever hear you so much as insinuate that I got where I am today due to anything other than my own merit and hard work, you are fired. Do I make myself clear, Harris?" she hissed, her voice a mere whisper compared to his declaration of her alleged whoredom.

He nodded so fast he resembled a rag doll flopping in the reckless hold of a young child.

"You are on your last chance in this department. You will not raise your voice to me again. You will meet every damn deadline I tell you to, no matter how ridiculous you think it is. If you can't meet that deadline, you will receive a write-up. I am not going to tolerate your sexist insubordination for another second. And I'll remind you that the reason you don't have my job is not because I slept around for it. It's because you're a dick, Harris. Nobody is ever going to respect you unless you straighten yourself out. So wise up immediately, or leave. This is the last time you will ever get the choice."

With that, she turned away from him. She walked back to her desk and took a seat. After drawing in a calming breath, she folded her hands together and looked up at him.

"Now. I want you to run background checks on Amy and Adrian Mallory. You'll have it to me by the end of the day tomorrow, whether I am sitting at my desk or not. If I'm not here, I want the results emailed to me before six p.m. If they arrive at six-oh-one, you are fired. Do I make myself clear?"

Another frantic nod and an echo of, "Amy and Adrian Mallory."

"Good. Now go back to work."

As Harris scuttled off, she looked around to find the majority of the on duty staff crowding the hallway leading to her area. The second she turned her scathing glare their way, they dispersed like rats fleeing a sinking ship. She noted the Chief shoving his way through the group as he made a quick path for his office.

Only Stilinski remained, grinning at her.

"What?" she snapped.

He laughed and shoved his hands into his pockets. "Nothing," he shrugged and shook his head. "It's just—damn, Faye. That was impressive."

He left her alone then, and she slumped into her chair. Her head dropped against the back of it before a quiet groan tugged from her throat. Thanks to Harris, her headache had returned with a vengeance.

14.

STARK HONESTY

As it turned out, forty-eight hours was not enough time to clear the smell of pot from Kayla Simmons's apartment. Lily could tell by the way the musk assaulted her as she entered the dingy cement hallway of the hostel-styled housing that not even a lifetime of airing out the building would be enough. The sinking feeling that accompanied the understanding of inevitable demise rolled through her stomach as she stepped into Kayla's apartment and realized the hallway smelled like fresh mountain air in comparison to the oversized trash bin she stood in now. This interview needed to be hasty.

The amount of junk stacked in the living room rivaled that of the aftermath of a college party. Somewhere buried under milk crates, boxes, crumpled fast food wrappers, and cigarette butts stood a tattered and stained couch that looked like it had been rescued from the curb on garbage day. Ratty clothing riddled with holes was strewn on every surface, almost blocking a small, boxy, television from view in the corner. A thick hoodie with a gaping hole in the sleeve half covered a suspicious glass pipe sitting on top of an unzipped sleeping bag behind the couch.

"Sorry for the mess," Kayla said as she walked through to the kitchen, every footstep causing a loud rustling noise as she stomped over old wrappers. "I can make coffee if you want."

The last thing Lily wanted to do was contract a disease on the job, which she was sure to do if she ingested anything inside this building. She didn't follow Kayla through the piles of toward the kitchen, but hung back in the living room to gape at the mess. The last time she'd seen this much garbage inside a residence, she had been busting a crack den with her team. After a moment of stupefied staring, she found her voice to answer Kayla's question.

"No, thank you. Where would you like to conduct the interview?"

"Can go out on the balcony if y'want. Not a bad day."

"That sounds great," the detective confirmed, all the while mentally praising God for fresh air. "Lead the way when you're ready," she added in a louder volume to Kayla.

The girl walked back with an open bag of pretzels and tilted it toward Lily. The detective raised a hand to decline and uttered a thanks for the thought. Kayla shrugged and shoved her hand into the bag, digging around for as many twisted pretzels as she could grab. She led the way to the open, screen-less window and ducked out onto the fire escape.

Lily followed suit and leaned against the stone wall of the apartment. It wasn't nearly as warm as Kayla seemed to think it was, but the sun was finally shining through the haze that had threatened rain earlier in the day. She dug into her coat pocket for her phone and asked, as she always did, if Kayla would mind her recording the conversation.

"Fuck yeah, I mind," the woman scowled and started digging into her own pockets. "Don't want any of this shit on tape. Can't you write it down?"

"I can, but again, I'd like to remind you I'm not here to prosecute you," she assuaged as her wary gaze turned to Kayla's hands. "It just helps jog my memory later when I'm trying to put all the pieces together."

"No recording," Kayla asserted as she sat on the fire escape, dropped her bag of pretzels, and tugged a lighter and pack of cigarettes from her coat. "You want a smoke?"

"No thanks," Lily relaxed when she noted the objects in Kayla's grip didn't include a weapon. She put her phone back in her own pocket and amended, "I'll just take notes, if you don't mind."

"That's fine," Kayla said, although she continued to glare until the detective produced a notepad and pen.

"Thank you," Lily said through a tight smile. This was going to be a long interview. "Could you start with your account of what happened the night you found Jessica Anderson on the street?"

"Yeah, sure. If you're not gonna record it."

"I'm not recording, Ms. Simmons."

Kayla lit her cigarette and took a long drag. She puffed it back out as she explained, "I was at a club on West 3rd."

"Oh, yeah," Lily frowned as she tried to recall the unique name of the club she'd seen in passing. "The Pussycat? Something like that, right? I've been."

"Shut the fuck up. *You* go clubbing?" Kayla gawked. "You're a cop!"

"I'm sure lots of cops party," she chuckled. "I don't go all the time, but I had a date once. Anyway, you were there for what kind of occasion?"

"Yeah. A party." Kayla took another drag before continuing, the smoke unfurling from her mouth and floating away in a breeze so slight neither woman could feel it. "So I was there with friends for a while and then they decided to go out back and do a couple lines, so I took off. Not fun anymore once they pull that shit out, y'know?"

Lily nodded without conveying whether she believed Kayla or not, and asked, "Do you remember around what time you decided to leave?"

"I don't have a clue. Pretty early in the morning, I guess. We didn't even get there 'till one, so sometime after that."

"Any sense of how long you were at the party? At all?" The last thing she wanted to do was lead the witness but it had been confirmed that Kayla found Jessica around three a.m., so Lily wanted to trace out Kayla's steps in as much detail as she could before that point.

"Couple hours, maybe? I really dunno. Sorry."

Lily shook her head. "No problem. Just helps establish the timeline. It's not required information. So what happened when you left the party?"

"Started walking home. Pretty nice walk once you get out of the club district. Nice and quiet, you know?"

"I didn't know a quiet place in New York City existed."

"Guess if it gets late enough, it does. I go past a bunch of apartments. There's a nursing home or rehab or something on the way, too, and they all close up real early in the night."

"I see."

"Yeah, but anyway, I heard some yelling. Kinda freaked me out so I stopped and waited until it stopped. Kept walking after I figured it was safe and found the girl."

"Do you remember who you heard yelling? Was it a man or woman?"

"Musta been the girl. Kinda shrill, screaming about being stabbed."

Lily's hand froze as the statement sank in.

"So you heard someone screaming about being stabbed and hung back until it stopped?" she asked.

"Guess so," Kayla sighed.

"Did it occur to you then to call the cops?"

"Nah, not really. I don't remember. But it's the city, you know? That shit happens all the time. I didn't want to get involved. Not like I could help, anyway, and I sure as hell didn't want to be the next one screaming about being stabbed."

Wasn't that what all the witnesses from the Kitty Genovese case stated when questioned all those years ago: that they didn't want to get involved? The lack of progress over the decades made Lily's throat tighten and her facial features pinch together in disgust. How had so little changed?

"I can understand the safety concern," she said at last. She didn't understand not calling the cops, but not wanting to die, she got. "But you did get involved after, didn't you?"

"Not by choice," Kayla defended. "I didn't ask to find her dying on the sidewalk!"

"Of course you didn't. Nobody would ask for that," Lily assured. "Ms. Simmons, I'm not accusing you of anything here. I'm just trying to understand what happened. Can you describe the events immediately following your discovery of Ms. Anderson? What condition was she in?"

"Bad condition. She was stabbed a buncha times. Just lying there by the time I found her." Kayla stared at the building looming across with vacant eyes, preoccupied by thoughts that belonged on another plane of existence, not in her everyday life. "There was blood everywhere. I thought she was dead, but while I was lookin' around to see if the guy was still in the area, she groaned."

Lily interjected, her confusion getting the better of her. "You were looking around for the man who attacked Jessica? What inclined you to do that if you didn't want to get involved?"

"I don't know, okay? Told you I wasn't really thinking right. Nothing I did made sense. Anyway, I heard her groan and kinda whimper again for help but it sounded like she couldn't breathe much. Once I figured she was still alive, I called 911."

Thank God someone finally had. No matter how morally questionable Kayla was otherwise, she had decided to try saving someone's life that night. That was more than Lily could say for the other witnesses.

"What happened then?" she prompted quietly.

"Couldn't do anything else, could I?" Kayla said.

She crushed the stub of her cigarette against the railing of the fire escape and flicked it off the side of the building. Both women watched as it spiraled to the ground and touched down on the gray concrete. The witness lit another.

"Sat there and told her it'd be okay. I thought help was gonna be there soon and she'd pull through. It wasn't. She died."

And there was the most revolting part of Jessica's death, that she could have survived if help had arrived on time.

The breeze picked up, whistling faintly past Lily's ears. Car horns blared on the streets below. Lily found herself staring at a couple walking hand in hand down the sidewalk. A series of hypothetical questions with dismal answers cropped up in her mind as she followed their progress. If anything were to happen to that couple right now and she called for an ambulance, would it arrive in time to save their lives? What if something happened and she decided not to call for help? Would anybody else save them?

She used to think somebody would. Now, she wasn't so sure.

"Ms. Simmons, why didn't you remain at the scene of the crime after Jessica died?"

"I did 'till the ambulance showed up," she said. "They asked a couple o' questions and kept asking if I needed medical attention. I didn't," she added in the sudden, sharp sting of mistrust. "I told 'em that, and I thought they could take care of everything else, so I gave 'em my contact information and went home."

"You weren't concerned about walking home alone after you'd come across a woman who'd been knifed down in the middle of the street?"

Kayla shrugged. "Dunno. Guess I didn't really think about that part of it. Wasn't really in my right mind after—," she paused mid-sentence to puff at her cigarette again. "After some chick died in my arms," she exhaled in a thick gray cloud.

The witness's defensive behavior regarding her activities that night made Lily less inclined to believe Kayla's impaired mindset was due to the trauma of watching someone die. She had been in a sober enough state of mind to realize that letting a paramedic check her on the scene would reveal her drug use. It seemed more likely that Kayla left to avoid being arrested for substance abuse.

"Of course," Lily said instead of arguing. She wasn't there to arrest Kayla, after all; persecuting her would only hinder the murder investigation. "I can see how that would be a mind-altering kind of experience. It's horrible to endure."

Kayla's dilated pupils shot back to the detective. She squinted and asked, "Someone die on you before?"

Lily wet her lips and stared hard at one of the thick blue lines running across her notepad before answering, "Yes, they have."

Kayla gave a solemn nod. "Fucking sucks, don't it?"

Lily found an odd sort of comfort in the stark honesty. It expressed just about everything she felt. She nodded again and began to jot the key points of Kayla's story down.

"It really does."

15.

DELGOTTI

Lily had one more interview before she could return to the station for the day, and she was thrilled that it would be at a bar. Perhaps it was the subconscious association between the smell of weed and unequivocal hunger, but the detective had never started salivating as quickly as she did when she stepped into Jessica's former workplace. The combined scent of canola oil and searing beef enveloped her and began to erase the stench of pot as she walked up to the bar.

The bar had only been open for a few hours by the time Lily stepped in for her interview with its owner, but the place was packed. The late afternoon on a Friday was the worst possible time to find seating. Patrons were either licking their wounds after a long workweek or reveling in the last few hours of freedom they had before clocking in for late night weekend shifts. Then, there were the typical day drunks, who remained firmly in their seats as if they'd grown into them since sitting down the moment the doors opened.

Luckily, Lily had an in today. She forced her way between a couple, who were leaning so close to each other, they may as well have shared one chair. She ignored their irritated and colorful complaints as she leaned over the bar to speak to the bartender.

"Hey, I'm looking for the owner."

"Oh yeah? You his best friend, too?" the guy asked with a crooked half grin. "Trying to get a drink?"

"What? No, it's not like that. We have a meeting. I called yesterday and set it up with him."

"Prove it," he challenged.

Lily stared at him for a few seconds before brushing her unzipped jacket away from her hip to reveal both her badge and gun. Both halves of the couple stole indiscreet glances toward the area. She let the jacket fall back in place.

"Is that proof enough, or do you want me to make a scene and scare off all your customers?" she asked.

"No need for that, lady," he chuckled and began preparing a drink for another customer along the bar. "You want the guy, you got him."

Lily squinted a little before stating, "You're Mr. Delgotti."

"Hey, you're pretty quick for a detective! Friends call me Bob, but I guess you can be formal if you feel like it," he said. "What's your drink?"

"Oh. No, thank you. I'm going to grab some food once I can find a seat but I'm not drinking."

He slid the drink to a man four chairs down and nodded at the detective. "What d'ya want? I'll put the order in and bring ya to the back so we can talk in the office."

"A burger with everything on it and some ch—fries."

Why was that still such an automatic reflex? Ordering chips would not get her what she wanted here.

"Burger and fries. Got it."

Bob stepped out from behind the bar and led her through the cramped kitchen. He paused long enough to shout her an order for two burgers and fries. A short cook promised it was coming up before the owner led her back to his office, which was a thin closet of a room packed with a long shelf for a desk, two chairs, a computer, and a ton of paperwork. Bob pulled a small stack of receipts off one chair and indicated for her to sit.

"Sorry 'bout the mess," he said as he set the papers aside and cleared off the desk in front of the computer. He sat in the vacant chair next to hers and sighed, "Haven't figured out Jessie's system yet. She used to keep this place spotless."

That was as good a place as any to dive in. "So she wasn't just a bartender?"

"Hell no. She did everything for us," he answered. "She liked bar the best, I think, but she took care of the money when I wasn't here, too."

"Sounds very helpful," Lily said. "And hard to replace."

"No kidding. I haven't even started looking. Can't really bring myself to, you know? We all knew Jessie real well. She was family."

More so than her own family, perhaps. It would make sense, if this was where Jessica spent a large portion of her life.

"I know how hard it can be to move forward from this," she said. "Especially if you two were close. Did you work together often?"

"Couple days a week," he shrugged and swung side to side in his chair. "I don't have a set schedule so I just come in whenever I gotta do stuff. She took care of the day-to-day crap for me. We started working the same shifts this past week a lot, though. You know, before she..."

He trailed off and let his gaze slip to the floor. Lily knew that look, and it was dangerous to the interview process. While she wanted to be respectful of his grief, she couldn't let it derail him this early.

"And you said the bar was her favorite spot?" she redirected. "Why's that?"

"Yeah. She was a real people person. Just liked being around 'em. She was good with all of 'em, too. Real friendly, and a hell of a memory. You had a customer come in here one time, she'd remember their drink a month later."

That seemed hyperbolic, given the constraints of short term memory, but Lily tried to look impressed, for his sake.

"Wow. I'm guessing she was a favorite with the regulars, then?"

"Oh, yeah. They loved her. Most people never had a problem with her at all."

"Most people?" Lily inquired, quirking an eyebrow.

One of the cooks stepped into the office before Bob could answer.

"Sorry to interrupt," he said as he reached over to set their plates on the desk between them. "Let me know if you need anything else, boss."

"Will do. Thanks, Nate."

Bob sat forward to grab a couple fries from his plate as Nate walked out of the office.

"Yeah," he said and popped the fries into his mouth. "Most people liked her just fine but she had a couple problem customers, I guess you could say. Mostly drunk guys hittin' on her. We never thought it was anything serious. Nothing that would actually hurt her."

"Can you recall what their behavior was like?" she asked. "Were there specific incidents she mentioned?"

Bob swallowed his food and thought aloud: "Well, there was this one guy who was always in here. Got a Jack and Coke. She had it ready as soon as he sat down almost every time he came in, and I think he took it as more than it was. They all get confused sometimes, but this guy was something else. He'd get drunk off his ass and start promising her all kinds of stuff. To take her on trips and buy her a car for a graduation present. Stuff like that."

"I see. Do you have any idea how he knew she was in school at the time?"

"Not with him specifically, nah. But she told guys about it all the time. It was one of the things she used to get 'em to tip higher. Anyway, none of 'em bothered her except this guy. I think he freaked her out a little. There was just something funny about him. You know the type."

"I do," she agreed as she picked up her burger, taking advantage of his willingness to talk to wolf down as much food as she could manage.

She'd developed a well-honed instinct to detect those kinds of men. They were typically middle class with delusions of grandeur, married and trapped in a perfectly nice life they realized far too late they didn't want. In her experience, they promised more than they could provide. It seemed typical for most women not to put any stock into those promises.

"Yeah, so one of those. She told me about all the stuff he'd been saying to her and promising to buy for her. Sounded like he was just looking for a hookup without taking his chance on paying for one off the street, if ya ask me."

"I'm sure she was used to that, though. He can't have been the first drunk to hit on her like that."

"I've seen guys like him loads of times, but he was the only one she mentioned. Sounded more persistent than the rest, I guess."

"That'd make sense, if he was that interested in her. Still creepy," she empathized. She swallowed a few more bites before asking, "So she told you about all this after he came in a few times? When she did, did you get the feeling she was concerned about continuing to serve him?"

"Never because of the alcohol. That's usually how it goes when we refuse service. It's 'cause they're drunk off their asses. But she could tell when they've really had enough and when they're just being a jackass. We gotta sober 'em up before we kick 'em out. She tried to boot him a couple times, but he just kept saying he was too drunk to be walkin' around. He knew his way around that law real well, apparently."

"What made her so worried, then?"

"Just got that feeling from him, I guess. Maybe worried is the wrong word. She wasn't scared or anything but she didn't hold back her opinions real well either, so she was just venting a few times and mentioned him. She said other guys hit on her and all but this one made her feel weird. She saw him take off his wedding ring a couple times and try to hide it real quick like if she was looking at him. Like he didn't want to get caught with it."

"Like he seriously thought she didn't already know he was that kind of guy?"

"Yeah, right?" he snorted and grabbed a few more fries. "Anyway, I told her I'd keep an eye out 'cause she was one of my best, you know? Gotta watch out for your people. I had it all worked out to talk to the guy next time he came in when she wasn't here. We even switched around some of her shifts so he couldn't learn the schedule. It didn't work. He figured it out anyway, and he stopped coming in when he knew I was in here."

"But Jessica reported that he was still coming in while she was working and bothering her?"

"Oh yeah. It was every day she was here, basically. She said one time she asked him why he wasn't at work in the middle of the day and he said he couldn't stay away from her. That's when she really got creeped out."

"Yeah, that'd do it. That sounds he was stalking her, at the very least," Lily noted as she sat back and picked at one of the remaining fries on her plate. "So, you mentioned you started working the same shifts as her in the last week. Because of this guy?"

"To see if he would leave her alone. It worked for a couple days. He'd always figure out when she was working alone, but the day he saw me working the bar with her, he took off. We didn't see him for three days after. But Tuesday night…"

Bob paused to look at her, but she held her silence so he could continue.

"It was already real late when the guy came in. Early, I guess. Little before one-thirty, probably. I wasn't up in the bar with Jessie 'cause it was almost the end of her shift so we thought we were in the clear. I heard some yelling, a glass broke, and my cooks started shoutin' for me to get up front 'cause some idiot was giving her a hard time.

"So I ran up there and found him halfway across the bar, trying to grab her. I guess he knocked a glass over when he tried to come over, but she managed to get far enough back so he couldn't reach her. The second he saw me, he backed up and started stammering about how he'd just tried to touch her hand and she freaked out. He tried to make it sound like it was nothing and she was overreacting."

"And you didn't buy it."

"Hell no, I didn't! Not when I knew how he'd been acting before. I got behind the bar and stood between them. Told Jessie to go to the back while I handled that piece of shit."

"What did you do once she went to the back?"

"I had to kick him out. He didn't come in to drink anything, so I knew it would be safer to get him out of there. Couldn't risk him coming after her again, so I kicked him to the curb. Thought I was doing the right thing, you know? That was maybe an hour before her shift ended. She was still kinda shaken up by the time she clocked out, so I told her I'd drive her home so she didn't have to walk all by herself…" His voice spiked in pitch before he broke off and hung his head. "I shoulda just drove her home."

"Hey, don't do that to yourself, Bob." Lily leaned forward and set a comforting hand on his knee. "There was no way you could have known. She'd walked home before and was fine, even after this guy started bugging her. You had no reason to think it would end differently this time."

"No, but I knew it wasn't good. I knew he'd be back," he said as he rubbed his eyes with his thumb and index finger. "I knew he wouldn't leave her alone and I just let her go."

Lily sat with him and gave him a little time to ride out this wave of regret. There was nothing she would be able to say to comfort him in the throes of it, so she waited until he sat back and dabbed a napkin over his face. When she was convinced he was beginning to collect himself, she asked the question she had been itching to get the answer to since the start of the interview.

"Bob, are you concerned that this customer is the one who killed Jessica?"

"Concern's got nothin' to do with it, Detective," he answered and looked up at her, his eyes sunken and bloodshot. "I know that's who did it."

16.

STRIKE TWO

Bob's tears signaled a hard stopping point for the interview. Despite his best efforts to collect himself, he hadn't been able to do so long enough to give Lily a solid description of the man in question, and she couldn't leave fast enough once he started crying. She assured him those were the only questions she had for the day, then promised to follow up with him tomorrow for the description of the suspect. She showed herself out after that.

Lily barely managed to exhale her relief when she almost ran headfirst into her next challenge of the day: a tall woman with predatory eyes and an eagle's beak of a nose. She was dressed in an open black blazer, a royal blue blouse, a black pencil skirt, and black boots that were far too tall to look anything but trashy with the skirt.

Lily pulled up short, her eyes wide and irritated as she caught a glimpse of the man behind the reporter, who appeared to have sprouted a large black lens from his shoulders instead of a head. He was clicking furiously, as was the eyelid-like shutter on the lens.

"Detective Faye? Alyssa Spencer from the New York Post. I've left several messages at your office."

"And when I have time, you can be sure I'll return them," Lily said and tried to sidestep the woman.

"We're just looking for a quick interview, Detective. No more than twenty minutes at most," Alyssa pressed. She let Lily pass, but followed her down the sidewalk.

"I apologize, but I don't have time at the moment," Lily stated, her accent thickening in her annoyance as she dug through her purse for the keys to her squad car. "I am attempting to pursue a lead on a confidential case."

"I understand, of course," Alyssa promised with a wide smile that looked too tight to be authentic. "But I'm sure you can understand the citizens of New York are demanding answers."

"And when I have them, I'll hold a press conference. For now, I have work to do."

Not one to be deterred, the reporter began her questioning, anyway. "Do you have a drinking problem, or do you have reason to believe someone inside that bar may be responsible for the murder of Jessica Anderson?"

Lily flipped a scathing glare at the woman, although she couldn't answer as quickly as she would have liked. She wasn't aware the victim's name had been announced yet. Then again, maybe it hadn't and Spencer was looking for official confirmation. Lily would need to talk to Alcarez about that when she returned to the station, which, at this rate, seemed unlikely to happen within the next few minutes.

"Ma'am, I am in the middle of a criminal investigation," Lily warned as she caught her keys and ripped them from her purse. "We are working as diligently as possible night and day to deliver accurate and swift justice, which we will not be able to do if we are derailed by a media circus. Now, if you'll excuse me—."

She attempted to step off the sidewalk toward her car, but the photographer stepped in her way this time. The shutter's clicking stopped but he didn't angle the camera away from her.

"Detective, be reasonable," Alyssa drawled as she drew a red pen out of her coat pocket. "All I want to do is get an honest reporting on the people behind this case. The public wants to know they'll be safe. I'm sure you can understand my motivations, from one investigator to another."

"Don't you *dare* call yourself that again," Lily snapped as she rounded on the journalist, her teeth clenched together and bared at the woman. "I don't care what you think you contribute to society by berating me with questions when I need to be focusing on catching a murderer at large. You are not an investigator. Right now, the only thing you are is a pain in the arse. Don't you dare cheapen the work I do keeping our citizens safe and at peace by deigning to think you and I share a title. You print gossip. I actively solve and prevent crimes. Do you understand?"

Alyssa stood her ground throughout the tirade, although her eyes grew larger with every vitriolic sentence the detective spat at her. It took her a few seconds to react once Lily ran out of steam, but she finally drew in a breath and puffed her chest out like a gorilla defending its territory. She adjusted her blazer by giving a sharp tug on the bottom hem and set her pen back to her notepad, a defiant smirk curling onto her lips.

"Can I quote you on that?" she asked in a clipped tone and held the detective's murderous gaze.

Lily's eye twitched as any victory she felt during her rant drained out of her body. She'd had too little sleep and far too much social interaction to deal with the New York Post's personal brand of leech right now. She was working for justice for a corpse, a person who had been living and breathing and walking the streets last week, and who had been murdered in one of the most savage and heartless manners Lily had ever seen. This was not the time for media interference.

"No," she growled.

"What happened to your forehead, Detective?"

"None of your business. Now move."

"We only have a few questions," Alyssa persisted, smirking as Lily began turning purple with rage.

Fortunately, the reporter was spared from her imminent arrest for hindering a police investigation when the detective's phone rang. She turned away from Alyssa and the photographer to answer. As she hit the green circle on the screen, she noted Stilinski's name.

"Faye," she greeted.

"Hey, it's Stilinski. Are you free? We need you down on Seventh and Main ASAP."

"I'll head that way now," she assured. "What's the situation?"
"We found another body."

Lily's stomach dropped so fast, she was sure it had migrated to her feet. She had feared this phone call since the start of the investigation on Jessica, but had been enjoying the luxury of focusing on only the complications that came from a single murder. Now there would be another set of family to inform, another round of interviews and background checks to conduct, and another motive to find. If the two bodies weren't connected, it meant two separate investigations that would divide her team and detract attention from Jessica's murder.

Of course, if the two bodies were connected, they had something far worse to deal with.

"What's the COD?" she asked, holding her breath and hoping he wouldn't deliver the news she was dreading.

"Same injuries as the last one," he said to confirm the fears she had yet to share with him. "You don't think they're connected, do you?"

"Dammit," she breathed out. "I don't know yet. I'll be right there. Thanks," she said and clicked off. She turned back toward the car and nearly ran into the photographer again. "All right," she snarled. "Now you're in danger of being charged with an obstruction of justice. Get out of the way or I'll arrest you both and make sure you don't see daylight until I retire."

Alyssa waved the photographer back to her as if summoning a dog. "Have a great day, Detective!" she called with a cheerful grin as Lily ducked into her car and peeled away from the pair, lights flashing and siren screaming.

Lily arrived on the newest scene within minutes. She walked over to the crime scene and grabbed the pair of officers standing there.

"We need a tent set up," she told them in a quiet undertone. "Do that now before the media gets any shots of the body." She didn't need to look back to know that Alyssa and her lackey had trailed her here.

"We may be too late for that," Stilinski said as he joined the three. "But I'll get started on it now."

"Not you," Lily shook her head. "You two go," she told the first pair before turning to Stilinski. "You responded to the call again?"

"Yeah, I was running patrol when the report came in. Same style, but we actually had someone call it in this—uh, Faye? Why do you smell like pot?"

"The witness I interviewed earlier reeked of it. Never mind that," she waved it off. "Someone reported the crime in progress and we didn't get here in time to stop it?" she reiterated. "Why the bloody hell not?"

"It wasn't that simple," Stilinski said. "The witness said she walked past the alley, saw a couple engaging in what appeared to be public, uh, sexual activities."

"You're nearly thirty, Stilinski. If you can't be more descriptive—."

"She was giving him a blow job," he stated with a conscious effort to maintain a stoic expression.

"Oh my," Lily grimaced at the deadpan delivery. "So, she walked by, saw that, and presumably continued on her way?"

"Sure. Wouldn't you?"

"You'd better believe it."

"Exactly. She went to a pizza place down the street for a date, which didn't go well. She left early and came back this way to get to the subway, and by that time, it was too late. She heard muffled crying and found the woman partially stripped and bleeding out in here in the alley."

"So she called us as soon as she found the victim?"

"Yes and by the time we got here, it was too late," he sighed. "So we did respond immediately. I was here within five minutes of getting the call and the ambulance arrived thirty seconds later."

Although the statement should have reassured Lily, fury bubbled inside her head like lava inside an active volcano. They had failed to prevent the second brutal and blatant homicide within a single week, all because people didn't pay attention to their surroundings or didn't care about the sufferings of anyone but themselves. It was absolutely despicable.

"Okay," she said at last. "You've taken her statement, then? Did you record it?"

"I didn't," he frowned. "Do we have to do that?"

"No. I just prefer it when I'm interviewing. It helps to review their inflection sometimes."

"Well, if you want to interview her again, she said she'd help however she can," Stilinski nodded toward his car. "I warned her to hang out until you got here. She's in my car."

"Good instinct," she agreed. "I'll go speak to her after I look at the body."

"Thanks." He glanced back toward the street, where the media stood at the ready like sharks anticipating a feeding frenzy. "I'll make sure they don't get any closer. The photographer and evidence team is on the way."

"Perfect," she nodded and glanced down the alleyway. All she could see of the corpse was a pile of dark colored clothing. "At least the weather was on our side this time. There should be a decent amount of DNA evidence left on the body."

"I hope you're right. We should be able to find ID on her, too."

"Good. That'll speed up the process, too. Can you see if you can verify the witness's alibi with the cashier at the pizza shop?"

"I'm on it," he promised and began to turn that way, but hesitated. "Hey, before you go over there… about the pot smell—."

"I wasn't smoking, Stilinski. It shouldn't even be that noticeable anymore," she frowned and sniffed the collar of her jacket, which smelled more like greasy food than pot now.

"No, no! I didn't think you were," he shook his head. "It's just... the victim reeks of it, too."

The familiar sensation of dread crept up the back of her neck, as if someone out of her line of sight was about to strike her. Her heart beat spiked as she tried to rationalize her fears away. It was coincidence, surely. Marijuana wasn't uncommon in the city. It hadn't been before its legalization, but now? A person could hardly walk a block without smelling it.

"It's probably nothing, though. Just a coincidence. People smoke pot all over the place here," Stilinski pointed out before heading down to the pizzeria.

As soon as he walked away, Lily darted into the alley. She slowed as she neared the crumpled corpse. The renewed scent of marijuana hit her, now mingled with the metallic addition of pints of spilled blood. She pressed her sleeve against her nose and drew in a slow breath through her mouth to steady herself before she closed the distance between herself and the corpse.

The first thing she saw was the last expression of terror Kayla Simmons had ever made.

17.

CONNECTED

"You okay?" Stilinski inquired of Lily as they watched Charlie zip Kayla into a shiny black body bag.

Lily felt like someone had tied strings to her eyeballs and attached the other ends to Kayla; she couldn't look away even after the coroner closed the body bag over the victim's white face and purpled lips. The detective crossed her arms and hunched forward, as if trying to root around inside her core for a warmth that evaporated long ago. Even the sun shining high above them couldn't penetrate the chill settling over her entire body, as if she had stepped into a box of impenetrable ice.

"It's just...hard to believe," she explained in a dragging, soft voice that sounded every ounce as drained as she looked. "I only spoke to her four hours ago."

"I'm so sorry, Faye," Stilinski frowned. "She was the one who found Anderson, right?"

"Yeah."

Unintelligible mutterings filled the empty air around them as the press reported on the details they'd managed to decipher so far. Their voices echoed down the alleyway and bounced back toward the cops. The agitated screeches of car horns sounded in the rush hour traffic a street over.

Despite the noise, Lily had never felt so isolated.

"So these homicides are connected," Stilinski spoke at last, and willingly placed himself in isolation with her.

"More so than they were before," she confirmed. "The M.O.'s the same, the COD is the same, the public setting is the same. It has to be the same killer. And his motive's easy for this one."

"Trying to silence the witness. Simmons was the only one who Anderson could have told the killer's identity to before she died. So she was the only one with that information. He's trying to cover his tracks."

"Only Kayla didn't have that information," Lily said. "She was drunk, at the very least, when she found Jessica. She confirmed she'd been out partying and didn't remember much except for the victim dying after she called the ambulance. She never mentioned anything about Jessica speaking to her, never mind about telling her the name of her killer."

If Lily's interview with Bob Delgotti made her believe both the patron bothering Jessica and Jessica's killer were one in the same, Kayla's death pulled her in a different direction. Supposing the two were the same person and the killer was trying to eliminate witnesses to Jessica's murder, he would have gone after the bar owner who had seen his face numerous times. The only reason Lily suspected he may not have targeted Delgotti was that doing so would break the M.O. established in the first murder.

"Hang on," Stilinski interrupted before she could connect the crucial final dots in her train of thought. "Did the killer even see her at the time of Anderson's murder?"

Lily ignored the pang of irritation that shot through her chest and head and answered, "It's not likely. Kayla told me she heard screaming down the street and stayed away from the area until it stopped. She never mentioned seeing the attacker, which probably means he was long gone by the time she finally found Jessica."

"So if he didn't see her that night, how did he know she was our primary witness?"

"Excellent question, Stilinski," she exhaled and looked over at him. "Honestly, I don't have a clue. He shouldn't have been able to find a connection. Kayla's name wasn't even in the papers yet."

He frowned back at her but nodded. "Something else to look into, I guess. Did you need to do anything else here before we finish up?"

"S'pose not," she said and cast a final glance around the scene to make sure. "I'll go talk to the witness so you can get out of here." She made the short walk to his car and knocked on the window before she opened the passenger door. "Ms. Dennings, yeah? Chelsea? Which do you prefer?"

The woman shrugged, picking at her cuticles so she didn't have to look up.

"Chelsea's fine."

"Brilliant. Hi, Chelsea. I'm Detective Faye. Officer Stilinski said he's taken your statement, but I was hoping we could speak for a few minutes?"

The woman, a dye-job redhead with dirt-brown roots, nodded as she abandoned the work on her cuticles. She finally looked at Lily with huge brown, bloodshot eyes. Her cheeks dripped with black mascara from her lower eyelashes. She raised one hand to scrub away the marks, but her efforts only distorted them.

"Great, thank you so much," Lily smiled and knelt down to meet the woman at eye level. She pulled out her notepad and assured, "I'll keep it short so Officer Stilinski can bring you home. Could you explain what happened, starting with your trip to the pizzeria?"

Chelsea's recounted the event almost exactly as she had depicted it to Stilinski the first time through. The only discrepancies were a few colorful words about the date who had stood her up and a truncated version of sitting with Kayla while they waited for help.

Lily jotted the main points down and asked, "Did you know the victim before today?"

"N-no ma'am," Chelsea sniffled.

"Okay, and you mentioned she was with a man in the alley when you first walked by. Did you know him?"

"No… I-I don't think so. I didn't get a good look," she explained and wiped her eyes on her sleeve. "With what they were doing, I mean…"

"Absolutely. I wouldn't stare something like that down, either," Lily shivered. "I know you didn't get a good look but did you happen to notice anything about his appearance? Build or race or height? Anything at all?"

Chelsea dropped her hands to her lap and went back to picking at her cuticles.

"He was tall," she recalled as she looked toward the alley. "Had kind of a bulky coat on. I'm pretty sure he was a white guy."

"Tall, bulky coat, white male," Lily echoed as she wrote that down and underlined the race, gratitude for the fact swelling in her chest. "Got it. You didn't happen to notice a hair color, did you?"

"He had a hat on. Just a black cap, I think. Like a beanie or something."

"Okay. Anything else?"

The woman shook her head and rubbed at the back of her neck. "I-I can't remember anything else… I'm sorry."

"No, it's okay. You've given us some great information already," she soothed. "Here, let me give you my card, and you call me if you think of anything else, okay? Can you do that for me?" she asked as she dug a business card from her jacket and brandished it.

"Yes, ma'am." Chelsea took it and withdrew her phone to input the number.

"Great. Thank you so much, Chelsea. Officer Stilinski is going to take you home now, if that's okay."

Chelsea nodded. "Thank you," she said, staring at the card.

"And do me a favor. Make sure you're not alone for a bit, yeah? Especially if you go out at night."

"Wait, why?"

The instructions snapped the witness out of her quiet, complacent state. Wide eyes stared up at Lily. The card slipped out of Chelsea's hold and fluttered to the pavement.

"It's precaution, that's all," Lily assured and stooped over to pick up the card. "It's good practice in the city anyway, but it's especially pertinent until we wrap up this case. Can you do that for me?"

"Y-yeah… but, Detective! I'm not in any danger, right?"

"We have no concrete reason to think you would be right now. But call me if you sense anything is off and we'll take care of it for you, yeah?"

"All right," Chelsea frowned, glancing around the scene as if expecting an attack in that very moment. "Detective Faye? There is one more thing…"

Lily took a step back so she could see Chelsea's face under the roof of the car, although the witness's gaze was fixed once more on the business card. "What's that?"

"That woman? She was pretty out of it when I got to her, but she said something while we were waiting for the ambulance," Chelsea said. "Right before she died." She bit her lip and glanced up at the detective through short, stubby lashes. "I think it was your name."

A small crease appeared between Lily's eyebrows as she frowned down at Chelsea. "My name? Are you sure?"

"Yes, ma'am. Your last name, I think. At least, it sounded like she was trying to say Lily." Chelsea's gaze rose again and flickered toward Stilinski. "Or… well, I don't know. The I-L sound, definitely. I guess it could have been either of your names."

Lily followed her eye line and studied Stilinski for a moment. Why would Kayla's last word be one of their names?

"Okay," she said. "That's great information, Ms. Dennings. Thank you."

Lily waved Stilinski over and watched him like a hawk while he slipped into the driver's seat and pulled away from the scene. Only when the car had turned the corner did Lily begin her own trek back to the station. The ride was silent. There were no calls coming in over the CB radio for a change, and Lily never listened to music in the car. Even the traffic surrounding her as she navigated the height of rush hour seemed muted today. It felt as if the universe noticed it had pushed her too far for one day and now sat in sheepish silence, awaiting either wrath or forgiveness.

Lily had nothing to offer the universe in return except questions. What if Kayla hadn't been saying Lily's name at all? What if she had been trying to give Chelsea the name of her killer?

There were plenty of reasonable explanations to all of her concerns, but habit in the field taught her not to rule any theory or any suspect out until she had solid evidence or an alibi. Individuals were always innocent until proven guilty in a court of law, but they were guilty until proven innocent in detective work. Nothing definitive pointed to or away from Stilinski as a suspect, and the inability to clear someone Lily worked so closely with left a bitter taste in the back of her throat.

Her mood did not improve when she returned to the station. Alcarez hailed her into his office as she attempted to walk past. She took a deep breath to quell the irritation flaring in her stomach and changed course.

"Chief, as much as I love our little conversations, I'm not in the mood for a pep talk right now," Lily frowned as she stepped in. "Just give it to me straight. What's the problem?"

"Fine. Your PR work is a nightmare," her boss answered before she had managed to so much as take a seat. "What's the problem with you and Alyssa Spencer?"

"What are you talking about, what's the problem?" Lily's brows slanted inward. "She accosted me in the middle of a homicide investigation while I was trying to gather information that could lead to the capture of a dangerous criminal. I can't sit around and answer press questions while I'm trying to catch a killer."

"The time you spent with that reporter, with any reporter, can make or break your credibility with the public," he pointed out and sat on the edge of his desk. "If they don't trust the people conducting the investigations, they aren't going to feel safe no matter what kind of progress you make on the case. If you become known as the detective who pushes the media around, people will be calling for your head in droves. And if that happens, I'll have to take action."

"Action that reinforces the inappropriate behavior conducted by the media? You know what kind of work Spencer does," Lily retaliated. "She's hardly a real journalist. All she does is try to defame police officers."

"And that's the climate we're in. It blows, but public opinion matters now more than ever. You can't have the people in this city turning against you, especially while you're in a position of leadership. If you're discredited, your entire team is, too."

"I can't be discredited! Defamed, yes, and if it comes down to that, I can get a cease and desist on her. But her mudslinging has no bearing on my record. Do you realize how many people I've put behind bars? How many people I've testified against? How many criminals could walk if you take me off cases because of public outcry?"

"If the media draws enough attention to your negative behavior and the Mayor has to start investigating, I won't have a choice. I know you do good work and get results, but that won't be enough to protect you if this gets worse. You need to tread carefully around these people."

Lily squared her jaw and turned her gaze across the glass room. As much as she hated to cater to tabloids, the Chief was right. If the Mayor got involved, none of her previous work mattered. They would have to open an investigation on her, and her entire team would suffer for it. She couldn't afford to let that happen in the middle of this case.

"Fine," she exhaled and drew in another slow breath. "I'll be more careful. But I swear, Chief, if she attacks me in the field like that again, I'm arresting her."

"If she gives you cause, I'm fine with that," he shrugged. "But don't do it when you're angry and don't make it public. If she impedes the investigation, I will take care of her. But if all she's doing is being a nuisance, you don't touch her. Understood?"

Lily pursed her lips and looked back to him. "Yes, Chief."

"Good. Now get back to work. I want this wrapped up as soon as possible."

"Yes, sir," the detective uttered in a gravelly tone before walking back to her desk.

Wrapped up? He wanted the investigation wrapped up, just like that? He knew how long one homicide case took, and now she had two on her hands. How was she supposed to wrap things up the same day they'd found a second body?

She kneaded her face with her fingertips, beginning with the temples and working her way down her jawline. For a few uninterrupted seconds of glorious silence, she sat. She closed her eyes and counted up to ten, then down to one. Then, she took a breath, opened her eyes, and went back to work.

As soon as she opened her email, she searched for all messages from Harris. It was well past six by now, and it wouldn't have surprised her to realize he hadn't sent her anything. When the results loaded, one unread email sat at the top. It was time-stamped at 5:51 p.m.

"Huh. Nice job," she murmured under her breath.

She replied with a simple thank you. Unfortunately, the Mallory hearings took a backseat to her main case right now. A small click of distaste sounded in the back of her throat at the thought of Harris's reaction the next morning, when she would have to tell him that she hadn't even looked at the information he sent.

"Too bad, mate. That's how it goes," Lily said before turning to the case folder to examine the statistics compiled on the homicide suspect's description.

It was a bulky file that contained all the reports from officers canvassing on the night of the first homicide, so a few papers slid out of it onto her mailbox tray as she lifted the folder. When she reached over to collect the strays, her fingers brushed against an envelope she didn't remember receiving the day before. She frowned and tugged it out of the stack, breath hitching at the sight.

"QUIT!" the front of the envelope screamed at her in red Sharpie.

That was it. The rest of the envelope was a crisp white, yet to be vandalized by stamps, postal markings, or an address to indicate who or where the letter came from. A mail carrier would have left the letter at the front desk with Maggie, but Maggie wouldn't have known to set it in Lily's box because there was no hint of who the envelope was meant for.

And if it hadn't come through the postal system or from Maggie, that meant someone had deliberately placed it in her box.

That meant the killer had been here.

"Faye?"

Lily startled so violently, it made her old chair pop in protest. She set the envelope face down on her desk and looked up to see the Chief approaching.

"Yes sir?" she asked in a warble.

He didn't notice her tone, too focused on straightening out the collar of his jacket.

"I'm heading out. Just wanted to make sure I didn't miss anything before I left. Did you get any new intel after visiting the crime scene today?"

Lily glanced down at the envelope while her heart tried to leapfrog out of her throat. This couldn't be considered intel since she had no idea what it contained, right? She hadn't even opened it. That meant there was nothing to report; she couldn't tell him about information she didn't have. So, she pushed the envelope under her keyboard and looked up at her boss.

"No, not that I can think of," she said with a tight smile. "Nothing new, sir."

18.

CLOSE RANGE

The implications of Kayla's last word simmered at the back of Lily's mind until she walked out of the station that evening. They burned as vividly as a flare and scrawled across the open air ahead of her as she walked to her car. Try as she might to think about anything else, she couldn't. The possibility that someone she worked with was a sadistic, sexually motivated killer dominated her thoughts throughout the night. It cropped up over and over again, most prevalent in the quiet moments when she finally managed to drift into an uneasy slumber.

After tossing around so often that she ripped her sheets off one corner of the bed, Lily gave up on the idea of sleep and readied for her next shift. As much as she loved work, the idea of going back in on less than three hours of sleep made her stomach churn. She stalled as long as she could by stopping at Starbucks on her way in. She drank a full venti macchiato in the shop before she decided to go in. She paused only to purchase a refill and a hot chocolate, and then proceeded to the station in a groggy haze.

She walked inside with automatic, stiff movements and stopped in front of Stilinski's desk. Somewhere in the back of her mind, she recognized he was sitting in his chair but she didn't look at him and didn't speak. The caffeine and sugar from the first of her drinks had yet to kick in fully enough to snap her out of her fog.

"Anything I can do for you, Faye?" the younger cop asked as he swiveled to face her.

He spun a little too exuberantly and smacked his knee on the side of his desk. His hand shot out to cup around his knee.

"Ow—fudge it all," he muttered under his breath, and then tried to smile at her.

A hint of a smile twitched onto her lips. She waited a beat longer in lieu of making a comment that would draw attention to his typical awkward demeanor or his sudden aversion to swearing outright. Instead, she set the hot chocolate on his desk and answered his question.

"I brought you hot chocolate," she said, and logic returned to her just in time to mentally question why she purchased that specific drink. "I don't know why I picked that, really. I just remembered you don't like their coffee, and I wasn't awake when I ordered. That's just what came out of my mouth, so I hope you actually drink hot chocolate. But if you don't—."

It was his turn to hold back a smirk as he cut her off by confirming, "I do. Thanks. I'm impressed you could remember anything about my Starbucks order before you drank yours."

"I've had a cup already. But if we're being honest, I'm impressed I can string a full sentence together right now," she said as she leaned against the side of his desk. "I got no sleep last night."

"Yeah? Yesterday really sucked."

"Easily one of the worst days I've had on the force," she agreed and blinked. Her eyes only opened a little more than halfway as she added, "And that includes the time I got shot."

"Whoa! Hold on. You got shot?" Stilinski's entire face elongated as his mouth dropped open and his eyes ballooned to cartoonish proportions.

"A couple years ago, and it wasn't major," she explained. "It was just a graze, really."

"Still. You've been shot, and you're still here," he said as he leaned forward to clasp both hands around his cup. "That's incredible."

She smiled at the awe painted on his face. It reminded her how rare life-threatening situations were for rookies on the job. Officer Isaacs had trained him on their department's procedures and taught him how to proceed with traffic stops of all sorts, but Lily doubted he'd ever seen an active shootout. That was the kind of on-duty action the entire precinct heard about. The idea of coming out of a life-or-death situation with little more than a graze seemed to shock him.

Yet, he appeared unfazed at the homicides involved in this case. He might have looked a little green after recovering the first body, but he'd adjusted to corpses with surprising swiftness. Was that an indicator that he wasn't as much of a novice as he tried to appear?

"Yeah. I suppose I am," she agreed. "Speaking of being where we're all supposed to be, you got Dennings home okay yesterday?"

"Yeah. She was still kind of freaked out, which is understandable. I'm still freaked out."

"Are you?"

"You're not?"

"Should I be?" she countered with a cocked eyebrow.

"Okay, you look really creepy when you're half asleep and trying to study me," he grimaced. "And are you really asking if you should be freaked out at the sight of two dead bodies in a week?"

She rolled her eyes but let her facial muscles relax so she wasn't giving such a harsh glare. "Are *you* really asking if I'm—?"

"Shut up!" another female cop called over to the two from her desk.

Lily's gaze didn't move from Stilinski's as she scoffed, "Back off, Isaacs. We're working."

"No, *I'm* working. *You're* flirting."

Despite her first instinct to vehemently deny the accusation, Lily couldn't form the words for even a weak defense. Her ears and cheeks heated. Her neck craned toward their female colleague. She made a few false starts at an explanation before Stilinski put her out of her misery.

"Detective Faye has better taste than that, Isaacs," he said with a light grin at his own expense. "And you wouldn't recognize flirting if it hit you over the head with a baton. That wasn't flirting."

"Exactly!" Lily blurted loudly in her haste to form a coherent sentence.

"But it was an attempt to avoid a direct question," he added as he whipped back around to fix the detective with a stern, reprimanding stare.

"Oh…" Lily flushed a darker shade of pink that made her look like a ripening strawberry. "Erm, what was the question again?"

Stilinski snorted and took a long sip from his hot chocolate. His eyes remained on hers as he lowered the cup. He swallowed, then took another sip. Then a shorter one.

"Really? You're giving me the silent treatment now? Very mature," she huffed.

"I'm just trying to give you some time to return to your normal skin tone, actually," he teased and then relented. "I'd asked if you weren't freaked out by the bodies."

Ah, right. Teasing aside, Lily had to figure out whether or not he was bluffing. She knew that prior to this investigation he had a lot of free time outside of work and that he didn't have many connections in the city. It was plausible that he could have met Jessica at her place of work, but was it equally plausible that such a vibrant and lanky goofball like him could be a murderer? Unfortunately, she had seen less likely scenarios play out before. She would have to get to know him better to find out if he was capable of lying about something so severe.

"Oh. No, I'm not. I see a lot of dead bodies," she pointed out. "I guess they don't unnerve me so much as upset me, especially with a case like Kayla's. I mean, I spoke to her yesterday, you know? It happened so quickly, it's not sunk in properly yet."

"So nothing like this has ever happened before? You've never had a homicide where you've talked to the victim before the murder?"

"No. Contrary to popular belief, I don't work on only murder investigations. We don't see enough murders to do that every day, all year."

"Seriously? Even in the middle of the city?"

"Sure. You're forgetting we're in a particular precinct without jurisdiction over most of the city. Yes, we cover a heavily trafficked area, but it's not Times Square. That's where all the really weird stuff happens."

"Not to keep eavesdropping on your super discreet conversation," Isaacs spoke up, her eyes sparkling as she teased the two, "but you're forgetting all the higher crime areas in New York."

Stilinski almost managed to suppress his chuckle at the interruption. "Like what?"

"Like where, if we're being grammatically correct," Lily muttered. "But think about it for a second. The Bronx, urban Syracuse. Places like that."

"You can just say low income, Faye," Isaacs pointed out.

"Yeah, if I want to be slapped with a discrimination lawsuit," Lily retorted. "Nothing's safe to say these days, even if there is a factual and proven between income and crime rate."

"But if we don't deal in fact, we'd never get anything done," Stilinski countered. "We have to call it what it is, right?"

"And therein lies the paradox we face every day," Lily said. She took a sip of her macchiato before expounding, "Everyone wants others to be held accountable but nobody wants others to hold them accountable."

"That's insane. It doesn't make any sense."

"That's the world we live in," Lily shrugged. "Isn't it, Isaacs?"

"Sure is, Faye. Crazy fucking world."

"Crazy fucking world," Lily agreed. She took a few seconds to study Stilinski for a reaction before she straightened up. "Fun as that philosophical tangent was, I need to get to work. Stilinski, let's put top priority on Jessica and Kayla, yeah? We'll have to push dealing with the Mallorys until Monday."

"Can do. Need me to run a background check on Simmons?"

"Yeah, let's start there. See if you can track down what happened after I left. I need to know who last saw her alive, aside from Dennings."

"Sure. Any reason?"

"Because it might have been me," Lily answered before striding to her desk.

There was plenty of work to go around with the discovery of a second body, but Lily's focus veered back to the envelope sitting under her keyboard as she sat down. That made three threats total, and she had lost sense of the timeline thanks to the method of delivery for the third. How long had the envelope sat in her mailbox? Was it there before Kayla's death or had it been planted after?

The last portion of the timeline she remembered in regards to the mailbox was Harris toppling it over during their argument. Had he truly knocked the box off her desk on accident, or done so as a diversion for a more sinister action? If he hadn't planted the note, who else could have? He had been gone by the time she returned from the crime scene the day before, so the area was empty. It was possible the letter had been placed by someone else entirely, somewhere between Harris's departure and her arrival.

There were too many possibilities to consider. She needed to start narrowing them down.

She took a deep breath and tugged the letter out from under her keyboard. Maybe there was a handwritten note inside she could use for handwriting analysis to rule her coworkers out as suspects. With that hope in mind, she pulled on a pair of latex gloves stored in her desk drawer and used a letter opener to cut the envelope, hoping to do as little damage as possible to the potential evidence inside.

She withdrew something much worse than a handwritten note. A thin stack of pictures slid into her hand as she tipped the envelope over. This time, the subject of the photos wasn't one of the homicide victims, but Lily herself. The photos caught her from various angles during the canvassing after the first murder, sitting in the back of the ambulance after the Mallory attack, and staring down her computer screen in the office. They were all taken at close range.

She flipped through the stack a few more times to take in all the details before the most obvious one stopped her cold. Each photo had been taken within seconds of Stilinski arriving on the scene.

19.

FLOODGATES

Lily returned to her email in hopes of finding correspondence from Matt. She needed good news after being hammered by nothing but the bad for the past 24 hours. She combed through several sales emails from stores she frequented, and she located a half-hearted apology from Harris. Mingled amongst those stood anything but good news.

Her inbox was filled with a barrage of new threats from an anonymous sender.

"Did you get my email, Faye?"

Lily jolted forward to grab the closest piece of paper she could reach and yanked it on top of the envelope and photos. She spun her chair without pushing it back, which led to the same mistake Stilinski made earlier. Her knee thwacked into the side of her desk, making her double over as pain lanced through her leg.

"Wow. Sorry. I thought you heard me walking over," Harris said with his nose stuck higher in the air than usual. "Guess I snuck up on you."

"No, it's not your fault," she gritted out. "What did you need?" she asked, his silhouette distorted and dancing as she viewed him through watering eyes.

"I just wanted to make sure you saw my email," he reiterated.

Lily's chest tightened as if the question were a boa constricting flexing its muscles around her torso. She turned to face him fully and used her body to block his view of her monitor. Did he already know what sat on the screen? Could he possibly be so bold as to ask her face-to-face when the messages had all been anonymous?

"S-sorry? What email?" she croaked.

Harris shifted his weight and shoved his tongue against his cheek, resembling an angered chipmunk. "My…" His eyes darted around the room of empty desks before he managed, "My apology."

"Oh. That one." The constricting loosened and she inhaled fully for the first time since spotting the new threats. She cast a cursory glance to her open email and minimized the window. "Right! Yes, I saw it. Thank you. I do really appreciate that."

He nodded as his eyes slid from her computer to her gloved hands.

"You okay? You're jumping like a rookie on her first patrol."

"I am not jumping," she said. "I'm fine. I've just got a ton of stuff to do today."

"I can see that. Why do you have gloves on?"

"No reason. It doesn't matter, Harris," she said without looking at him.

"You're being weird."

"I'm not being—! You know what? I have a lot of work to do, Harris. I appreciate the apology, though. Thanks."

She swiveled away from him and opened her web browser. Although she didn't need to look anything up, she automatically navigated to the state government's main page. It kept her busy long enough for Harris to take the hint and walk away. Even after he was gone, she spent a few minutes clicking random links to make sure nobody was watching her when she returned to her email. She chose the first threat listed toward the bottom of her screen and clicked it open.

"You were warned to stay off the case. Since you don't seem to take my warnings seriously, I had to show you how easily I can act on them. I'm close."

The second email read: *"Have you seen the photographs yet? By now, you can see it's a hobby of mine. You make a lovely subject."*

She scrolled up to the next message and scanned it as she yanked her gloves off.

"You can't track me down by ignoring me, Detective. You will pay attention to me soon enough."

She hunched over her keyboard. Next email.

"Hope the trail isn't growing cold already. Not when I was kind enough to start a new case for you."

She grimaced at the paperclip in the corner of the next one and read: *"She photographed nicely, too. Not as well as you will, though. Judge for yourself."*

She didn't open the attachments.

After that: *"Don't worry about finding me, sweetheart. If you don't stay away from this case, I'll find you. Believe me; I'm looking forward to our next encounter."*

The final email simply read, *"I'll see you soon."*

Lily slammed her palms down on either side of her keyboard and shoved herself away from her desk. She abandoned her macchiato, exed out of her email, and stormed into the break room. There, she tore the coffee pot away from the inactive brewer and swore as it gave no resistance, light in its emptiness.

"Who doesn't make a new pot when they've finished one?" she seethed as she wrenched the brew basket from the machine and tossed the old grinds into the trash.

She continued muttering to an indifferent set of chairs as she made a new pot of coffee. Once it began to brew, she texted Matt for an update on the email and made a couple calls to wrap up loose ends.

"Hi Derek," she said when she got the first man's voicemail. "This is Detective Faye with the NYPD, following up. I realized we never got your alibi and I want to ask you a few more questions about the nature of your relationship with Miss Anderson. If you could give me or Detective Harris a call back within twenty-four hours, I would appreciate it. Thanks."

She placed a second call to Delgotti while she walked the length of the kitchen and back a few times. His voicemail message blared through the receiver after several rings. When the beep sounded, she left a message requesting a physical description of the patron who had tried to assault Jessica during her last shift. She ended the call and shoved her phone into her back pocket before pouring herself the coffee she had worked so hard to brew.

"Faye?"

The Chief's voice wasn't as loud or jarring as usual, but it caused her to flinch all the same. She swore as hot coffee sloshed over the sides of the cup onto her hand. More spilled in her haste to shove the cup onto the table and the coffee pot back onto the maker. She grabbed a paper towel and wiped her hand dry before shaking it in the air to cool the burn.

"Jumpy today?" her supervisor asked in the same oddly quiet tone as before.

"I am not jumpy!" she snapped and turned to face him. "Why does everyone keep saying that?"

He stared back with a somber frown. "Get any interesting emails lately?"

Lily straightened, clutching the damp paper towel as she met his gaze. "W-why would you—?"

"Because I got one we should talk about," he answered and turned his back to her. "My office, Faye. Now."

Lily gaped after him as a pit clenched and sank in her stomach. The emails she'd received were one thing, but to think the Chief had been a recipient as well? It made her heart thrum in her chest, the vibrations reverberating through her slender frame so powerfully they made her head throb.

Lily's legs turned from solid flesh and bone to quaking gelatin as she stumbled after him. She reached out to balance herself on her typical seat, then sank into it. Sending her threats was one thing, but sending them to her boss? If she hadn't believed this guy was serious before, she did now.

"You're strangely quiet. Something on your mind lately?" the man asked as he leaned over his desk toward her and crossed his arms.

"Just waiting to see what you needed me for, sir."

Surely, that disembodied voice wasn't hers. She didn't sound that hollow and weak. She was too outspoken to be so quiet.

"I was hoping you would be more transparent with me than this, Faye. I'm going to give you another shot before I have to take action, and I want you to be honest with me. You got it?"

Lily frowned. "Erm… not really," she confessed. "What are you asking?"

"Are you in danger, Faye?"

Lily's tongue ran along her bottom lip, though her mouth was too dry to be of any assistance to her chapping skin. The cut on her forehead had developed its own pulse that was beating out of sync with the generalized throbbing of fear which had overtaken the rest of her body. She glanced and realized she had carried her coffee in with her. She took a sip to steady herself, but the acrid taste made her shudder more. She reached forward and pushed the cup onto the Chief's desk instead.

"Danger?" she repeated, and the word fired enough synapses to jolt her out of her numbed state. "That's going a bit far, perhaps."

"But you have received threats."

"Why would you even ask me that?"

"It wasn't a question. I'm not guessing here. I'm trying to find out why you're hiding how serious this investigation is getting."

"What am I supposed to be hiding, sir? Yeah, I've had a couple of threats, but that's pretty standard for these kinds of cases."

"Is it standard for them to seek me out, too?" he asked and angled his monitor her way so she could see the email open on the screen. "Because I can't remember the last time this happened."

Whatever vestige of feeling had returned to Lily's limbs drained from her as she looked over the most blatant and hostile of the threats. It contained three image attachments and read:

"I warned your detective to stay off my trail. Now I'm warning you: if she finds me, she dies. If you want her to live, take her off the case and let it go cold. You have until noon to send your decision.

P.S. Take a look at those attachments. You know what happens to the prettiest flowers? They're picked first."

Lily stared at the last line for a long few seconds before an involuntary shudder wracked through her body.

"I wouldn't be nearly as concerned with that if these homicides didn't contain an obvious sexual component," she rasped, her throat so dry it seemed like her vocal chords had sprouted barbs that were trying to ensnare her voice.

"But they do. I don't know how close you are to finding this guy, but he's making his position pretty clear. We don't have the upper hand anymore."

Try as she could to disagree, Lily knew he was right. She didn't have the killer's identity. Even if she did, it would hardly reduce the chance of being attacked unless they were ready to make an immediate arrest. There was no way to ensure her safety unless they had the guy behind bars.

"Okay," she conceded through a hard exhale. "So what's our next move?"

"You won't like it, but keep in mind I've got about three hours to make it," he warned. "I need you to take the day off."

The likelihood of Lily disconnecting from work was equal to the likelihood that a balloon would remain intact while attached to a porcupine. Still, she nodded instead of putting up a fight.

"Short term solution, yeah?" she verified. "So he thinks I'm off the case?"

"So he knows you are," he corrected. "It won't go on your file or anything, but I don't want to give him any reason to think you're still on his trail."

"You think not being here will be enough to keep him from coming after me?"

"Are you worried it won't be?"

She hesitated and took her cup of coffee in hand again. "I don't think it's a risk I want to take. I've gotten a few emails myself."

The confirmation made his eyebrows rise. "So you do think you're in danger."

"Not immediately, no. But I see the potential for it."

"I guess that's a step up from denying it," he sighed. "Okay. You want a detail?"

She nodded and chewed the inside of her cheek as she thought through her options. "Yeah. I'd like Stilinski."

"You sure? He could stay here and work on the case."

"No, it's fine," she said. Worst case scenario, it would prevent him from falsifying anything in her absence. Best case scenario, she would be able to mark him off her list of suspects. "I only have a couple leads. Grunt work, really. Harris has been vying for more to do, so I'll pass it off to him for the day."

"If you're okay with that, sure," he said before he sat back. "Faye, do you have any leads? Anything that can push us the right way?"

"I have suspicions, but they're nothing I can prove. Certainly nothing I want to act on yet."

"Anything I can act on?"

She shook her head. She was covering Stilinski. If Harris had a hand in any of this, he would show it in the work he did after she gave him the case. There was nothing for the Chief to do.

"Faye, do you have any reason to suspect anyone at this station?"

"Chief…" Her weary gaze locked on his face and she noted he looked as aged as she felt. "I have reason to suspect almost everyone right now."

20.

BUGGED

When Lily left the Chief's office, she popped by Stilinski's desk. She let him know Alcarez wanted to see him, and then she returned to her desk clump to find Harris. Her steps were silent as she walked behind him and glanced over his shoulder to find him playing solitaire instead of working.

"Slow morning?" she asked.

It was his turn to jump. He closed out of his game and turned his chair so forcefully, he almost tipped himself out of it. He steadied and looked up at her, his visage pale.

"No, I was just taking a break," he blurted.

She held up a hand. "Don't worry about it. I know I haven't given you much work lately, but that changes now, yeah? I'm being pulled off the double homicide for now. I know Stilinski was the primary on the scene but we need a detective heading this up. I can either give it to Jordan when he comes in, or you're free to take it, if you think you'd be interested."

Harris's eyes grew as wide as golf balls, and he nodded so quickly Lily worried he might detach his head from his neck.

"A-are you sure?" he asked. "I can do it, but really? Where are you going? Why aren't you staying on the case?"

"I'm sure," she chuckled. "The Chief just wants me to focus on another case for now. So here's what I need you to do…"

She tasked him with interviewing Derek to get his alibi and warned him that Delgotti would probably be calling back with a suspect description. It would need to be cross referenced with the descriptions provided in the summary of the canvassing reports. If he did it properly, it wouldn't take him all day to complete those tasks, so she also told him to go interview Amy and Aiden Mallory at the prison.

"I think that's everything for today. Make sure you're checking in with Stilinski regularly, though. He's still working the case, so keep him informed."

"You got it," he agreed. "Hey, boss? Thanks. You're not going to regret stepping off the case."

Lily took note of his wording and fired back a less subtle warning of her own: "See that I don't. Have a good day, Harris."

"Oh, I will," he grinned and turned to craft a new email.

Meanwhile, Lily gathered her personal belongings and headed back to the Chief's office.

Stilinski stepped out to meet her and gave a tight smile. "Hey. Let me grab my coat and we'll take off."

"Yeah, perfect. I'll meet you up front," she said as her phone pinged.

She yanked it from her pocket, hoping to connect with one of the witnesses she'd called earlier. Instead, she found a text from a six-digit number. The preview didn't instill warm feelings, but she opened it all the same as soon as Stilinski walked back to his desk.

"*I hear you've been pulled off the case,*" it read. "*Too bad. I was looking forward to getting to know you more intimately.*"

She stared at the screen for a second before poking her head into the office again.

"Hey," she said. "Keep an eye on Harris today, will you?"

He nodded and didn't ask questions. "Yeah, I will. Have a good day off, Faye."

"Thanks, boss," she nodded and met Stilinski at the front desk.

"Ready to go?" he asked.

"Yeah," she smiled, pocketing her phone as she walked out with him. "I need to make a quick stop before we go to my place, though."

"Sure thing. Just tell me where to drive."

She directed him to the forensics lab and nearly jumped out of the car as it rolled to a stop.

"I'll be right back," she said before elbowing her way into the lab. Matt, I need a favor. Do you have a second?"

"Do you know where I work? Of course I don't. And I haven't found the source of the emails yet," Matt said as he looked over. One glance at her flustered expression made him change his tune, and he added, "What do you need?"

She dug her phone out of her pocket and handed it to him with a note she'd written out before walking into the building. It read:

"I think it's bugged. Can you x-ray to confirm?"

Matt frowned as he took the phone and scanned the note. He looked back up at her, searching her eyes.

"Lily…"

"I know what it sounds like, Matt. I didn't come in for a commentary. I just need to know you can do it," she cut him off.

"Yeah, I can," he said as he got up. "Follow me."

She walked down the hall with him and entered a small lab filled with steel tables and microscopes. The pair stopped in front of what looked like a common household printer and scanner. She set a hand on the metal table to prop herself up as she leaned over the tech's shoulder.

"How long until we find out? Stilinski's waiting in the car."

"Within a minute. It's a simple scan," he assured as he hit a switch on the side of the machine and placed the phone face up on the flat metal plate.

"Good," she let out a breath and straightened up, giving him a little space to work. She took to pacing behind him instead, arms crossed and gaze fixed on the floor.

Matt began scanning the device but paused as he flipped it over to look at her.

"This is really starting to get to you, isn't it?"

She stopped pacing and looked up, staring at a metal shelf across the room. She chewed on her bottom lip and bobbed her head, not in confirmation but as if bracing herself to answer the question. After a slow breath, she murmured her answer.

"You know what a detective's worst fear is?"

"The unknown."

"Exactly. I can handle the threats. I can handle the homicides. I can handle interviews with the victims' families and writing up the reports and getting into tight spots for the sake of discovering the truth," she said. "What I can't handle is this." She pointed at her phone.

"The unknown," Matt repeated. "Don't take this the wrong way, but you're sure it's not paranoia?"

"Uh, yeah. I'm sure. This guy's texting me now, Matt. Besides, you're the one who freaked out when I got the first email. What are you trying to say now, that I shouldn't be concerned?"

"No, you should be, especially if you've been getting more messages. But sometimes you project onto the wrong target. You get the right thought but apply it to something uninvolved."

Lily frowned at the back of his head, bent toward the machine.

"Matt, you know as well as I do that's no way to solve an investigation. And in case you haven't noticed, I've solved plenty. Why would I find a lead and follow it in the wrong direction?"

"Maybe you wouldn't," he admitted. "Maybe you do it because it's not the unknown that terrifies you; it's the truth."

He straightened and handed the phone back to her before beckoning her to look at the scans. Nothing unusual showed up. The only thing the x-ray revealed was the circuit board.

"The phone's clean," he added as he looked sideways at her. "You have good instincts, and fear is a pretty strong indicator when something's not right. But don't reject the warnings just because you don't know how to make sense of them yet. Lil? I mean this, so listen to me," he insisted as he tried in vain to meet her distracted gaze. "If you don't feel safe, do something about it. I've never seen you this worried about a case before, and I don't like it."

Lily didn't take her eyes off the scan. It *had* to be her phone. There was nothing else she carried on her person constantly except her notebook, and she would have noticed a bug in that. It would have been too difficult to conceal anything against such flat surfaces. Someone was watching her and accessing information very few people knew. If they weren't bugging her phone, how else were they learning all of this? The only other possibility was too terrifying to think about.

Because the only other possibility was that the person threatening her worked in the same room she did.

Maybe Matt was right. She was too afraid of the truth to admit it, even if doing so helped her follow the right lead.

"I don't know what to do, Matt," she whispered and blinked faster as she stared down at the table. "I feel like I'm going crazy."

"You're not going crazy. You just need to take a step back. When's the last time you slept?"

"Last night," she said in the same tone a toddler would take while resisting a nap.

"When's the last time you got good sleep?" he amended.

She pursed her lips and maintained her position. "Not that long ago."

"Sure. Yeah, that's what I thought. Go home, Lily. You need to take a break from this, or you're not going to be able to help anyone."

There was no use arguing with Matt. He had always been her voice of reason, especially in her early days in the homicide division. She had always abhorred the idea of slowing down before she found the killer, never knowing what one night's sleep would add to the body count on her cases. It was always Matt who managed to calm her fears and talk her into taking care of herself throughout the investigations, as he did now.

"You're only doing the killer a favor if you're not at your best," he prompted when she didn't answer.

"I know."

He left it at that and reached over to switch off the machine.

Lily took a deep breath and stepped away from the table as the scans disappeared.

"Okay," she said at last. "Thank you, Matt. Really."

"Anytime. You know I'm here for you."

"I appreciate it," she said and stuffed her phone back in her jacket pocket to rest next to her badge. "Hey, can you do me a favor?"

"Keep this on the down low?" he guessed.

"I'm supposed to be on leave today," she said, as if that justified her request. "The Chief's gonna kill me if he finds out I was doing any digging."

"If you promise to go home and get some sleep, I'll keep it between us."

"Deal." She could at least attempt to hold up her end of that bargain. If she couldn't manage to sleep? Too bad. She could say she tried.

"Good. Now get out of here, Detective. I've got work to do."

"You got it," she chuckled and thanked him again before showing herself out.

Stilinski was still waiting in the car at her insistence. He may have been assigned to protect her, but she didn't know if she could trust him yet. The last thing she needed to do was tip him off to the fact that she was still investigating if he was the one they were fooling into thinking she was off the case.

"Everything okay?" he asked when she ducked back into the passenger seat.

"Yep," she said as she buckled. "We're good."

The killer found out about her removal from the case within minutes of her leaving Alcarez's office. If her phone wasn't bugged and the killer wasn't listening in on her conversations, that meant it had to be someone close to her. The three people she'd worked closest with over the last few days were Stilinski, Harris, the Chief, and Jordan.

She ruled out the Chief and Jordan after only a minute or two of reflection. She couldn't picture her boss playing a role in any of this. He had supported her ever since her start in the precinct, and she couldn't see any major changes in their relationship that would have jeopardized that. Jordan had roughly the same level of technological understanding as she did, so she doubted he would be able to send advanced anonymous emails and texts. Besides, he wasn't in the station when she was removed from the case, so he couldn't have known about it so quickly. That only left her strongest two suspects, one of whom she was taking to her home.

At least if anything happened to her today, the Chief would know who the killer was.

Stilinski and Harris were her two strongest suspects, but it was no secret that Harris was the more likely of the two. He had the motive to want Lily out of the way, although she had no idea what would have linked him to Anderson's and Simmons's deaths. Stilinski had a more obvious link to the deaths but not necessarily to the emails.

Was that enough? She hadn't seen evidence that he was prone to anger or violence, his record was clear of questionable actions in the line of duty, and he was generally helpful. Even more than that, he was a good, dedicated cop.

Still, he had been the one on duty at the time of both murders, and he was young and tech-savvy enough to know how to anonymize messages and texts before they came to her. The real question was whether he had a secretly ruthless personality or a tragic backstory that could make a guy snap.

"So, where to now? Anymore top secret errands to run?" he asked.

Lily connected gazes with him and realized the car wasn't moving yet. Of course he was waiting on directions from her. How long had she been sitting in silence, glaring at the radio?

"Oh. No. I think I'm just going to head home and try to get some rest. Might as well make use of the time off if the Chief is forcing me to, right?"

"Might as well," he agreed. "Just tell me when to turn."

She gave him the first few streets and turns to get him started, then spoke up again when the silence made her squirm.

"Thanks again for doing this. I know you kind of got stuck with it, but I appreciate you being willing to babysit."

"It was either this or filing old case reports. Tough decision," he added, throwing a light smile her way. "But I figured you might be at least marginally more interesting. Besides, I can't sit still that long without Adderall."

"Oh, yeah," she grimaced. "That's got to be tough, considering most of the work we give rookies is desk stuff."

"It sucks," he agreed. "But I don't mind paying my dues, you know? All rookies do it. At least I'm not interning somewhere for no money."

"Wow. You've got a much better attitude than most of the rookies I've dealt with. They're usually pretty entitled when they graduate from the Academy."

"I was just happy to be out of there and to get a job in a real station," Stilinski said. "I was never that good at school stuff."

"Really? I always sort of fancied you'd be the top of your class or something. I just thought you were too humble to brag."

"Oh, no. My grades weren't great. If I hadn't had a recommendation and an awesome interview with the Chief, I never would have landed a job."

"You're smart, though. How is that even possible?"

He shook his head, trying to detract attention from his bashful smile. "It was a focus problem, I guess. Couldn't stare at a board for that long. The field stuff was a breeze. That's where I can really concentrate, you know? That's real life stuff."

"And it's often life or death these days."

"Right," he agreed before glancing over at her. "Wait, no. We're not thinking about that today," he warned. "No death talk right now. Let's talk about something other than work, maybe."

There was her opening.

"That's fine with me." She fixed him with an intense, purposeful stare. "Let's talk more about you."

21.

RIFT

Within the hour, the two officers were discussing their life stories at Lily's kitchen table while they waited for a pot of coffee to brew. The only thing the car ride revealed was how much the two had in common; it did nothing to alleviate or confirm her concerns that he could be the one sending death threats to her. They each had one sibling, Lily's older and Stilinski's younger. They agreed over favorite sitcoms and movie genres. They loved the same books. Neither of them truly knew many people in the city to connect with. They had both grown into a love of true crime due to tragic circumstances.

Stilinski had lost his father from medical complications that resulted from excessive drug use. The elder Stilinski's habits spiraled the family into financial ruin and split its members into even but opposing sides. He had decided before his father's death that he could become an officer to crack down on the growing market for hard drugs, but the loss kicked him into gear. He signed up for the Academy the day after the funeral.

Lily had done the same shortly after the funerals of both her parents.

In short, she had made no progress on the case itself, but found several more reasons to enjoy his company.

She watched him open the fridge and stage a successful search for the creamer. She didn't notice how intently she was focusing until he leaned in and waved a hand in front of her face.

"Why are you watching me so carefully?" he asked as he passed her the creamer.

"What?" she replied and shook head minutely to draw herself back into the moment. "I was just spacing out."

"That was not spacing out. You're more relaxed when you space out, but that stare was intense. You were studying me."

"I study everyone. It doesn't mean anything, necessarily."

"It doesn't? You're not trying to find out if I'm a suspect?"

The gurgling of the coffee maker swallowed any chance she had to reply, although the ability to do so escaped her, anyway. Her lips parted and hung slack as she waited for the noise to stop. When the kitchen fell silent again, she realized her brain had, too. How was she supposed to defend that?

"Sorry," Stilinski broke the silence as he poured himself a cup. "That didn't come out the way I wanted it to."

"N-no, it's… I'm just not sure why… Why would you—?"

"It's okay. You don't have to do that," he cut her off without looking at her. "I get it."

He added a small amount of cream to his mug and stirred it into the coffee. The metal spoon clacked against the ceramic mug a few times before he removed. He set the spoon on the counter next to the pot.

"For what it's worth, I don't think you're trying to kill me."

"You don't? Because you've been acting weird since we left the station."

"Yeah, of course I'm being weird. I'm investigating a double homicide that I've received a death threat for. Forgive me for being a bit twitchy."

"So you do think I'm a suspect."

"That's not what I said."

"It's what you're thinking, though."

"What, so now you're an authority on what I'm thinking?"

"Why won't you just tell me? I'm giving you the opportunity. Now would be the time to come clean with it."

It would be the time to come clean. But she had already dug her heels into her argument to the contrary. Her only options were to admit it to him now and risk compromising the investigation or to continue lying and hope he dropped it.

"Bloody hell! Would you relax?"

"I think you're the one who needs to relax, Faye," he bit back. "And stop lying to me like I'm stupid."

"I don't think you're stupid! I wouldn't even be working the case with you if I thought that."

"Right, like you were given a choice on whether you got to work with me or not."

Lily stared back at him, unaware that she'd stopped breathing. This was exactly the sort of altercation she'd been hoping to avoid, but he seemed bent on seeing it through. Why was he pushing so hard?

"Look, I'm sorry if I've done anything to give you the wrong impression—."

"It's not the wrong impression, Faye," he growled. "Why won't you just admit it?"

"Because what good would it do?! We're working well together! Why are you trying to ruin that?"

"I'm not trying to ruin anything. I'm trying to figure out why you won't trust me."

"I do!"

"You don't, or we wouldn't even be having this conversation!"

"I don't know why we are having this conversation!" She stood and joined him at the coffee pot, her cheeks pinkening with the heat of the argument. "What do you want from me?"

"I want you to tell me the truth! That's it!"

"Would that make you feel better?" she demanded and slapped a hand against the granite countertop. "If I told you I'm looking at you as a murder suspect and trying to figure out if you're going to kill me the next chance you get? Would that really help anything?"

"At least I'd know you were just doing due diligence! How am I supposed to do my job—which is keeping you safe, by the way—if you don't trust me to do it?"

"I can't believe you're even trying to have this conversation right now!" she said through a laugh of disbelief. "You're absolutely mad, you know that?"

"Mad enough to kill?" he asked at a quarter of the volume most of their argument had been conducted in.

The sudden shift in volume and tone sent a shock of goosebumps up her spine. She cocked her head to the side in an attempt to flick away the phantom feeling that someone was reaching for the back of her neck. A sudden, irrational flare of raw panic clawed from deep within her stomach like a rat trying to escape a sinking ship, and the breath she hadn't had to spare earlier now stuttered out of her mouth.

"Stilinski…"

He set his own coffee down and pushed it away from the edge of the counter. A small trickle of coffee sloshed over the side and streamed down, forming a pool on the countertop. He took half a step toward her, but stopped when her hand swung back toward the gun on her hip. He leaned away and raised his hands in surrender, even as his jaw squared.

"Just tell me," he murmured.

She swallowed around the golf ball sized lump in her throat and nodded.

"Yes. Okay?" she breathed out. "I've had more threats than I've let on, and one of them absolutely had to come from within the station, so every man at work is a suspect right now. I can't afford to not be that thorough. You have to understand that."

He stared back at his mug, though he made no move to pick it up.

"I get it," he murmured and turned his back to her. "I, uh, am gonna have Chief call Isaacs to stay with you tonight. I'll be in the car until she gets here."

"What? No, you don't have to—."

"You're not comfortable with me here, Faye. Don't worry about it." He pulled his jacket off the back of his chair and tugged it on. "Have a good night, okay? Stay safe."

"Stilinski, this is ridiculous," she protested, although she stayed rooted in place until he walked out the front door.

Lily made it as far as turning the coffee maker off before losing interest in the task of cleaning up. She spent the remainder of the day and most of the night on the couch, where the only altercations taking place were between her and Netflix. She played an episode of a sitcom before she dozed off, and every time she woke in sporadic increments throughout the night, the screen read, "Are you still watching?" Each time, she smashed the select button on the remote a little too hard to play the next episode, and then attempted to fall back asleep.

When she watched the clock on the television flip to five-thirty, she gave up on sleep. It was late enough in the morning to justify getting ready for work. So she pushed herself off the couch and straightened out the crumpled uniform she hadn't changed out of from the day before. Then, she staggered to the front door and peeked her head out.

"Isaacs?" she called with a sleepy wave toward the car in her driveway.

When Isaacs stepped out of her car and walked to the front door, Lily said, "I'm going to get ready for work and head in soon. You don't have to hang out until your shift ends, if you don't want to."

"You going to be okay to get there without an escort?" Isaacs asked in a soft tone that didn't carry.

"Yeah, I'm good. Thanks for hanging out. Sorry it was so boring," she gave a half smile.

"I would rather it be boring than have to scrape your brains off your front door," Isaacs considered. "All right. See you later, Faye."

"Lovely," Lily muttered and wrinkled her nose.

She waited until Isaacs ducked into the car and drove off before she slipped back into her house. She locked the door behind her and trudged up the stairs to get ready. If she couldn't survive on her own for the next hour and a half, she had no business being an officer.

Before she left for work, she made a pit stop in the kitchen to clean the mugs from the day before. She hadn't bothered taking care of them after Stilinski left. The coffee he had spilled hardened into a sticky stain which she had to scrub away with a sponge. She did so with mounting fury with the situation, then hurled the sponge into the sink and stormed out. Her drive only exacerbated her foul mood, which was at an all-time high when she arrived at work.

She had gotten no sleep, had no coffee yet, and she was on terrible terms with the only officer she'd been getting along with this week. It was not going to be a good day.

She walked through Stilinski's area and frowned when she saw his desk empty. Rather than risk missing the opportunity to talk to him and clear this whole mess up, she sat in his chair and waited for him to arrive.

When he walked in twenty minutes later and saw her at his desk, he stopped cold.

"What do you want, Faye? I've got work to do," he said as he closed the gap between them tugged his coat off the back of the chair, despite the resistance she created by leaning against it.

"I want to talk to you. Where are you going?"

"I'm on patrol today, and I don't want to talk."

"Don't be a child, Stilinski," she insisted, trailing after him into the parking lot. "I'm sorry I offended you but I have to be realistic here. If you didn't want to know, you shouldn't have asked."

"You don't think I have a right to know that I'm being considered a suspect for a double homicide and a plot to kill the officer on the case?" he hissed, eyes darting around the lot to make sure they weren't being surveilled. "Never crossed your mind that I might be able to help you out a little by proving I'm not doing any of this?"

"Internal investigations aren't that simple, Stilinski. Let's just say for argument's sake it was you. Theoretically," she snapped before he could argue with her. "Now that you know I think that, you're of course going to do everything to prove it's not you, including altering a pattern of behavior I've been observing for the duration of the investigation. If the killer knows he's being watched, all the variables change and I am that much farther away from figuring out who's threatening to kill me. That's a bad enough scenario when the killer is a civilian I'm not interacting with every day. Now imagine it's someone I have to put my entire trust in day in and day out. See how messy it gets? And we're obviously already seeing the results of what happens to the coworker relationship when suspicions are directed at the wrong person, aren't we?"

His keys jangled as he swung the ring around his finger, considering her speech.

"I'm not angry you suspected me. I'm pissed that you lied about it," he said once her point sank in. "But now that I know, will you at least give me the chance to prove it's not me?"

"Of course I will. Believe me, the last thing I want is to think you're involved in any of this."

"I'm not involved in it, so thanks."

"Can we not do that, though?" she requested with a wince. "We don't need to be rude about it. We're supposed to be working together, yeah?"

He shrugged. "I'm not just going to stop being mad, Faye."

"I don't need you to stop being mad. I need you to work with me, so we can clear your name and move on from this whole mess. I should have done that ages ago and I'm sorry I didn't. I'm sorry I lied about it, too. So, can we talk when you get back from patrol? I can conduct a proper interview and have it all on record."

He nodded. "Yeah, I'll be back eleven. Is that good?"

"It's perfect. Be careful on patrol, okay? No more bodies."

"Trust me, I never want to find one again," he muttered and walked out.

22.

MENTAL BLOCK

Lily was on her third cup of coffee within two hours when the Chief shouted for her. She groaned into her styrofoam cup and carried it with her as she walked across the station. She stopped in her boss's doorway and tried to assert her authority to be back at the station by speaking before him.

"Anything interesting happen yesterday?"

"Come in. Shut the door," he said. "I want to talk about those threats again."

Her nose wrinkled as she stepped in, shut the door behind her, and took a seat. At least he wasn't kicking her out yet.

"Newberry called for you yesterday," Alcarez started. "A few times. Said he's been tracking the location of the messages, and it's moving."

Lily perked up at that. "Wait, what? I only gave him one message to trace."

"Yeah, and I gave him remote access to your desktop yesterday. So we know about all the messages you've been lying about."

"Chief! That's—."

"Within my right as your supervisor who is trying to keep you safe," he cut in with an enraged glare that had her shrinking back in her seat.

"You said the location's been moving?" she muttered, staring down at her coffee. "That means some of the emails are being sent from a laptop, right?"

"That seems likely. They're mostly coming from one IP address, which we can't trace unless we submit a subpoena to a specific individual. But it does look like that's a laptop, based on the way it's been moving around," the man answered and slid a list across the desk. "I looked up the coordinates Newberry sent based on the IP addresses, and it looks like the emails have been sent from a few different Starbucks, a public library…" he paused and glanced up at her. "And a couple from the station."

She nodded as she scanned over the paper, but didn't react otherwise. The punch he'd expected he was delivering was common knowledge to her at this point.

"You knew that already, didn't you?"

"Not about the additional locations," she said through a clenched jaw. "But I knew some of the threats originated in the station."

"How?"

She shook her head. "It's not relevant."

"The hell it isn't, Faye! We are past the point of keeping secrets. I want to know everything, now, or you're off this case permanently."

"I got an envelope," Lily cracked under the threat. "With pictures of me at crime scenes and around the station. It wasn't postmarked and it didn't have my name on it, so the only person who would have known to put it in my box was the one sending it."

He sat back in his chair and eyed her. His entire torso expanded as he drew in a deep breath, then dispelled it. After he started and stalled on an attempt to speak, he massaged the bridge of his nose and tried again.

"Until this case is solved, you tell me if you get so much as a dirty look from anyone here. Anymore emails, envelopes, or pictures—you tell me about them. Instantly. If this has already escalated to the point of the killer reaching out to me, I don't know how much longer we can hold him at bay before he makes a move." He folded his hands together on the desk and leaned over them. "But I need to know now so I can help you: who are your suspects?"

"I haven't been able to rule anyone out yet," she confessed. "It's been kind of secondary to the murders. This information will help, though," she added and waved the paper she held.

Alcarez glowered. "I feel like I'm going to regret asking this but what were you doing with your time off yesterday?"

"Investigating Stilinski," she confessed and tried to switch tracks before he could react. "So, about these locations…"

"Dammit, Faye! That was supposed to be time off so you could rest," he growled. "Not time to conduct your own background check on the person I tasked to protect you!"

"But I'm making progress!" she insisted. "Chief, you just said yourself that the killer is escalating. You know I couldn't just sit around and do nothing yesterday. I'm going mental!"

"You know how this stuff works, Faye. These circumstances are exactly the reason I needed you to be resting," he held firm, jabbing his index finger against the desk to punctuate his point. "You know the killer could be waiting for you to wear yourself down before he attacks, especially if he knows that's what you usually do in these cases. And if he does that, what's going to happen to you then?"

Lily ground her teeth together and gritted out, "You really have been talking to Matt."

"The kid has good sense. You should listen to him once in a while," the Chief said. "Moving forward, I need you to rest."

She took a sip of her coffee to stall, but finally admitted, "You're right."

"You're damn right, I am," he said as he sat back. "Okay. So, what did you find out about Stilinski?"

"Well, based on this list, I don't think it can be him."

"Why not?"

"He hates Starbucks, for one. He barely knows where the New York Public Library is, say nothing about smaller libraries in the area. I know that's not enough to give him a solid alibi, but I'll get one soon. I'm interviewing him over lunch."

"You're...interviewing him? Does he know he's a suspect?"

"This has been a really weird investigation, okay? He was not supposed to find out. He guessed and I didn't have a good enough recovery line. That's why he sent Isaacs over yesterday and didn't stay with me. He's pissed."

"I'm sure he is," he sighed. "Do you have it under control, or do you need some help?"

"No, I can handle him. The locations help a lot. I'll just confirm it during the interview and we'll be safe to cross him off the list and move on."

"Good. Were you worried it was him before?"

"I really hoped it wasn't," she admitted. "But I didn't have much to help rule him out, either. Now I do. Thankfully. We work well together. I would have been pissed if I had to give that up because he was a murderer."

"Good thing he's not, then. I'm glad I picked the right guy to guard you yesterday."

"If I recall correctly, I requested him, but sure. You did," she nodded. "Chief, I swear I'll get some rest tonight. But I have leads I need to follow today. Can I please finish out my shift?"

She held her breath as he scrutinized her for what seemed like an hour. Her death grip on her coffee and the bags under her eyes didn't inspire much confidence, and she knew his concerns were reasonable. Still, she had momentum now and hoped he could see that was more important for the time being.

"Yes, you can finish the shift," he conceded. "And keep me updated if you find anything. You give me a name and I'll take care of the guy, got it?"

"Yes sir," she said before stepping out.

His concern was nice, but she felt a strange swell of irritation at the offer. Would he have offered to deal with the killer if she was at her peak mental and physical capacity? Her frustration clouded the historical evidence that he had made similar offers; she could handle this without her boss intervening to do her dirty work.

In fact, she had been handling it. She would have continued to do so without interference if Matt had reported these findings to her in the first place and upheld his promise to keep her inquiries quiet. Instead, he'd dragged the Chief into it and undermined her in the process.

When she got back to her desk, she flipped the list facedown so nobody walking past would see it. Instead of looking over the details to find a pattern straight away, she texted Matt.

LILY: *You told my boss? I said this was confidential!*

She continued to fume until he replied a few minutes later.

MATT: *You lied about how serious this was. You don't get to be mad at me about this.*

LILY: *Like hell, I don't! You breached confidentiality. I don't have a clue who I can trust right now, Chief included. What happened if the person you looped into this was the person coming after me?*

MATT: *I don't think you'd be texting me right now.*

LILY: *That's not funny.*

MATT: *I wasn't trying to be. You need to start taking this seriously. You made me check your phone for bugs and almost had a nervous breakdown. Do you remember that?*

MATT: *I'm not losing my best friend because you're too damn stubborn to take care of yourself.*

She started to type that she was not stubborn, but he sent another message before she could hit send.

MATT: *And yes you are stubborn.*

She pursed her lips and deleted her message.

LILY: *I am taking care of myself, okay? I know my limits and I know when I have to take a break. I'm never going to stop arguing that, so you might as well trust me when I say I've got it under control.*

It took him so long to respond this time she thought he'd admitted defeat. She checked it off as a victory and started to look over his report. She found two potential patterns to the locations of the computers before her phone buzzed again.

MATT: *I just don't want to stop arguing with you anytime soon.*

Lily stared at the text long enough to let the impact of it set in. This wasn't a game. She'd proven that much by storming his office with her personal side projects and showing him how much her inability to come up with answers scared her.

The idea of her fear pushed his words from yesterday through her mind again.

It's not the unknown that terrifies you; it's the truth.

If she couldn't overcome the mental block preventing her from seeing the truth, she wasn't going to be able to stop the murderer in time to protect herself. Only, she didn't know how to dissolve that block. Her own stubbornness was going to get her killed.

23.

MISTAKES

Stilinski was still on patrol when Lily remembered she'd instructed Harris to leave yesterday's findings on his desk. She took a cursory look around her area before walking through the station. She found the file in question next to her colleague's keyboard and scooped it up. As she walked back to her own desk, she began to thumb through its contents and found Harris's additions to be both sizeable and impressive; he had taken more initiative once she gave him free reign.

At its forefront, the file contained a status report on the background checks of the Mallorys. Harris's accompanying note stated it was in progress and he would update the file as soon as he received word back. The next several pages contained the header "2nd Interview - Derek Williams" and had been typed like the script of a play.

An inaudible sigh escaped her lips as her posture straightened, as though the thought of interviewing the man who hit on her had been sitting on her shoulders like a barbell stacked to its limit. The transcript was a little thicker than her initial interview, so she settled in at her desk and began to scan through it.

The first page crushed her hopes that the size difference in transcripts meant Harris had gotten more valuable information from Derek than she had. The document reported little more than cringe-worthy small talk. Page two began with a stunted remark about the weather and didn't show signs of improving. Page five began to give way to slightly relevant details about Derek's family life and dating history. Page twelve was where it got interesting.

"I thought I left that on Stilinski's desk," Harris said from behind Lily.

She held up a hand to make him wait as she devoured the rest of the page, lips moving silently at a frantic pace.

"You're not supposed to be on this case anymore," he persisted. "You *just* gave it to me."

"Chief put me back on it," she told him, internally chiding herself even before she finished speaking.

The whole point of appearing to be off the case was to convince the killer not to move forward with his own plan of attack. Since she hadn't ruled Harris out as a suspect, it would have been smart to come up with a cover story before she blurted out that she was back on the case. It was too late to backtrack now, though. She just needed to finish reading before she could think of an excuse.

"Will you please be quiet for two seconds? We can discuss this in a minute," she added.

"No! I want to discuss it now. If this isn't your case, you shouldn't be looking through it. That's confidential material, you know. Give it back!"

Lily tensed at the demand, her eyes halting in the middle of the sentence she was reading. "Harris, you've done amazing work here. Really. Don't undo that by whining." She turned toward him and said, "I'm not taking it over completely, all right? I know you have a lot in progress, and I'm not going to get in the way of those tasks. I'm just an extra pair of hands so we don't get overworked. Unless, of course, you've solved the whole thing already."

"Maybe I have."

Her expression didn't falter as she stared him down and said, "Then tell me who the killer is."

Harris's jaw slackened and his eyes darted back and forth as he scrambled for an answer. After a couple of seconds, he declared: "Aiden Mallory."

Lily exhaled and folded her hands together on top of the case file.

"It can't be Aiden Mallory, Harris," she explained, her patronizing tone thinly veiled. "He was in custody at the time of the second murder."

At least this much seemed to have occurred to Harris, because he had his rebuttal prepared: "He has an accomplice."

"Look, it's not impossible for that to be true, but it's highly unlikely at this point, and I think you know that," she pointed out. "Harris, I really need you to stop butting heads with me on this one. We've got too much to do and not enough time to do it, and I don't have the energy to argue with you about this every single day. Please go talk to the Chief if you have issues with this decision. Otherwise, let's just work on it together and get on with our day, yeah?"

Harris held her gaze without moving for so long she wondered if he'd frozen that way. His lips pressed into a thin line of fury and his thick eyebrows slanted so low, all she could see of his narrowed eyes were his black pupils. Movement just below her line of vision told her he was clenching and unclenching his hands.

"I will go talk to the Chief," he said at last, his voice warbling and quiet. As he turned away, he added, "Someone needs to teach you how to keep your nose out of everyone else's business."

His unsettling words stuck with her as she continued through the case file. Harris had cross-referenced every witness description of the killer with the interviews Lily conducted and narrowed it down to a useable profile. His conclusion stated the killer was a Caucasian male between his thirties and forties. His approximate height was six feet tall. He had either been wearing a brown hat or had brown hair.

The description didn't match Derek, but it did fit Lily's coworkers better than she'd hoped. Although Harris was half Hispanic, his lighter skin tone often caused people to confuse him for Caucasian. But would Harris's own report fail to rule him out as a suspect if he truly was the killer?

With that in mind, Lily returned to the transcript of Derek's interview and scanned it from the beginning. This time, she kept her eyes on Harris's questions instead of Derek's answers. If her detective was the killer, it would make sense for him to ask leading questions that tried to pin blame on Derek. If Harris wasn't the killer, the questions would be more pointed for the sake of gathering the truth about Derek's living situation with Jessica.

The transcript read:

DETECTIVE: So what kind of relationship did you have with your roommate?

Lily noted this assumed there was a relationship, and that Harris didn't use Jessica's name. A sign of remorse? Killers tended to dehumanize their victims by refusing to use their names, except in the case of sociopaths who had no capacity for remorse.

SUSPECT: We were just roommates, man. I mean, I liked her. Don't get me wrong. She had a lot going for her that a lot of guys thought was attractive, you know? She just had that kind of personality that sucks you in, too.

DETECTIVE: The kind of person you just want to be around, right? Spend time with?

SUSPECT: Yeah, as much as you can. It sucked because our schedules were so different. We got to hang out sometimes living together but I didn't see her as much as I wanted to. She was an awesome person.

DETECTIVE: You said you liked her. Just for my own clarification, can you specify? Liked her how?

SUSPECT: [pause] Maybe it's the wrong word. I guess there was a time where I thought I loved her, even. But how do you really know, right? We never dated or anything, so it's not like I had a chance to figure it out.

DETECTIVE: Really? All that time living together and you never told her how you felt? Didn't even ask her out? Nothing?

That wasn't what Derek had said. It was an odd misdirection, but a misdirection nonetheless. It gave Derek an easy opportunity to lie.

SUSPECT: Hell no. I didn't want to ask her out so she could turn me down. It would make things weird, you know? I liked her but I didn't want risk her moving out because I'm an asshole who couldn't keep his mouth shut.

DETECTIVE: Hey, I get it. Dating sucks. It's tough. So if you didn't do anything about it, what happened? Did she ever figure out you liked her?

SUSPECT: I don't know. It doesn't matter if she did now, anyway, does it?

DETECTIVE: It actually does.

SUSPECT: Look, man. I already told the other detective I have an alibi. I would never do anything to hurt Jessie.

DETECTIVE: Not even if she rejected you?

SUSPECT: I just said she never rejected me because I never asked her out.

DETECTIVE: So let's get your alibi on the record and clear this up right now. Where were you that night?

SUSPECT: I was working. We shut down at two and it takes about an hour to clean up, so I left a little after three and got a drink with a couple coworkers. I can have them call you and vouch for me.

DETECTIVE: I'll follow up with them if you leave their names. How long did you stay out?

SUSPECT: A couple hours. I got home around five thirty and went straight to sleep.

DETECTIVE: And you didn't check on your roommate before you went to bed?

SUSPECT: I never do. It was five thirty! I wasn't gonna wake her up.

Lily skimmed through the rest of the transcript, but conversation dwindled from there. As soon as Harris stopped pretending to be his friend and acted like a cop, Derek's factual demeanor turned defensive and his answers yielded no further information. Despite the shutdown, Harris managed to acquire the contact information for Derek's coworkers. At the bottom of the last page of the transcript, Harris scrawled a handwritten note that read: "*Alibi confirmed by three witnesses on 5/15. - HH.*"

A high pitched ringtone sounded from the corner of her desk, and Lily reached over to her answer her work phone. She didn't look away from the report as she pulled the receiver to her ear. Her eyes were already glancing through the transcript one more time for any details she may have missed.

"This is Faye."

"Do you really want to be pissing Harris off right now?" Alcarez's voice reached through the other end.

"Sir, it is not my job to coddle my team. Harris is going to have to suck it up."

"What if he can't?" he pointed out. "What if you're giving him more motive?"

"Whoever's doing this clearly already thinks they have motive," she pointed out. "If I start acting differently around anyone at this point, they'll think I'm onto them."

He grunted and warned, "Just be careful."

"You got it, Chief," Lily said and waited a beat to make sure he wasn't going to add anything. The line clicked and disconnected instead, so she hung up and went back to work.

Not thirty seconds later, the phone rang again. She took a deep breath and answered, again without looking at the caller ID.

"This is Faye."

"Head Detective Faye?" a woman asked.

Lily bit back an audible grumble as she scribbled a note to herself. *'CHECK CALLER ID. ALWAYS!'* She underlined the last word three times.

"Ms. Spencer, isn't it?" she replied. "What can I do for you?"

"Oh. You seem much more accommodating today," the reporter said in a lilting tone that seemed to suggest she was grinning. "I was just hoping for a few minutes of your time to verify a couple of facts for an article I'm writing."

"What's the article about?" Lily frowned.

"The recent homicides, of course. Before you object, I know you can't confirm anything about an ongoing investigation, so I won't ask. I just wanted to include a little bit of your biography. Maybe your motivations for police work. Readers have a hard time remembering that the names in print are representative of actual people, so I'd like to have something to help remind them."

"I'm not making any comments," Lily warned. "But if you make it fast, I'll give you some yes or no answers. Five questions, max. Then I'm off."

"Thank you, Detective. I really appreciate it. First, are you originally from Surrey, England?"

"Yes." That wasn't hard-to-find information.

"And you moved here about nine years ago?"

"Yes.

"When you were twenty?"

"Yes."

"And was that immediately after your parents were both killed?"

Lily's lips pressed into a tight line and her fingers curled around the phone until her knuckles went white. After flexing her hand for a moment, she relaxed it and drew in a slow, silent breath.

"That's what you were trying to get at? Is that what you really wanted to know?" she asked in a lower octave than usual.

"It is a point of interest to readers, yes."

Lily exhaled her answer: "Yes."

The reporter's voice softened so it nearly sounded genuine as she said, "I'm so sorry to hear that. And that was what motivated you to become a law enforcement officer?"

"Yes. And that's five. That's all the time I've got, Spencer."

"That's all I needed. Have a great day, Detective!" Alyssa chirped and cut the call before Lily could retort.

24.

GOTCHA

Lily didn't have much time to recover from the brief but jarring conversation with Spencer before Stilinski's interview. She carried her previously neglected drink into the interrogation room to wait for him. She sat still and silent in the cold, concrete box of a room and swirled her red plastic stirrer around in her beige beverage. It created a small whirlpool in the middle of the cup until it built enough momentum to tug the stirrer out of her tentative grip and spun it around the cup on its own.

As the whirlpool slowed to a stop and the stirrer stilled again, her mind wandered back to the many unsolved questions she had yet to deal with. Was there any possibility Kayla's death was unrelated to Jessica's? It wasn't likely. Did that mean the killer really was making his way through witnesses to the crimes? What was the point in stalking the detective in the process? If the motive was as simple as getting away with the first murder, wouldn't it be more prudent to stay far away from the head detective on the case? What did the killer want with her? And how did the Mallorys fit into any of this?

Lily tsked to herself, the sound creating a faint echo in the empty room. All that the line of questioning did was add to her nerves. The killer was doing a good enough job setting her on edge; she didn't need to help the process along by working herself up in her downtime. She exhaled and fidgeted with her phone, flipping it over and back a few times. When that didn't do anything to distract her, she unlocked the phone and opened her Facebook app.

She hadn't checked it in several days, but she only had five notifications and a couple dozen new posts to look through on her feed. The only friends she had tended not to post much. In the corner of the app's screen, a red bubble popped up with a white number one to alert her of a new message. Her thumb hovered above it for a second before hitting the notification.

This rerouted Lily to the messenger app, but there were no new conversations listed when it opened and loaded. She frowned and navigated to her message requests, where she found the source of the notification. There was a new message from an account titled with her full name that used her photo from the station's website as its profile picture.

The message contained only the taunt, "Gotcha."

Before shock could set in, Lily pulled up the Facebook app again and checked her privacy settings. Friends only for everything. No friends of friends, no public settings. That explained why the notification had popped up in her message requests instead of conversations.

She cradled the phone with both hands and stared at the screen until it dimmed from her inactivity. This was the first concrete lead she had linking the killer to someone with a presence in her life, and it had to be a staggering presence if they knew she had a Facebook account. Once again, she was hit with the breath-snatching realization that a trusted ally was trying to kill her.

"Faye? Hey, you okay?"

Lily looked up from her phone to find Stilinski standing on the other side of the table. She closed the app on her phone and set it screen down on the table.

"Hi. Yes," she said and pulled a tight smile when her words didn't seem to convince him. "I didn't hear you come in."

He nodded, a light frown etching across his lips as he examined her. Rather than saying anything, he took a seat. He held himself in a rigid posture and stared at the table. If he had been a suspect, that behavior might have suggested guilt, but Lily had a feeling it had more to do with the tension lingering between the two.

"I should have told you I'd be in here," she said. "Glad you found me."

"Wasn't hard to guess where you'd be," he shrugged and continued to avoid her gaze.

"Right," she said and tried to think of a decent way to transition into the interview. When she couldn't find one, she just made the rough switch and said, "Okay. Before we get started, I want to let you know this is nothing personal. It's due diligence."

Lily adjusted her own seating to face him more directly and folded her hands on the table as she looked to him.

"Some of the information we'll go over is stuff I already know about you, but I'd like to have it on the official record so we don't have to come back to this. That okay?"

"Expect redundancy. Sure, go for it," Stilinski said and mimicked her seating by clasping his hands together on the table.

Lily knew he hadn't done anything. She had enough plausible deniability to clear him, but if this case ended in a trial, she wanted to have her progress well documented. A jury wasn't likely to side with her if she had played favorites by letting her coworker slide with a shaky alibi. She needed it to be airtight.

"Mind if I record this?"

"Seems like that would be smart."

Stilinski's attitude wasn't helping. Usually, interviewees were either overly cooperative or openly hostile. There wasn't an overlap like she was sensing now. Her typical strategy would have to change.

"Where are you from, Stilinski?" she asked once she'd hit record.

"Florida. Starting off strong, huh?"

"Where in Florida?" she pressed, ignoring the jab.

"Sarasota. My family's from there."

"And you were the only one who moved to New York?"

"Yep. There aren't many of us left. Just my mom down there now."

"What prompted you to move away from her?"

"I wasn't trying to move away from her," he defended. "An opportunity opened up here, so I took it. You know what it's like. You go where the work is."

"I do know what it's like," she agreed. "I wasn't attacking you, Stilinski. Just getting this on record."

He flexed his interlocked fingers to crack his knuckles before he nodded. "Right. Sorry."

"I get it," she said. "It's a tense situation. Lashing out is our natural defense. But we're in this together, remember? We're here to help each other out."

"I know," he murmured and splayed his fingers out flat on the table. "It just stings, you know? I thought you trusted me."

"I do trust you," she frowned. "But how would it look in trial if it came out I had suspected you and then never followed up? I'll look negligent, and that would destroy my credibility. Maybe enough to let the killer walk. I've seen it happen before and I'm not going to let that happen now. That's the last thing either of us needs. Right?"

"Right." He sat back in his seat, shoulders slumping and his back arching against the metal chair. "I know. Sorry. I'll stop being such a dick."

"I'd appreciate that," she teased and sat back as well. "Okay, let's get into the good stuff and stop wasting our time, yeah?"

"Yeah, sounds good."

"Yeah," she smiled, glad to note his posture was relaxing. She started recording and asked, "Can you describe when you became aware of this investigation?"

"Last Tuesday, right around three-thirty in the morning," he said. "I was on patrol about six blocks away when I got a call regarding a stabbing across the street from Montview Apartments. I was the closest officer in the vicinity, so I headed over and found the victim."

"And when did you update your patrol log to reflect the change in your route for the evening?"

"Right after you and I spoke at the scene. As soon as I went back to my squad car, I entered it. I called Chief to let him know what was going on, too, so he can verify."

"He already has, but thank you. When you found the victim, what state was she in?"

"She was dead by the time I got there. The paramedics called it a minute after I made it to the body. So I set up a perimeter to preserve the scene the best we could in the rain and spoke to the witness, Kayla Simmons."

"At what point did you send Ms. Simmons away from the scene?"

"I didn't send her away, but I had no reason to hold her. I interviewed her to get her account of the story, like I told you when you showed up, but it was pretty obvious she was intoxicated and wasn't processing what she'd found. The paramedics verified she wasn't injured to the best of their abilities—she wouldn't let anyone near her to really confirm—and then we let her go home. That was probably five minutes before you showed up."

Lily nodded and moved to the next murder. Stilinski easily explained his presence there as well. His patrol log confirmed his alibi, as it detailed what parts of the city he had been during the times in which both murders crimes had been committed. With that out of the way, she could get into the more personal aspects of the case.

"You're not much for social media, right? Do you have a Twitter or Facebook, or anything?"

Stilinski shrugged and shook his head. "I mean, I like social media but I don't have a ton of time to use it. No Twitter. I have a Facebook but I haven't had much time to check it. It's been probably two weeks since I logged in at all. I have that Instagram, too, but I really only post pictures of my Starbucks cups when they get my name wrong."

"So you haven't been on Facebook lately? What do you usually do with your time between shifts?"

"Nope, not lately. And that depends on the day, I guess. Ever since this investigation started, I've been going straight home and sleeping after work. I try to get eight hours, and then I get up to work out for about an hour. Then I grab something to eat and then go into work."

Lily sat forward to ask, "What kind of places do you usually eat at?"

"Nowhere healthy," he snorted. "There's a pizza place and a pub I like on my way home from the gym, so I've been going between both of those. If I get really desperate, I'll stop at the market next to the gym and grab crackers or something I can eat on the way back to my apartment."

"What, no Dunkin Donuts?" she teased.

"Only if I want to go three blocks out of my way on the walk home," he mused, but smiled at her teasing. "That's what makes me mad about Starbucks. I swear there are six of them on my way home, but if I want Dunkin, I have to go halfway across the city."

"Naturally. I suppose I've been dragging you into Starbucks enough to last a lifetime lately."

"Yeah, I've been there more this week than I ever have before. I mean, if you want to keep going there, I don't mind it, but I don't walk in on my own."

That was what she'd suspected. "I appreciate you putting up with my unsatisfactory coffee habits," she smirked at him. "Okay, last question. You're not much of a reader, are you?"

"News, sure. Books, or something? Just those true crime ones we talked about. Books are too expensive, anyway."

"You know we have a ton of libraries around here, right? You could just borrow."

"Yeah, and that would be a lot easier to do if I knew where any of them were."

Lily grinned at the confirmation and reached for her phone. "I'm sure it would be," she agreed. "And we're going to fix that problem and acquaint you with some of them, I assure you. Okay, I think that's all I had for you. Thanks." She cut off the recording and saved it before tucking her phone away. "You're officially cleared."

"I am?" he asked, eyebrows popping up to wrinkle his forehead. "Just like that?"

"Just like that," she confirmed as she stood. "See how good I am at this? You didn't even know you were giving me an alibi."

"I kind of knew," he defended as he rose and followed her out of the interrogation room. "Man, I'd hate to be in there with you if I actually was a suspect."

"Good. Keep that attitude and we'll never have this issue again," she joked and nudged him when they paused to linger in the hallway. "Thanks for putting up with that, though. I feel a lot better having it on the record."

"Yeah, I guess I do, too," he admitted. He fidgeted and rubbed the back of his neck before asking, "Are we good now?"

"*I'm* good. Are *you*?"

"Yeah," he smiled. "I gotta get back on patrol… but if you want, I could bring something back for dinner? You know, so you don't have to wait until you get off work to eat. Who knows when that will be, anyway?"

"You know this job well," she chuckled. "That would be awesome. Thanks. Just give me a call and let me know where you're going, and I'll place my order then?"

"You got it," he nodded and took a few steps back toward his desk. "I'll see you later, Faye."

"See you," she echoed, her gaze lingering on him until he disappeared from the hallway.

Her stomach clenched up as soon as the comfort of his presence disappeared. Ruling Stilinski out as a suspect should have been a huge relief. It might have been, without the newest threat looming over her head.

She stepped forward to walk out of the hallway, but her knees buckled before she made it too far. Her hand slapped against the concrete wall to prevent herself from toppling sideways and slamming her head against it, but her legs didn't stop shaking. She pressed her back to the cold stone and slid down to the dingy tile as her breathing quickened. The straight lines in the concrete bricks across the hall dissolved and began to slither down the hall in a continuous serpentine motion. Nausea clawed at her stomach and throat. She swallowed bile and dropped her head into her trembling hands, heels pressing hard against her eyeballs until they burned white hot from the pressure.

It was time to face the truth.

25.

STRIKE THREE

Harris was nowhere to be found after the earlier altercation, much to Lily's relief. It had taken her a solid twenty minutes to stand and drag herself out of the back hallway to her desk. Her body still shook as she dropped into her chair and rested her heavy arms on either side of her keyboard. Her head hung as she tried to take regular breaths. Every inch of her felt like she had been struggling against someone holding her underwater.

Breathing had only just become a regular occurrence again when Harris returned with a brown paper bag bearing the name of a restaurant a block away. He gave her a curious look as he sat at his desk.

She had no idea how disheveled her appearance was after her panic attack and didn't feel like discussing it. Her phone rang just in time to prevent him from asking what was wrong with her, and for a second, she was grateful for the distraction. The feeling was squashed by dread as she read the name on the screen, but she answered the call anyway.

"Please, please tell me you're just calling to get my dinner order early," she whined into the receiver.

"I wish. I jinxed it," Stilinski groaned back. "I'm so sorry, Faye. We've got another body."

She yanked the phone away from her ear and fumbled to mute her side of the call. She barely managed to do so before she shouted so loudly that Harris jumped and spilled part of his soda down his uniform. She didn't take time to apologize, even though he sent her a dirty glare as he patted his shirt dry with napkins bearing the restaurant's logo.

She unmuted the phone and growled, "You have got to be kidding me."

"I really wish I was. And I know this makes me look suspicious but I've got my driving log and the dispatcher to give me an alibi. How soon can you be here?"

"I'll leave now."

"Okay, good. But, I need to warn you before you get down here, Faye," Stilinski's voice took on an urgency she hadn't heard from him before. "This one's probably going to be a little more shocking."

"What makes you say that? The other two were pretty gruesome," she grimaced as she shrugged her jacket on and walked out of the station in a hunched, defeated posture.

"Yeah, but…" he sighed. "Just get down here."

"I'm on my way. What aren't you telling me?"

"I don't know if you'll want to come down if I do."

"It's my job, isn't it? I'm coming one way or another." She received nothing in response to her logic but silence. "Stilinski, what is it?"

"I'll brief you when you get here," he said at last. "See you soon?"

"Yeah," she relented with a frustrated sigh of her own. "Send me the coordinates and I'll be there ASAP. Just make sure the scene is cordoned off and nobody's close enough to mess with the evidence."

"Will do. We've got the markers out, and the photographer at work already."

"Okay, thanks. Good work," she said. "See you soon."

She hung up and hit the parking lot. Once she made her way to a squad car and began pulling onto the street, she flipped the lights and sirens on so she could push her way through the city traffic a little faster. It was still too slow a journey for her liking, but having the extra level of authority helped.

As she battled her way through the busy streets and often perilous intersections, her thoughts clung to Stilinski's warning. What on earth would be so shocking about the third body, so different that she wouldn't want to come to the scene anymore? Did this mean the killer had given up on his copycat ways? Maybe it had been a rush job. But she wouldn't really consider that shocking, and certainly not to the point of driving her away. It had to be more personal than that.

Stilinski had sectioned off the crime scene with surprising attention to detail, making sure that not only were the press too far back to tamper with the evidence, but that they weren't even able to see the body. He'd had a white tent installed over the part of the sidewalk the crime occurred on and was standing watch outside it while the forensic photographer took pictures of the evidence within.

"Detective!" a familiar, grating voice shouted as Lily got out of her car and slammed the door shut.

Lily gritted her teeth. She didn't need to look to know that Spencer was here, too. Couldn't she just leave well enough alone? Instead of acknowledging her, Lily kept walking toward the scene.

"Detective!" Alyssa shouted after her anyway. "What can you tell us about the rumors that you're the killer's next target?"

Lily's feet stopped before her brain warned her torso to do the same, and she jerked forward. After teetering a moment to regain her balance, she whirled around to face the reporters, lips pressed into a hard line. She walked a few steps back toward the cluster of cameras and locked eyes with Alyssa.

"Where the hell did you dream that up, Spencer?" she demanded.

"Haven't you been following my coverage on the case?" Alyssa asked in mock surprise. "I had a tell-all run in with someone very close to you, who informed me you've been receiving threats to stop the investigation."

Someone close to her? Lily gritted her teeth as she tried to formulate a response that wouldn't allow the media at large to interfere with the case.

"Who?" was all she could growl.

Anything else she could possibly say would end up twisted in the headlines by that evening if she spoke it.

"Oh, detective. A good journalist never reveals their sources," Alyssa smirked. "So you're not denying that someone is trying to threaten you into abandoning this investigation? Are you going to leave it in the hands of a more capable detective?"

Lily's eyes widened. "More c—I am the Head Detective on the force, Spencer!" she snarled. "I have earned my place there just like everyone else on the squad. And I will not stop this investigation no matter who or what forces try to make me. Now, I am going to do my job and examine the crime scene. Move, before I charge you with obstruction of justice!" She only waited a beat to watch the smirk slip from Alyssa's face before snapping, "That's what I thought."

She stomped over to the tent and reached for the flap to duck inside.

Stilinski side-stepped to block the entrance and grimaced. "Before you go in there—."

"Stilinski, not now," she warned. "I need to get out of their sights and start doing my job."

"Faye, I really think I should warn you before you do," he began to protest.

"Move!" she growled and stepped around him, ducking into the tent.

As soon as she laid eyes on the body of Chelsea Dennings, she regretted not listening to him.

This victim was the only one who'd been stripped completely. Chelsea's head had fallen to the side to reveal a gaping hole where her throat had been slashed. Her vacant stare greeted Lily's as the detective entered. For a few moments, Lily stared into at the dead, startling, emerald eyes, too stunned by the sight to look away.

When the detective managed to survey the rest of the victim, her stomach twisted so violently that she suspected she might throw up. The killer had left one last threat to verify how personal the case was now. A single word had been etched out of the sheet of now dried blood covering Chelsea's bare torso:

"Faye."

26.

ABSENCE

"Is she okay? She hasn't moved since you brought her in."

"I have no idea. She's been like this since she saw the body."

The Chief and Stilinski were both leaning against the Chief's desk, bent forward to study Lily. Stilinski had returned her to the office and sat her down in her usual chair, and she hadn't moved since then. She had barely blinked.

"Was it that bad?" Alcarez frowned as he straightened up to look at Stilinski. "I've never seen her like this."

"It wasn't pretty. I tried to warn her before she went in, but she pushed past me and the next thing I knew, she was screaming," Stilinski reported as he watched the detective. "The killer made it pretty damn obvious he's coming for her next."

The words made Lily gasp, and the two leaned back toward her. Both men held their breath while they waited, but Lily made no further movements or sounds. Stilinski exhaled and rubbed the back of his head.

"I don't know what to do, Chief."

"We'll figure something out. She's probably just in shock. Lily?" the Chief asked. "Can you hear me?"

It took a few seconds before she nodded, her clouded and unfocused gaze fixed on the desk between the two men.

"Okay, that's a good start. Can you talk? Are you all right?"

Lily didn't speak.

"Faye, if you don't say something, I'm pulling you off the case," he finally threatened. This kind of paralysis was understandable but unaffordable.

"N—I—," Lily tried to protest a couple of times before shaking herself out of the daze enough to speak in a full but sluggish sentence. "Sh-she didn't...have green eyes."

Stilinski frowned at the Chief for translation, but Alcarez shook his head.

"Faye, what are you talking about? Who didn't have green eyes?"

"The v-victim. Chelsea Dennings," Lily connected, speaking at the same speed of a sloth moving from tree to tree. "She didn't have...green eyes."

"She's got green eyes, Faye," Stilinski said. "They were wide open. We both saw them."

"No. The first time we met her—you can't tell me you don't remember," Lily insisted as she switched her gaze to Stilinski, and cognition flashed into her eyes. "She didn't have green eyes. She had brown eyes!"

"So what?" the Chief cut in. "What does it matter what color her eyes are?"

"It's significant!" Lily snapped and used the anger to push her weary body out of the chair so she could pace. "I-it means something. I mean, she's already a fake redhead. Why go through the trouble of mimicking my eye color— my exact eye color, by the way, which is shockingly uncommon—unless it was significant?"

"I'm pretty sure it just means you're the next target," Stilinski pointed out. "Which we could have already guessed from the, uh, writing."

"But it's overkill," Lily pointed out, swinging her hands into an X formation and slicing them out through the air. "I've always known the killer was after me, so what's the point in going through a step like that just to prove it some more?" She dropped her hands to her sides again and started muttering to herself, mind racing. "No. No, that can't be the only reason. There's something staring me in the face and I can't see it. I can't figure out what it is, but dammit, it's *there*!"

"Faye!" Alcarez barked. "I think you need to take a break."

"I don't need a break! I need to figure out why this is necessary!"

"I'm not asking, Detective."

The quiet but firm tone put an end to her frantic babbling. Lily stopped pacing in favor of looking at him.

"Chief, come on," she pleaded in the broken tone of an addict begging for one more hit. "I can do this. Nobody knows this case like I do. I just need a little more help," she admitted and looked between the two. "You know I can't take a break now. Who would even fill in for me? I mean, I've been working on this case nonstop. I-I've been tracking the emails, I have leads to pursue, I have a...a list of suspects I've barely been able to investigate—."

"Which is why I need you to keep working on it. Later. But you know I can't allow that to happen now if someone inside this station is putting your life at risk."

Stilinski's eyes widened as he looked to their boss, then to Lily, and asked, "What? I thought you'd cleared everyone here. Why wouldn't you tell me you still suspected an officer?"

"I didn't exactly have time between ruling you out and you finding Chelsea!" she snapped back. "And I couldn't tell you before. Not when I didn't know who I could trust."

"Given the circumstances, I don't think you can blame her for that," the Chief pointed out.

"I don't blame her for considering me a suspect. I just thought she knew me better than to lie to me about it," Stilinski said.

So they weren't as good as he'd said they were earlier. Lily couldn't fault him for letting the incident sting even if they agreed they were past it. The fact that she thought him a suspect was bad enough, but she hadn't demonstrated that her trust in him was restored once his name had been cleared. She should have told him she suspected other officers, even if there hadn't been time to do so. She should have found a way. Maybe if she had, they wouldn't be having this argument and resurrecting the tension they had started the day with.

She frowned as she hobbled back to her seat like an elderly woman after a hip replacement. She sank into her chair again, not sure if her physical or mental health could take another hit today.

"I do know you better than that," she sighed in a quiet tone. "And I didn't mean to lie to you about it. But you were on patrol most of the day. There really wasn't time."

"I get it. You don't have to justify it to me," he said, although he held her gaze too intensely for Lily to believe he was shrugging the matter off. "Besides, this isn't even what we're talking about. We have to deal with what happened out there."

"Agreed," the Chief interrupted. "I'm recommending a week off and a security detail until we catch this bastard. If it's someone in our force, we'll find out soon."

"We don't have time to deal with it," Lily said. "And I'm not taking a week off. I can't afford to do that right now. There are three dead women I need to investigate—"

"And we're not going to risk making it four," Alcarez glared. "We are not arguing about this anymore, Faye. Until I can get a better handle on the situation from inside the station, you are no longer on this case."

"Chief! Who the hell is going to solve it, then?"

"I'm taking point on it for now. All I'm asking is for you to take a few days off and reset before trying to come back to this. You've got a major conflict of interest in this case now."

"And nobody else except Stilinski to take care of it. Chief, all due respect, you don't know all the nuances of the case that we do."

"I'm sure I'll be able to catch up to speed with the work you've done so far. Seven days, Faye. That's all I'm asking."

"Like hell I'll take seven days off," she snarled and her hands clenched around the arms of the chair as if she had to physically restrain herself to keep from lunging at him. "I've barely been working the case that long and three people have been killed. What the bloody hell do you think is going to happen if I leave for seven days? I will give you two."

"Five."

"Two."

"Four."

"Three."

"I'll take it. Stilinski, make sure she actually gets some rest. I want you with her twenty-four seven."

Lily didn't bother arguing that time. If there was anybody she trusted now with her life, it was Stilinski and Stilinski only. She just hoped she could earn his trust back before something happened to her.

"Yes sir," the younger cop nodded. "I'll check in daily, and more than that if I see any suspicious activity."

"Good. Now I'm giving you an hour to wrap up whatever you're working on and take off for the day," the Chief warned. "Both of you. Any questions?"

"No sir," Lily muttered and looked down at her lap.

"Good. Make sure you sign your firearm out. Get a box of ammo, too, if you think you'll need it. I want your weapon on you at all times."

Lily nodded. Maybe it was supposed to serve as a gesture of goodwill and trust in her ability to carry around her service weapon without using it in anything but self defense. That wasn't how it felt in the moment, though. It felt like an omen, a confirmation that she would be attacked. It was only a matter of when.

"Then you're both dismissed."

"Thank you, sir," Stilinski said as he began to follow Lily out. "You need any help packing up?" he asked her..

"No, thanks. I think can take care of it," Lily said and glanced over at him as they neared his desk. "I hope I didn't imply that I don't trust you in there. Because I do."

"You don't have to explain yourself," he murmured and averted his gaze to stare at a pencil on his desk.

"Maybe not, but I want you to hear it, because you seem like it's still upsetting you," she said. "You have to understand the frame of mind I've been in lately."

"I get it, Faye. I just wish you'd dealt with it differently, that's all."

"I should have," she conceded. "And I really wish I'd had time to. I can't imagine how you must be feeling after everything that's happened with us in the last couple of days. The last thing I want to do is be dishonest with you, because you really are one of the only people I can trust right now. I really hope that remains mutual."

"I don't know if we have time to talk about all that right now," he said before he flashed a secretive smile. "Especially if you want to walk out of this station with copies of all your case files."

Lily stared back at him with wide eyes. How had he known she was planning to take her case files with her? She opened her mouth, unsure if she was about to argue with him to save face or question him.

"See?" He nudged her before she could decide. "We know each other pretty well."

She snorted and nudged him back. "Okay, you prat. You've made your point. Go finish your work before you have to babysit me for three days."

"Yes ma'am," he chuckled and walked back to his desk.

She began the laborious task of gathering all the paper copies of her work, both within the case file and her personal notebook. She would leave the originals with the Chief so it looked like she had nothing to work on from home. While she was at it, she also printed out all the relevant emails she had received, including each of the threats and attachments.

The task ended up taking most of the hour. The printer was old and jammed easily. Each time it did, she had to figure out which documents hadn't copied correctly and try again. The attempts were coupled with paranoid glances over her shoulder toward the Chief's office. She didn't want to explain what she was doing and, thankfully, it didn't come to that. He stayed in his office and she finished printing off everything she needed to continue working through her mandated leave of absence.

She hid her copies in a nondescript manila folder and slipped it into her purse. Once they were stowed as needed, she boxed up the originals and delivered them to her boss.

"Sir? These are all the files you'll need to continue the investigation," she said. "I've also changed my email password and written down the new code for you, so you can see the threats for yourself, if you'd like. In case you didn't get them from Matt already. I also have a proposed schedule of investigatory events written in my planner, which I highly suggest you follow. There are a couple of leads I need to check on again but I would prefer to do that upon my return since I have established relationships with those individuals. Is there anything else you need to pick up where I've left off?"

"If you think I have everything I'll need in that box, I'll take your word for it," he said as he took it from her and set it on the corner of his desk. "What all is in there?"

"The case file, my notebook, my planner, and the lists of evidence, weapons, witnesses from the first two homicides. I also put the dates and times of the emails I've received," she accounted. "If you need anything or have any questions at all, Chief, please call me. I'll be relaxing as much as I possibly can but I won't be able to take my mind off this case."

"I don't expect you to completely," he said. "But you need some rest and time to recalibrate. Once you've had that, we'll talk. Now, have a nice leave."

Lily gritted her teeth but held back the arguments forming on her tongue and said, "Yes, sir. See you in three days."

She stepped out of his office and moved back to Stilinski.

"You ready to go?" she asked as she stopped in front of his desk. "I think I'm about thirty seconds away from being escorted off the property."

"I am ready," Stilinski said with an amused grin.

He stood and collected his coat. It looked as though he was just holding back a chuckle while he packed up and walked to the front desk to sign out their weapons. He was still grinning when they walked outside.

"What are you smiling about?" Lily demanded through a quiet laugh as they approached his car. "It's obvious you want me to comment on it, so please. What could you possibly find so amusing?"

"That. That's what I find so amusing," he grinned and held the door open for her. "Has anyone ever told you what a drama queen you are?"

27.

EYES

The adrenaline from the ups and downs of the day vanished the second the officers dropped into their seats and buckled in. The only conversation either could muster were directions and grunts of understanding. The DJ from the Top 40s station whispered through the speakers, but the subject matter didn't hold the attention of the current audience. Both stared blankly at the road ahead of them, exhaustion weighing heavy on their faces.

The conversation picked up for a full sixty seconds once they stepped into Lily's house. She reminded Stilinski where each room was, then showed him the drawer of take out menus and apologized on behalf of her empty fridge. She hadn't been able to grocery shop since the case began.

"I'm just going to take a shower and get ready for bed," she told him. "Feel free to watch TV or read, or anything you'd like before you go to sleep."

"Okay." His voice hitched as he used it for the first time in half an hour. He cleared his throat and asked, "You need me to clear the upstairs?"

They both looked toward the stairs and winced. The wooden blocks had never looked so mountainous before. It would be a trek to make it to the landing, let alone around the rest of the upstairs.

"Nah, I've got it," she promised. "If I scream, feel free to come running, but I can manage. I still have my gun, in case anything happens."
"Good. Shout if you have reason to use it," he said.

"I will. Have a good night," she added before dragging herself up the stairs and into the bathroom.

She made a thorough and irrational sweep of the area once she shut the door. She padded over to the shower and held her breath as she ripped back the curtain to find… absolutely nothing. An empty shower, as it should have been. But just to be safe, she left the curtain open while she turned on the water, then searched the shelves beneath the sink and even flung open the medicine cabinet. What she thought she'd find there, she wasn't sure.

Once she knew nothing could attack her from within the room, she locked the bathroom door and stripped out of her work clothes. After surveying the room for a few seconds, she placed her service weapon on the closed lid of the toilet so it was well within her reach in case of an emergency. She was not going to risk dying naked in the shower; there were few ways she would want to be killed if given the choice, and that was not one of them.

The shower itself washed away enough of the day's stress to make room for the subconscious thoughts she hadn't had time to deal with yet. She replayed the week leading up to Chelsea's death in a series of brief one-line summaries while she washed and rinsed her face. As she massaged shampoo into her hair, she recounted the day's events.

That was when it hit her. She knew why Chelsea's eye color changed, and why it was bothering her.

"Stilinski! I just thought of something!" she shouted as she jumped out of the shower and wrapped herself in a towel. She tucked it under her arms and sprinted into the hallway, the water still running in its stall. "Stilinski!"

"What? What is it? Where is he?" he demanded as he clomped up the stairs, his own weapon clasped between his hands.

He darted straight past her into the bathroom and spun in a circle on his heel to check for intruders.

"What? No, nobody's in the house," she clarified. "No. I just realized why it was bothering me that her eye color changed!"

"Who? Dennings?" He holstered his gun and stepped back into the hall to glower at her. "Faye, you are not supposed to be working on this. You're supposed to be resting."

"And I did for a little while! And then I realized Chelsea's eyes matched mine almost perfectly!" Lily explained with an excited grin.

Stilinski's face didn't change even after she explained the source of her enthusiasm.

"Yeah?" he asked. "And like Chief said, so what?"

"That specific shade of green is really rare. Something like two percent of the global population have green eyes at all, and most of those individuals have lighter hues. You have to special order contact lenses with my exact shade; they don't just come in that color. She wouldn't have had time between our first meeting and her death to send away for them. And what possible motive would she have to change her eye color, anyhow?"

"I mean, you can get a bunch of stuff off the internet now in less than two days, but still. Assuming she didn't do that…" Understanding sparked on his face and the slow flame of reasoning smoldered in gold flecks inside his hazel irises. "Hold on. That would have to mean…" he trailed off in thought.

"Yep! Finish that sentence!" she beamed and pointed emphatically at him. "Put it together."

"She's not the one who put those contacts in?"

"Right!"

"Which means the killer put them in after Dennings died."

"Yes! He would have already had those lenses. Which means he's made a premeditated move and won't be able to plead insanity on this last murder when we catch him."

"Oh, right. That definitely ups the chances of a life sentence, if not a lot more." Something sparked behind his eyes. "Wait a second. If the killer put those lenses in..."

"There you go. Back on track. Lay it on me."

"Could we get DNA off them?"

"It's possible! Especially if he put them in after she was dead." Her eyes would have stopped producing tears that could have washed the killer's DNA away at that point.

"Whoa! Did I just find a lead?"

"You did!" With her help, but hey, he'd made the connection. It wasn't bad work.

"All right!" he grinned and swooped in to hug her. He froze about two seconds after they embraced and realized, "You're wearing a towel."

"Yep, and there's soap in my hair still. I should probably get back to that."

"I'm gonna let you," he agreed and jumped away from her as if she'd turned into a giant hot coal. "And I'll call Charlie and tell him not to touch those lenses."

"Brill," she beamed, her entire face pink. "Really good work, Stilinski."

"Not bad, either, Faye," he complimented before returning downstairs.

Lily stepped back into the shower and rinsed the shampoo out of her hair, still grinning.

Not bad at all.

28.

THE SUN STILL RISES

The stillness brought by early morning gave Lily the time she needed to reflect on her situation. Thanks to last night's progress, she and Stilinski were closing in on the answers they desperately needed, but how did she keep herself safe until they arrested the killer? She would need to keep Stilinski close, now that he was the only officer she'd cleared.

It wasn't wise of her to slip out of the house before the sun even rose, but she didn't go far. She perched on a large rock in her cramped back yard and turned her focus toward her breathing. The case had consumed her thoughts ever since Jessica's death; it was time to stop thinking. Surely, her guard would understand that she needed get out and meditate.

She didn't look back when she heard Stilinski's boots squishing against the rain-saturated grass. She kept her gaze on the dark, spiky patch of grass in front of her and counted down three more deep breaths. Then, she spoke up.

"I should have left a note, but I figured you could find me. I didn't go far."

"No, and I appreciate that," he granted in a muted, sleepy voice that warmed her insides despite the chill in the air. "But given the situation, it might have been helpful so I didn't freak out when I woke up to an empty house."

"If you're looking for an apology, you aren't going to get one," she warned as she shifted on the large rock she had turned into her seat.

"I don't want one. I just want you to be safe, Faye. Sneaking out makes it kind of hard for me to keep you safe."

"I'm not on house arrest, Stilinski. It's not sneaking out," she sighed and crossed her arms. "I came outside to clear my head because I couldn't sleep. That's it. I have every right as a free American to sit outside my own home when I feel like it."

She expected more of an argument, but he asked, "Do you have dual citizenship or did you cross completely over to the dark side?"

She glanced up at him and frowned. "Why is that relevant right now?"

"It's not, but I'm not here to babysit you," he shrugged. "You can defend yourself if it comes down to it, so I'm not going to lecture you. I just want to have a conversation that doesn't involve the crap we've been dealing with for a change."

"I guess it's been a while since we talked about anything else."

"Yeah, it has," he agreed and nudged her arm. "Move over. You didn't answer my question, by the way."

Lily scooted over on her perch so he could sit next to her.

"I have dual citizenship," she answered. "Which is an even more difficult process than simply switching, by the way. The ceremony is odd."

"It is?" he asked as he took a seat and looked out across the small yard with her. "What's odd about it?"

"They make you denounce the Queen!" she grimaced. "Which is incredibly awkward if you're remaining an English citizen, too. It's not like I've really denounced the Queen. I agree with the monarchy far more than I do the system of government here, after all."

"Wow…" Stilinski blinked a few times. "That is… quite the opinion to have before coffee."

"Sorry. I've been up for an hour."

"You should have woken me up. Told me you couldn't sleep."

"I thought you weren't babysitting."

"I'm not. Just letting you know that waking me up is an option, so you're not alone if you want company."

"I wasn't alone. You just weren't conscious."

"That makes it sound like you were standing in my room. Do I need to request a lock on that door?"

"There *is* a lock on the door, and for the record, I wasn't watching you sleep, you perv," she snorted.

"Good. It would be really awkward trying to navigate around the office if I had a restraining order against you," he joked.

"No kidding. That would suck," she chuckled.

"I'd hate to have to do that, anyway. So much paperwork, you know."

"Right. It's terribly inconvenient. How dare I even make you think it?"

"How British of you."

"What?" she laughed. "How is not thinking about inconveniencing others British of me? If anything, that's American."

"Wow. You're slamming both of your countries right now."

"Let's change the subject before I become downright treasonous, then," she snorted. "You're right; we should not be having these conversations before coffee."

"Guess not," he grinned. "Want to head in?"

"I guess. In a minute," she said and looked back out to the horizon. "We'll miss the best part if we go in now."

"The best part?"

"Trust me," she smiled.

The sky turned lighter shades of blue as the sun crested over the horizon, then mixed into a rapid succession of violet, red, and yellow hues.

Stilinski didn't move a muscle until the sky settled on a misty gray-blue and the sun was visible in all its circular, gold splendor. Then, he shifted to glance at her.

"I guess trusting you pays off sometimes."

"Looks like it does," she smirked. "Imagine that."

"I don't have to imagine anymore. I just saw the proof."

She looked over and smacked his bicep, laughing, "Come on, you prat. Let's go make coffee."

"Now you're talking," he grinned and hopped up. "What were you doing out here, anyway?"

"Meditating," she said as she walked back toward the house with him. "I like to watch the sunrise when I can. It helps me get perspective."

"How so?"

"It's just a good reminder that my problems are temporary. No matter what happens, life goes on. The sun still rises. It's still going to set at the end of the day, regardless of what goes on in between."

"All right. You're getting back into the territory I can't function in before coffee," he smiled and stepped away to grab two mugs from the cupboard.

"Hey, you're the one who started this conversation. You should be able to track with me by now."

"I was only up for fifteen minutes before I found you outside. Enough time to check my email. Oh, but that reminds me: Charlie got back to me about the contacts."

Lily peered sideways at him while she poured a cup of coffee.

"Did he manage to pull anything off them?"

"We got a partial but it was pretty washed out," Stilinski reported and set his cup next to the coffee pot. "Chief's putting in a request for the manufacturer of the contacts, though. He's gonna see if he can get a listing of anyone who bought them in the last couple of weeks in our area. It's kind of a long shot, but you said they were pretty specific contacts, right?"

"Yeah, not ones I think many people would order. Anyone who wants green eyes usually goes for a darker shade than mine," she said as she poured coffee into his mug as well. "So that's...something, anyway. We could also try to figure out what color hair dye was used on Chelsea and track the killer from there, but that's a much larger pool to narrow down."

"And we're already on it. Charlie locked in the color and brand last night. I think either Harris or Jordan are following up on that today."

"Brilliant," she nodded and thought it over for a few seconds.

For the first time in the investigation, it looked like they had a lead that could produce a name and a direct link to the killer. If they could trace the contacts purchase back to a credit card, an arrest could be made by the time Lily returned to work.

The realization brought a slow, relieved grin onto her face as she raised her gaze to meet her partner's.

"Then we almost have him."

"Yeah." Stilinski returned her smile with a smaller one of his own. "Almost."

29.

MUD-SLINGING

The momentum petered out after the first day of Lily's short-term vacation. Neither she nor Stilinski had the ability to follow up on the most promising lead in the case to date, so they spent the entire second day on nothing but cooking, naps, and Netflix. By the third day, Lily's energy returned in full and made it impossible to sit still, so she took to pacing in the kitchen.

Although she didn't voice her discomfort, it hung in the air as thick as fog. Aside from the aimless wandering, she alternated between wringing her hands, picking at her nails, fiddling with her necklace, and playing over a scene in her mind that seemed to be miles away from the kitchen floor she was glaring at.

"I don't get why you're so annoyed," Stilinski told her from his seat at the table, where he crouched over the remains of a syrup-soaked waffle and half a strip of bacon. "You're going back tomorrow."

"I'm not annoyed. I have cabin fever," she grumbled. "There's nothing else we can work on. You don't find that annoying?"

"I don't think a three-day vacation is annoying. I haven't had three days off in a row since I started working here," he said as he got up to brew a pot of decaf.

"Exactly! That's why I like this job, because I don't have to stop. I can't just turn off being a detective when I'm not in the station. Some of my biggest breakthroughs on cases come to me on my days off."

"So why is this break any different?"

"I was forced to go on leave because someone wants to kill me. It's not a fun little holiday," she pointed out before striding into the living room. "Besides, we already had the breakthrough. I want to do something about it now."

"Oh, come on. Now you're just trying to hurt my feelings," Stilinski grinned as he followed and watched her collapse on the couch. "You're not having fun? Am I boring you?"

Lily rolled her eyes and swiped a copy of the New York Post from the growing stack of papers on the coffee table. Stilinski had been collecting them off the front step every morning but Lily had yet to read through them. Part of her hadn't wanted to, since she figured Alyssa Spencer had printed plenty about her in the past three days, particularly after Lily's breakdown at Chelsea's crime scene.

"You know my irritation has nothing to do with you," she said. "But I'm going mental. I've gone over the case files ten times this morning alone, and I'm not finding anything new."

"Because they're covering the main leads we have at the station. There's nothing else for us to do right now."

"Well, I want there to be something for us to do," she grumbled as she flipped through the paper, looking for any headlines relating to the case.

"There will be tomorrow. But taking a break has been awesome for the case so far. If continuing to rest is the most helpful thing you can do right now, do it. Chill out and try to remember what it's like to be a normal person for a few more hours."

Lily glowered down at the paper with pursed lips. A quiet, whistling exhale escaped from her flared nostrils before she sighed.

"How are you this smart? It's irritating."

"Only because you're used to being right all the time," he joked. "I'm messing with your home turf now, aren't I?"

"Yes, you are. Cut it out."

"Yes, Your Majesty," he snorted.

He ducked back into the kitchen as the brewer bubbled at the end of its cycle, leaving Lily to read her paper.

A low growl formed in the back of her throat when she found the article she'd been searching for. Spencer's line of questioning felt like it occurred weeks ago, not days. Yet, the date of the paper's publication was marked for only four days back, the same date of the phone call and Chelsea's murder. Lily wasn't surprised to see Spencer had capitalized on the immediate opportunity to slander the detective's reputation.

"This is bloody insane," she muttered.

"What is?" Stilinski asked.

He approached the couch in a slow crab-like walk as his long legs moved independently from the rest of his body. From the torso up, he was still as a statue to prevent spilling the two full cups he carried, one in each hand. He stopped at the coffee table and bent at the knees to set the mugs down. Once he managed the feat with a surprising amount of grace, he flopped back onto the cushion next to her. The springs creaked in protest at his sudden lapse in control over his full weight, but Lily hardly looked up.

"The article Spencer wrote about me before I took my leave," she frowned. "She called me a few days back and asked to confirm some facts… I was wondering how she'd twist them."

"So what did she write?"

"Unfortunately, nothing I can demand a retraction on since I've confirmed some of the facts she wrote about. She talks about how long I've worked for the NYPD, how long I've been Head Detective, why I moved from England… she really twisted the typical tragic backstory angle and made me sound awful, though. Listen to this:

"Head Detective Lily Faye joined the NYPD after fleeing from her hometown in Surrey upon the mysterious deaths of both parents—"

"Whoa. Hold on," he stopped her there to squint at the paper. "Why's she making it sound like you had something to do with that?"

"She's a gossip columnist pretending to be a reporter," Lily rolled her eyes. She tossed the paper aside and reached for her laptop instead. "She only has a job as long as her stories can cause a scene. I wonder what other rubbish she's been saying about me."

"Lily, come on. We don't need to worry about her right now," he protested. "You're supposed to be relaxing, remember? We should watch a movie or something."

"I don't want to watch a movie. I want to find out how else she's been slandering me," she said and navigated to the paper's website. "Here we go. Wait, Harris and Jordan are in this article," she frowned at the picture connected to the headline and clicked into the article. "She's going after my team while I'm not there? Really?"

"What?" Stilinski leaned against her to read over her shoulder. "Well… Harris does have the case right now. It kinda makes sense if she's following it."

"Yeah, but why pull Jordan into it, too?" Lily asked as she scrolled through the page. "Okay, let's see… She says, *'Detectives Jordan and Harris are well versed on homicide cases…'* blah blah, years of service, background information, Jordan's dissertation, Harris's gun collection... Oh, here's something:

" 'However, neither police officer seems versed in decorum. While attempting to obtain an interview with Head Detective, Lily Faye, who has been conspicuously absent since the discovery of the last murder victim,'—that bitch. Of course I'm absent.—*'both Jordan and Harris became belligerent and hostile, to the point of threatening the reporter, who was eventually forced to leave for fear of her safety.'* What?" Lily's eyes widened in outrage.

"'The nature of this attack on the media is egregious and indicative of a failure on the part of

the justice system to uphold the safety of our citizens. Now, more than ever, we must demand increased accountability from our police officers and ensure that such corruption is permanently weeded out."

Lily slammed the lid of the laptop shut with such a loud snap, it made Stilinski jump. She leaned forward to drop it on the table, which shook and caused her coffee to slosh and run down the sides in tiny rivulets.

Stilinski leaned away from her to put a safe distance between the two and regarded her with raised eyebrows.

"Who does she think she is?" she seethed. "It's one thing to call my competency into question with the way this investigation has gone, but to attack my detectives like this? Nobody goes after my team and gets away with it!"

"Okay, well… what *are* you going to do about it?" he asked as he studied her arms for any signs she might take a swing at him. "Not to sound like a jerk, but what *can* you do?"

"Nothing," she growled and tapped her foot against the floor. "I can't do anything until I'm back to work. Then I'll solve this case and put the rumors to rest."

"Exactly. When we get back to the station tomorrow, you can fix this. But for now, it's not a big deal," he soothed. "It's media, Faye. Mud-slinging. It'll blow over the second a more interesting headline pops up."

"Yeah?" she questioned as she glanced back to the laptop. "Well, unless we catch this guy soon, a more interesting headline is exactly what we're going to get."

30.

ELECTRIC REVELATIONS

"What the bloody *hell* were you two thinking? Do you have any idea what kind of attention this has drawn to this investigation?"

The scene Alcarez watched from his safe space behind his desk would have been comical, were his Head Detective not so hell-bent on terrifying her subordinates. For the past ten minutes, he had been watching in silence while Lily paced back and forth in front of Jordan and Harris. Both men were larger and older than Faye, yet they sat slumped so far back in their chairs, it looked like they were trying to crawl under them to avoid her withering looks. For every minute of silence, they seemed to lose another inch in stature.

Now that she finally snapped, both detectives jumped as though she had shoved a taser against their ribs. With all the grace of a synchronized swim team, their heads dropped and they mumbled a feeble apology.

Lily came to a halt in front of them and set her hands on her hips, blocking Alcarez's view of Jordan's and Harris's cowed expressions.

"What is the first rule when dealing with the media?" she demanded.

Harris and Jordan exchanged glances, then shook their heads at one another as subtly as they could. Jordan lost in the end. He grimaced as he glanced up at her.

"Everything's on the record?"

"Everything is on the record!" Lily confirmed, each word punctuated with its own exclamation point. "What's the second rule?"

Jordan shot a glance to Harris, who went pale at the silent election. He looked up and floundered for a few seconds.

Lily let him.

"*Don't* talk to the media!" she snapped when his gaping started to grate on her. "I should be able to trust two grown-arse men while I'm gone for three damn days not to put the entire station's reputation at risk! What do you have to say for yourselves?"

More floundering ensued, and Alcarez covered his mouth with a hand to hide his grin.

Lily held a hand up and grimaced when that didn't make the sniveling stop.

"Okay, shut up!" she insisted. "I've heard enough out of you two. You're both cleaning up the records room for the rest of the day. Just stay the hell out of my way so I can fix this mess."

Harris's eyes widened and he leaned over in his chair to look at the Chief.

"She can't do that, can she?"

"She can," their boss confirmed and lowered his hand, the smile vanishing as he did so. "She's your direct supervisor. She can do whatever she damn well pleases with her team, especially when they're acting as dumb as the two of you did. Now, she's got work to do. I'd say you know better than to keep her from doing it."

"Yes sir," Jordan muttered as he got up. He grimaced as he looked to Lily and added, "Sorry."

"We'll talk about it tomorrow," she told him. "Thank you."

"This is not fair," Harris protested as he stood and followed Jordan out. "We were trying to help."

Lily crossed her arms and turned back to the Chief once the two were out of earshot.

"How hard do you think I'd have to push before he applies for a transfer?"

"I don't think you're going to have any luck there. He's about as stubborn as you, only he's stupid about it. You can't fix that kind," the Chief grimaced. "Are you sure sentencing your entire team to records is the best way to go right now? Don't you need some help?"

"I'll be fine for a day. I'm sick of them undermining my authority. If this is what it takes to get a little respect, so be it."

"All right. But you know you're a hypocrite, right? I gave you another chance when you messed up with the media."

"You did and I appreciate it," she agreed. "I also don't have a history of behavior issues."

"Neither does Jordan."

"Point taken, but if he stayed up here, I'd be babysitting him all day. He wouldn't do a thing without asking me if it's okay first, and I don't have time for that right now."

"Some people might call that respect, you know. It's a hell of a lot better than what Harris is giving you."

"Is it?" she frowned. "They're both annoying as hell."

"Maybe, but they're your team."

"For better or for worse, I suppose," she huffed and walked out.

Jordan was gone by the time she returned to her area, but Harris was lingering. He hopped up when he saw her and opened his mouth, but she held up a hand to stop him.

"I don't want to hear it."

"No, it's not about this," he insisted, then glanced around the station. "I just want you to know something before I head down there. It's about Amy

Mallory," he said and waited to make sure she didn't cut him off again before he finished, "Someone bailed her out."

"What?" Lily's stomach twisted at the news. "When? Who?"

"Yesterday afternoon," Harris said. "I looked up the record and put a copy in your ingoing. Just… it's pretty weird. You might want to check it out sooner than later."

She nodded, her mouth scrunching into a puzzled frown. Since when had he decided to be helpful? Was he trying to mislead her and pull focus by directing her to an unrelated task?

"I will. Thanks."

He leaned against the door to the stairwell and nodded as if the knowledge they shared was conspiratory. Then, he pushed the door open and disappeared.

As soon as he left, Lily snatched the stack of papers from her box and sorted through them until she found the report of Amy Mallory's bail. She scanned through the typed up statement, eyes jumping to the name of the officer who had submitted the report. Then, she checked to see who had signed to let the woman walk.

The names were identical.

All the breath escaped Lily's lungs with a soft "whoosh" as she sank into her chair. Her eyes darted between the two signatures. Her thoughts zipped back and forth until she caught a snippet of the one she needed. The emails.

She dug through the case file for Matt's initial documentation on the location of each of the emails. When she searched for geographical patterns before, she had included the station. What happened if she removed that and only counted the Starbucks and library locations?

With a hopeful half grin, she pulled open the bottom drawer on her left and tugged out a laminated copy of a Manhattan city guide. She flipped to the map, grabbed a dry erase marker, and scribbled a star over each of the locations'

coordinates. Then, drew an X over the sites of all three murders.

"No way," she whispered as she sat back to look at the map, which now

contained a prominent, perfect circle of stars and exes.

As Lily could finally see with startling clarity, the shops from which the

threats originated and the placements of the second and third murders formed a

perimeter around a significant landmark in this case. She circled the area and

capped the marker. The longer she stared at the map, the further her mouth fell

open.

In the dead center of the circle stood the Montview apartment building,

in which the Amy and Aiden Mallory resided.

"They're accomplices," she whispered.

The weight of the electric revelation sank in as she took a deep, cleansing

breath. That was when another odd thought occurred to her and forced the hairs

on the back of her neck to rise. It felt akin to lightning striking in the same spot

twice.

The station smelled like flowers.

She had noticed a different scent as soon as she walked in, because the

station usually reeked either of body odor and coffee or disinfectant. She had

only dismissed the observation in her hurry to ream out her detectives, but she

understood its significance now. This was not a place that should have smelled

like Amy and Aiden's apartment.

She rocketed out of her seat and followed the scent, clutching the city

guide in one hand and Amy's release form in the other as she circled the room.

She wandered through the entire station, sniffing like a bloodhound on the hunt.

The scent was strongest next to the exit, so she tried to trace it from there back

to its point of origin.

"Uh, Faye?" Stilinski asked as she walked through his area for the second time, her eyes narrowed and scrutinizing. "Whatcha doing?"

"Shh. I'm sniffing. Do you smell flowers?" she replied as she straightened up, sniffed, and then repeated the motion while bending her knees.

"I guess a little? It's probably Maggie's perfume."

"It's not perfume," she said as she walked out of the room. "It's laundry detergent."

"Okay…" Stilinski pushed himself up from his desk and followed her back to her own area. "And that's a problem because…?"

"Because," she said and paused to take another deep breath. "It smells like the Mallorys' apartment."

She glanced back to see the impact her words made on him, and her shoulders slumped at his blank expression.

"Come on, man. I was trying to have a dramatic moment like they do on TV but I need you to keep up if that's going to happen."

"Sorry. You lost me on this one. So what if it smells like their place?"

"Stilinski, the murderer works here. We know that. And someone just bailed her out of prison, which she was in for plotting with her son to attack the detective searching for information on Jessica Anderson's homicide."

He bobbed his head twice, slowly.

"Which means… she was trying to cover for the killer by planning to get rid of you?"

"Maybe. But it at least means she was in the company of the murderer. Recently," Lily corrected. "Because she sure as hell hasn't been to the station lately. But the person who bailed her out has been. And yes, that could mean she was probably covering for him that night. But more importantly than that…" She thrust the report of Amy's release toward him with a wide grin. "He slipped up, Stilinski. He finally showed his hand. We know who it is."

She finally understood which officer was using the psychology behind the Kitty Genovese murder to get away with his own killings.

All of a sudden, she found herself in the presence of the dramatic moment she'd been reaching for moments earlier. She swallowed hard as sweat beaded along her forehead and her heart slammed viciously against her ribs. Now, she wished she didn't have the opportunity to deliver the line.

"I know who's going to try to kill me."

31.

SAFETY

Stilinski didn't so much as bat an eyelash after Lily gave a somber explanation of who was after her and how she knew. If he was at all skeptical, he didn't show it. He didn't question her suspicions, either. Everything from the flower smell to Spencer's article pointed to the same conclusion she'd drawn.

"Okay," he said simply once she finished giving her explanation. "You're right. It all adds up. So what's our next move? Do we arrest him? Take this to the Chief?"

"I think we at least need to talk to the Chief first. We still need to make the connection between him and Amy Mallory, but I think I have a hunch there. I just don't have proof for it yet. But we have plenty of cause to make an arrest. I just need to get a warrant drawn up and signed. And I think I'd feel better if he was the one to make the arrest. I can't be the one to do it, if I'm the next target."

She stopped to draw in a slow breath, but the reality of the sentence shoved the wind out of her lungs. It felt like she had discovered the killer was one of their own weeks ago, but it was a different matter altogether to have the evidence to prove it. Now, she knew beyond a shadow of a doubt.

Stilinski kept careful watch on her throughout the explanation and noted the way she'd changed from drastic excitement over cracking the case to what he could only describe as realization. The color drained from her face as she fell into a semi-catatonic state in which she stared straight ahead without blinking. So he leaned forward and snapped his fingers in front of her face, then grimaced when that method didn't yield any results. She'd done this in front of him before, so he knew it could happen, but he wasn't sure there was a good way to snap her out of it.

"Faye? Come on, you can't do this to me right now. We need a game plan."

"N-no, I know," she shook her head but still didn't blink or look at him. "I just…" she exhaled hard and took a couple of quick breaths. "It's kind of hard to tamp these kinds of feelings down once you let them come up. Sorry. You're right. Game plan. I just need a second because I'm working my way up to a panic attack and if that happens, I'm going to be useless for the rest of the night."

"Hey, keep breathing," he frowned and reached over to clasp her hand in both of his. "Faye, look at me. This sucks. I get it. I know that. There's no denying that this is a horrible situation. But not breathing is only going to make it worse, okay?"

Her wide eyes darted around the room before settling on his face. She nodded and drew in a slower breath this time, trying to match his own breathing pattern. It took a few rounds before she could speak again, but she nodded once she got to that point.

"Sorry," she whispered. "I'm fine. I'll be okay now."

"Are you sure?" he asked with a sympathetic smile and held her gaze. "Need me to get you some water or coffee or anything?"

"No, I'm okay," she said and squeezed his hands, as if that somehow proved she was back to normal. "Thank you."

"Hey, that was all you. Way to get ahead of that panic attack," he said. "Let's figure out a game plan and then I'll give you a lift home. How's that sound?"

"Yeah," she nodded again and wiggled her hand to slip it out of his hold. "That'd be brilliant. I appreciate it."

"No problem," he said and released her hands as she moved away.

"I had my suspicions before this, you know? It's just... different when you finally find the connection and it hits you."

"Yeah, I bet. I can't believe you figured it out off the smell and the article, though. That's genius level detecting."

A natural, unbidden smile stretched across her lips as she studied his expression. All she seemed to see of humanity these days was the absolute worst it had to offer; Stilinski was a blinding reminder that there was a good side to people as well. The way he looked at her now with soft, understanding eyes and a confident grin was proof that despite what they saw every day, trust still existed. And for whatever reason, he trusted her.

"You know how long it's been since someone looked at me like that?" she asked in her own kind of awed state.

"Like what?"

"Like…" she shook her head and swallowed back the emotion to keep her voice from shaking. "Like you have complete faith in me. And like you want me to be safe, no matter what. And I know you probably know I can take care of myself—."

"Course I do. I'm just the rookie, remember?" he smiled. "You don't need me."

"No, and I would like that to be on the record," she said. "But you have no idea how much I appreciate you sticking around nonetheless. I would have gone mental the last couple of weeks without your help."

"You wouldn't have," he assured. "Yeah, I probably helped a little but it's like you said. You don't need me."

"Nope," she murmured and let the word linger between them.

Maybe she didn't need him, but she wanted him around, especially with the recent developments in the case. She'd grown attached to the idea of the safety he provided whenever he was around. Of course, the safety was the only contributing factor. It had nothing to do with the person. She could have felt the safety with almost any officer on the force. It just so happened that he had been the one working the case with her since the beginning. That was all it was. It had nothing to do with him, specifically.

"You used to carry yourself differently, Faye," he said with a gentle voice. "There was always this authority I looked up to, you know?"

"Confidence," she said. "It's confidence."

"I know. And it's really nice to see. I think you just needed this breakthrough to get a little of it back."

"This certainly helps," she smiled back at him. "Honestly, thank you. I needed the pep talk. Now, come on," she added as she climbed to her feet. "We have work to do."

"I'm coming." A deep laugh rumbled through his chest as he stood up. "Just give me a second to recover from the whiplash."

"What? I feel better," she shrugged as she glanced back to him.

"I know you do. I just didn't think my pep talks were that effective," he grinned.

"Well, this one was. Good job," she teased.

Maybe it had nothing to do with the pep talk after all. Maybe she wouldn't feel the same safety with any old officer. Maybe it had everything to do with him.

Her phone rang before they could travel to Chief's office, and she stepped off to the side when she saw who was calling.

"Matt? I thought you might have dropped off the face of the earth considering you haven't called or texted me in the last few days," she pursed her lips. "To what do I owe this pleasure?"

"Sorry." Ever the man of few words, he cut to the chase: "We found out who bought the contacts Dennings was wearing."

Lily thrust her hand in front of Stilinski's face and snapped for him to listen, despite the fact that he was already staring at her with rapt attention.

"You traced it back to a card? Whose was it?" she demanded as she put the call on speakerphone. "Contacts purchase," she whispered to catch Stilinski up.

Matt's voice boomed out of the speaker; there was no chance of misunderstanding his answer.

"The card belongs to Amy Mallory."

32.

PALPABLE

The next two days dragged by. Preparing a defense for court and figuring out the right time to make an arrest was hard enough on its own, but Lily had to do it all while the killer sat within ten feet of her. Both his twelve-hour shifts overlapped with hers, which meant dedicating the majority of her days to pretending to pursue the wrong leads. That left Stilinski and the Chief doing most of the real work while she distracted the killer. If he spotted any indication they were closing in, Lily would be dead before she could so much as reach for her weapon.

"Faye!"

"What now?" she growled. She carried her case file into his office with her and swung the door shut before pointing out, "We do have a phone system so you don't have to yell."

"I hope to God you're not trying to be funny at a time like this," Alcarez scowled. "We have more proof."

"You're kidding. What else did you find?"

The evidence had been stacking up over the past two days. As soon as Lily figured out who they were looking for, everything began to lock into place. It was more than enough to take to the DA, which she planned to do first thing in the morning.

"I signed off on a cybersecurity course for him a year ago," Alcarez said and handed her the form. "I called the instructor and asked what she teaches. Tracking anonymous emails was on the agenda."

Lily frowned and asked, "What did she do, show them how to create anonymous messages so they could track them from the source?"

"That's exactly what she did. We're figuring out how to fix that curriculum. But speaking of email, I got into your team's inboxes. There are some pretty interesting things in there, including a chain talking about how you were taken off the case. The first email was sent five minutes after you left my office that day."

Lily's cheeks puffed out as she exhaled.

"That idiot."

"I need an ETA on this, Faye," Alcarez warned as he leaned toward her. "I want to make the arrest."

"Can you give me until morning? Please? He's none the wiser and I'm so close to having everything wrapped up. If we make an arrest now, it's going to be all over the media by morning and I'll have to deal Spencer all day instead of taking this to the DA."

Alcarez scowled and stood to pace behind his desk.

"You're cutting it too close, Faye. We have enough to arrest him for a dozen crimes, three of them homicides, and you want to wait another night so you can tie up loose ends? I'm not doing that."

"I'm not asking you to do anything," she said as she hooked her hands together behind her back like a soldier standing at ease. "I've been sitting in the same room as him for two days, Chief. Trust me; he has no idea we're onto him. I've had him running interviews on the families of the victims all week. He thinks we're still in the early stages of connecting the third victim to the first, and I'm so close to being done." She watched him stride back and forth, her brow wrinkling as she implored, "The DA already left for the day or I'd agree with doing this now, but we have to wait until morning to get a warrant anyway, yeah? It's just one more night. If anything happens, you can suspend me for as long as you want. Fire me, even."

"I'm not firing you if you're assaulted," he said as he came to a stop behind his chair and squeezed the back of it, fingers digging into the padded mesh material. "You're sure about this?"

"As sure as I am that he's behind all three of these murders. Yes, sir. I wouldn't put my own life in danger if I thought otherwise, especially not in a case like this. And I promise, first thing in the morning, you can make the arrest. I'll be ready to handle everything by then, even the media. Even Spencer."

He didn't speak but stared at her with an intensity that she'd only seen him use twice since he hired her. It was the sort of gaze that made people believe in x-ray vision and left most people feeling cold and vulnerable in its wake. Exposed.

Lily shifted as she stared at the bridge of his nose instead of looking him in the eye. It was an old trick, one she preferred to sinking into her discomfort. The silence that passed between the two of them grew more and more pressurized until it surrounded her and made her head twinge from its force. Still, she said nothing.

"I want Stilinski with you until the arrest is made," he spoke at last. "Isaacs, too."

"Chief, I don't need—!"

"If you're going to be this stupid in light of an investigation that could lead to the end of your life, then yes. You *do* need them, Faye!" he barked. "I've given you more leeway than you deserve on this case and I am not going to let that fact get you killed! Do you understand me? You take them with you tonight or I make the arrest now. End of discussion!"

This time, Lily's lack of speech wasn't elective. She tensed her jaw to keep her mouth from falling open and tried to conjure up enough words to form a cohesive sentence. The Chief's sudden outburst seemed to have frightened even her thoughts, which had skittered into the unreachable recesses of her mind like mice startled by the clawed swat of a hungry cat.

"I'll take that as a yes," he said and straightened up. "Tell Isaacs to take you home and run a check before you go inside."

"Yes sir," she managed and retreated to the officers' desk clump. "Hey, Isaacs? Chief wants you to run a perimeter check on my place."

"He's having us babysit now?" Isaacs asked as she pushed away from her desk and grabbed her keys. "Or did you ask for it?"

"Of course I didn't. I think it's fine," Lily said. "Stilinski, Chief wants you on guard duty again."

"Sounds good. I've got a couple quick things to finish up, but I'll be right behind you two," he said.

"Great. Call when you pull up so I know it's you, yeah?"

"I will. See you soon."

She gathered everything she would need to put the finishing touches on her case before meeting Isaacs up front. It took longer than usual to get out of the city thanks to the bumper to bumper traffic. Neither female spoke as Isaacs navigated back to Lily's townhouse without needing directions.

"You got keys? I'll take a quick look inside and then walk the block to be sure," Isaacs explained when they pulled into Lily's parking spot.

"Yeah, sure," Lily agreed and handed them over.

She watched Isaacs disappear into the house and exhaled with deliberate slowness. As much as she may have resisted the Chief's orders, the knowledge that the house would be cleared before she walked in soaked her in relief. The phrase, "He doesn't know we're onto him" had been thrown around so many times in the last couple of hours, she was beginning to doubt its sincerity. The singular assurance she clung to sounded flimsier and less probable with every repetition. But Isaacs's sweep of the property would solidify the claim enough to get her through one more night.

She hoped.

Isaacs emerged from the building a few minutes later and gave her a thumbs up before walking down the street and turning the corner. The minutes dragged by after that, ticking off on the dashboard clock with excruciating slowness. Five wasn't so bad, but the block wasn't big enough for ten unless Isaacs had run into trouble.

The second the ten minute mark hit, Lily reached for the door handle.

Isaacs rounded the corner before she could get out of the car. The officer glanced around the street and to the front door one more time before waving Lily out.

"Looks like you're all set," she said. "Sorry. There were a few kids loitering on the other side of the block. Took me a minute to shoo them off."

"No problem," Lily assured, even though her heart was beating a little faster now. "Thanks. Stilinski should be here soon, so I'm covered for the night."

"All right. I'll radio and make sure he's on his way before I take off," Isaacs said and ducked back into her car.

Lily headed inside, locked the door behind her, and flipped on the light in the entryway.

She'd never noticed how sinister her place of residence could look. Nothing but darkness loomed beyond the entrance. The doorways leading to the living room and kitchen taunted her with their vacuums of blackness. Rational thought tried to replace her fears as she recounted the items she would find behind the void: a couch; a coffee table; and a television in the living room, and chairs; a dining room table, and a coffee maker in the kitchen. She knew that nothing more sinister skulked in the darkness. She just had to prove it to herself, no matter how creepy and stifling it all was.

One more night. That was all she had to survive.

She inched toward the kitchen, ears straining for any foreign noise. The heavy panting rising from her own lungs overtook her until she could hear little else, anyway. Her delicate and silent footsteps froze just outside the kitchen doorway, where she planted herself while she texted Stilinski.

LILY: *I'm psyching myself out. How close are you?*

STILINSKI: *Trying to pull out of the city now. I'll be there soon, OK?*

LILY: *Okay. Thanks. I'll be inside.*

She ducked into the kitchen at last, tossed her phone on the counter, and reached for the light over the oven. To her immediate horror, her hand connected with an uneven surface about three feet before she expected to reach anything. The plummeting of her stomach told her she'd hit the chest of Russell Jordan instead of her intended target.

Before she could wrench her hand back, his stout fingers coiled around her wrist so tightly, she could feel an instant bruise forming.

"Get off me!" Her shriek split through the silence as she swung her free hand back for her gun.

Jordan twisted her arm behind her back and shoved her into the fridge face-first. A sharp pain lanced through her shoulder as something cold pierced through her flesh. Her grip on her gun instinctively loosened as the nerve endings in her arm burned, and the weapon clattered to the tile floor.

It may as well have been miles out of reach.

"You're going to make this a lot harder on yourself if you fight back," he spoke as calmly as if he were reading from a textbook; he had probably said the same thing to dozens of criminals during arrests.

"You're the one who's about to have a hard time if you think I'm going to let you—."

He cut her off by slamming his hand against the knife handle, sending shooting pains through her entire arm and down the left side of her body. His free hand tangled in her hair to keep a firm grip on her.

"You know what your problem is, Faye?" he hissed in her ear, ignoring her newest shout as it tapered into a weak attempt to suppress a sob. "You don't know when to shut the fuck up. It's a wonder you got anything done on this case."

"It yields… a surprising… number of results," she gritted out through quick, shallow breaths.

"Clearly," he grunted and wrenched the knife from her shoulder.

Hot, thick blood soaked into her shirt as he spun her toward him and slammed her against the door. He pressed his forearm across the bottom of her throat to hold her in place and kicked her gun away. His other hand held the knife firmly in the air, its silver blade glistening with splashes of crimson.

Her vision went dark as he cut off her oxygen. Stars popped in front of her eyes against the black background as she tried to push him away, but the attempt to do so only made the tear in her shoulder burn. The pressure of his hold was too great to break even without injury.

"You...didn't have...me fooled," she choked out.

"Oh, but I did for a long time," he laughed as he moved his arm and pointed the sharp end of the blade toward her throat. "You've been a real pain in the ass, Faye. I might have gone a little easier on you, but you made it so much worse for yourself."

He reached up and clamped a hand on her shoulder, digging his thumb into her wound until she shouted.

"Now move," he hissed and shoved her toward the doorway. "We don't have much time."

33.

RECKONING

"There's still time for you to change your mind, Jordan," Lily warned without moving any further into the hall. Her heart hammered as if it knew it would never get the chance to beat again. "You've got a family to think about."

"Don't pretend you care about what happens to them," he snarled and tapped the flat side of the knife against her face, smearing her own blood onto her cheek. "If you did, you would have dropped the case when I told you to. Now, shut up and walk."

Did he know Stilinski was coming by tonight? How long had it been since Lily texted the officer? She was all too aware of how quickly time sped up in life or death situations and knew that it probably had only been a couple minutes. Stilinski could still be half an hour away. A massive lump rose in her throat, accompanied by a feeble whimper as she tried to breathe around it; she would be dead by the time he got here if traffic hadn't cleared.

"G-got it," she rasped as the tip of the knife pricked against her shoulder blades.

She stepped into the hall and let her gaze flicker sideways to the front door. Her window to escape would slam shut the second she walked into the living room with him; if she was going to make a move, she had to do it now. All she had to do was make it out the front door.

So, she took a deep breath and launched herself to the side.

Jordan lunged with her as if he had expected the move. He slashed the knife across her back, and she snarled as the new wound began to bleed. She fell against the door and managed to unlock it before he caught up. With inhuman reflexes, he swung his free hand out and caught her by the hair. He yanked her against him and pressed the blade back against her neck to silence another shout forming in her throat.

"What did I JUST say?" he hissed in her ear and kicked the back of her knee to force her to move.

A quiet whimper rose from her throat as she tripped forward, increasing the pressure of the blade against her neck. She grabbed hold of his arm and threw herself back against him. If she couldn't knock him off balance in the struggle, she needed to at least make sure she didn't impale herself.

Jordan didn't so much as tense as she threw herself back against him. Instead, he laughed and wrapped his knife-wielding arm around her waist, rendering her immobile. The blade poked against her ribs as he tightened his hold and dragged her toward the living room.

"There's that fire! It's more fun this way, isn't it?"

"You're... a freak," she growled as she flung her right hand out to catch the door frame. "Ah!" she cried as he wrenched her away from it, one of her nails snapping and her fingers stinging.

She took another opportunity to fight when he flung her onto the couch. She spun onto her back and kicked, adrenaline pounding so hard she couldn't feel the pain in her back or shoulder. Her foot connected squarely with his groin and a wave of triumph rushed through her as he doubled over with a grunt of pain. She started to sit up, but her moment of victory came to an abrupt halt as his fist slammed into her mouth.

Her entire head tingled as her bottom lip cracked in half from the impact. A sticky river of blood spewed down her chin, soaking into the front of her shirt as Jordan threw himself on top of her.

Bright white lights popped in front of her eyes again, and then her vision went dark as Jordan's chest pressed against her face. She sucked in a deep breath, only to choke on blood and the scratchy wool of his shirt. Her legs thrashed in an effort to throw him off balance as his rough hands clamped over her wrists and forced them together. She heard him drop the knife onto the back of the couch with a muffled *whump.*

"Stay...still!" he grunted.

She heard the teeth of handcuffs grinding together and felt the cold steel bite into both wrists simultaneously as Jordan locked them too tightly. A low sob broke from between her lips, the sound of it bouncing around the room as Jordan sat back.

He reached down and brushed a calloused thumb across her split lip. The resulting whimper it elicited made him grin.

"Never took you for the dramatic kind, Faye," he said as he leaned back and squeezed her thigh tightly until she stopped fighting. "There's a good girl. I think we both know this tantrum is beneath you."

Lily blinked a light but now constant flow of tears as she looked back up at him. She had to keep him talking if she had any hopes of getting out of this alive. Stilinski had to be close now.

He had to be.

"What d-did I do?" she whispered, the cut causing each word to carry its own ghost of a whistle. "I've a-always tried to help you."

"You know what you did." Jordan's voice brokered no sympathy. "Don't play stupid. First, you took a job everyone else in our division wanted. One you didn't deserve. Hell, I wasn't even considered for it. And then you stuck your nose into this case. If you'd left it alone like I'd said, none of this would be happening now But it's too late for that. So let's get it over with, huh?"

"Russell, p-please. You don't h-have to—."

He cut her protests off by grabbing her chin so tightly she felt her jawbone shift and constrict beneath his fingers.

"All I want you to do is nod. Now, I asked you a question. Do you understand?"

She had seen too many cases of sexual assault go south for the victim because of moments like these; answering in the affirmative now could later be argued as consent in court. If there was so much as a glimmer of hope that she could survive this and take him to trial, she was not giving him that defense. Instead, she spit at him and felt a defiant surge of satisfaction to see her blood spray across his face.

Yet again, her victory was short-lived. This time, it wasn't his fist that silenced her but the same knife that had previously driven into her shoulder. He jabbed the blade into her right side, as easily as slicing a hot knife through butter. Her eyes widened at the ceiling, and her whole body jolted as the hilt met her flesh. A feeble gurgle rose at the back of her throat.

"This could have gone so differently, Faye," Jordan sighed in the ensuing silence, staring down at her with a pitying smile as he yanked the knife back out.

"It's about to go a lot differently for you," a new voice growled.

A shot cracked through the air and Jordan twisted to the left from the impact as the bullet burrowed into his shoulder. Lily mustered her waning strength and tilted her hips to knock him onto the coffee table and living room floor. As he crashed into the furniture, she pulled her aching arms down to cover her chest and ignored the new inferno blazing in her stomach as she forced herself to sit up.

That was when she spotted her gun lying a foot away from Jordan, well within his reach if he noticed it, too. In the initial altercation, Lily had neglected to notice him pause to pick it up before he marched her inside. But she saw it now, and rolled off the couch to drag herself toward it on her elbows.

Jordan followed her determined gaze to the Glock as her fingers stretched toward it. As he raised his knife, another shot rang out from Stilinski's gun. The sleeve of Jordan's shirt tore open from the impact. Lily's hands closed around the gun. She twisted onto her back with a shout of pain and pulled the trigger.

Jordan staggered backwards, halfway between her and Stilinski. The knife dropped onto the thin carpeting with a thud.

The adrenaline that protected Lily throughout most of the fight vanished with shocking speed. Her vision swirled as her entire body pulsed with pain. Her focus went in and out with each throb of her heart, forcing her to watch the rest of the scene in snapshots, as if flipping through an old-school Viewfinder.

Jordan sinking to one knee. Stilinski pressing his gun to Jordan's temple. Red and blue lights flashing through the dark room. Stilinski pulling Jordan to his feet. The two vanishing from the room. Paramedics materializing from thin air. The living room flooding with pure white light. Stilinski emerging from the darkness and appearing at her side.

"Lily? Come on! You gotta stay with us, okay?" he pleaded.

He knelt down and unlocked the cuffs holding her wrists together. He flung them aside and shoved his hands against the wound on her stomach. When she shouted in pain and tried to flinch away, he winced but held tight.

"I know, I know! I'm sorry. But I don't have another way to pack it, okay? Just hang in there. You gotta stay with me."

"I-I'm h-here." Lily went through considerable effort to expel the words. Speech required oxygen and she had no ability to take in any right now, but the struggle was worth it for the flicker of relief that passed over his otherwise terrified expression.

"G-get..."

"I did," he cut her off and tried to smile, even though the effort only brought tears to his eyes. "I did. Isaacs has him. They're going to book him after surgery. Chief's meeting us there. So you rest, okay? We're going to get you taken care of."

Lily gave a feeble nod and let the paramedics take over. She heard mention of surgery as they loaded her into the ambulance. After that, it was only a matter of seconds before the cave darkness of unconsciousness swallowed her whole.

34.

PAIN

Weak flickers of memories defined the next few days for Lily. All she remembered were glimpses of consciousness: a swarm of doctors in light blue scrubs and white surgical masks, fluorescent lights flickering overhead, a hovering nurse with the softest-looking ringlets of brown hair Lily had ever seen, and a large blue balloon with "Get well soon!" written in a cartoonish scrawl. Underlying it all was the last thing she could remember hearing: *"You gotta stay with me. Stay with me."*

Her return to the land of the living was a slow affair. Exhaustion, trauma, and pain medication weighed down her limbs. When she first began to stir, all she could see, smell, hear, and taste was gray. It looked like a filmy haze, smelled like a wet basement long shielded from light, sounded like static on a disconnected television channel, and tasted like water draining from a rusty pipe. Gray was not a good place to be.

"Stay with me."

She forced her eyes open and drew in a sharp breath. The gray around her began to glow and form shapes.

"Hey, look who finally decided to wake up," a soft voice murmured from her left.

The shapes stopped shifting after she blinked a few times. Instead of gray, the room was a ghostly, dim white containing a few splashes of light from the hall and someone's phone screen. Several machines cast threatening shadows along the outskirts of the room, though the only one running was the heart monitor on her right.

She glanced to her left to see who the phone belonged to, and her half-alert gaze drifted upward to meet Stilinski's.

His lips quirked upward in a teasing smirk, but his eyes held no trace of humor. He studied her for a few seconds, waiting for her to recall the events responsible for landing her in this state.

"They said the surgery went really well. Nobody's sure how but the knife missed pretty much all your organs. You're probably going to need to stick with bed rest for a while, but there's no internal bleeding or anything," he explained.

"Good," she rasped.

The word stuck in her sandpaper-dry throat. She tried to swallow and got air with no saliva, prompting a brief coughing fit as a result. Sharp pains jabbed through her stomach, triggering flashbacks of the attack.

Raw, suffocating panic clawed its way from the stitched up wound, through her lungs, and into her throat. She heaved in a gulp of air and shoved the starchy hospital blanket away. She planted her hands on the bed with flat palms and tried to push herself upright, but the attempt ended as another punch of pain pulsed through her shoulder and back. She dropped onto the bed again and began to curl into a ball.

Stilinski remained seated but lurched toward her, his own eyes wide and reflective of her own panic.

"Lil! Hey, it's okay. You're safe," he promised. He stopped short of touching her and added, "You're in the hospital, and you have to stay still. You really don't want to pull your stitches."

Lily's eyes watered as her twisting yanked at the unyielding stitches in her shoulder, back, and stomach. She stopped moving and the flare of pain dulled to a steady aching instead. She only moved her head now, surveying every corner of the room.

"J-Jordan," she whispered, her voice hoarse and trembling. "Where is he? W-where's Jordan?"

"Not here," he said firmly. "He's in jail. They took him in as soon as they dug the bullets out of him." He studied her as she sank back against the pillows and promised, "He's miles away, Lily."

She nodded but continued to look around, studying the shadows to ensure nothing more sinister than the food cart lingered within them. The room fell quiet again. The beeping of her heart monitor slowed. Hushed voices carried down the hall and past her door. Matt entered a few minutes later with a nurse in white scrubs, who asked standard questions about pain levels. Lily forgot her responses as soon as they slipped from her mouth. The nurse injected more medication into the IV, admonished her to get some rest, and left.

Matt took a seat next to Stilinski and cleared his throat.

"Can I get you anything, Lil?"

"I think—," Lily began before her voice cracked in its attempt to travel over the desert landscape her vocal chords and throat had become. She croaked, "Water?"

"Yeah, sure," he said and jumped out of his seat to pour her a glass.

He delivered it and she swigged as much of it as she could in one go.

"Stilinski told me how you solved it," he murmured after letting her have a few minutes. "The dissertation connection? Genius."

"Thanks," she whispered. "Shouldn't have waited like I did."

"Let's not worry about that right now," Stilinski cut in. "Matt, you were talking to the nurse, right? What's our timeline looking like?"

"She said we'll reevaluate after a week," Matt replied, then gave Lily a pointed look. "Depending on how well you rest."

"What else am I gonna do, run laps?" Lily glared back.

"A week seems… a little soon. Doesn't it?" Stilinski frowned.

"The nurse said the most major wound is the abdominal one, and there were no complications in surgery. As long Lily doesn't do anything crazy, she should be good to go after a week."

"Oh. Well that's good news," Stilinski mused, although he looked to Lily for her reaction.

The morphine made it harder to think, but that worked in her favor here. It silenced her emotional response to the whole affair and left her with strictly analytical thoughts, for the time being.

"Well, where am I supposed to go, exactly?" she asked. "My house is a crime scene."

"Harris got it all processed, and we've all been pitching in to clean it up a little. It's mostly done by now."

She nodded but didn't respond. She picked apart her styrofoam cup and deposited the torn pieces from its vanishing cup.

"You can stay with me if you'd rather not go home," Matt offered after watching her for a few seconds. "As long as you need to."

Again, a nod.

"I'll need clean clothes at some point."

"We can make a stop. I'll pack some stuff up for you, if you make a list."

"Okay," Lily agreed and finally stopped mutilating the cup.

Stilinski glanced between the two and slurped his coffee to avoid letting another silence coating the room. Thankfully, it didn't take long for someone else to start making noise. The nurse with the brown ringlets walked in, armed with a clipboard and a soft smile.

"Welcome back, Detective. I'm Stryker. I'll be your night shift nurse until you can go home," she introduced as she walked around to check Lily's vitals and IV. "How are your pain levels?"

"I was stabbed a few times, so… above average?" Lily muttered and started picking at her blanket.

"Right. That's definitely fair," Stryker winced. "I mean, how are your levels considering the stab wounds? You seem to be partially inclined okay. Is that causing any extra pain?"

"I'm fine."

"That's not what I asked."

"Excuse me?" Lily's gaze finally rose to meet the nurse's, her jaw slack in surprise.

"You're not telling me how much pain you're in. While I can understand that given what you've been through, saying you're fine isn't really going to help me do my job. So I'm going to need an honest answer."

Matt and Stilinski exchanged bemused glances while Lily and Stryker stared back at one another. The stalemate didn't last long.

"I've got all day, Detective," Stryker said without losing the same smile she had when she walked in.

Lily tried to sit up a little straighter to show she wouldn't be challenged, but cursed quietly as the wound on her stomach twinged.

"Fine," she conceded. "It's not great, okay? Muted because of the meds but I'm in pain."

Stryker glanced back up, bangs bouncing out of her eyes with the movement.

"That's all I needed to know. I will be back for another check this afternoon. In the meantime, can I get you anything else?"

"Coffee. Please."

"I'm really sorry, but it's going to be a few days before you're cleared for caffeine again," Stryker sighed. "I'll get you more water for the time being," she assured and walked out.

Lily glared after her and waited for her to disappear before she huffed, "I don't like that nurse."

"Yeah, because she's as stubborn as you are and won't give you coffee," Matt snorted. "You two will be best friends by the end of the day."

Lily turned her glare on him briefly and then lowered it to the blanket again. Her eyelids drooped after a few seconds, and she raised her uninjured arm to stifle a yawn.

"I think that's our cue," Stilinski said with a fond smile. "We'll let you rest."

"We'll be right outside if you need us," Matt added as he rose to his feet.

She watched the two leave, fist clenching around the blanket as the doorway brightened. She leaned back to stare at the ceiling tiles and rubbed her eyes, glad that the yawning ruse had worked. A low, rattling breath slipped from between her lips before she squeezed her eyes shut and broke down.

35.

INSTRUCTIONS FOR CARE

If Lily had thought a three-day vacation at home was bad, it was nothing compared to an entire week confined to a hospital bed. She'd gone from daily workouts and vigorous shift work to lying in one place for the majority of each day. She could practically feel her muscles atrophying while her wounds healed.

Stilinski went back to work for a couple of night shifts, after visiting hours ended. He and Matt were with her non-stop otherwise. Alcarez visited on the third day, bringing a gift shop bouquet in a ceramic vase. Isaacs dropped in a few times with a variety of snacks to save Lily from the drudgery of hospital food.

On the fifth day, even Harris stopped by with his wife and their small son. The little boy toted a small stuffed bear holding a heart that read, "Get well soon!" Mrs. Harris held a new bouquet of azaleas. Her husband carried the best gift anyone could give, in Lily's opinion: a set of books.

"Harris… wow," Lily breathed after collecting the gifts. "This is so sweet of you."

"Yeah, well I have my moments," the detective shrugged. "Sorry it wasn't sooner. Little guy just got over a cold and we didn't want it to mess with you while your immune system is down."

"I should actually take him to the cafeteria," Mrs. Harris smiled as she scooped her son up. "It's really good to see you're doing well, Lily."

"Thank you," Lily smiled and watched them leave before looking back to her detective. "So… I owe you a huge thanks."

"Nah, you don't," Harris said as he took a seat.

"Yes, I do. And a ton of apologies. You really pulled through on this investigation, in a lot more ways than I have time to talk through, but thank you."

Harris nodded and looked back at her with the rarest sight she'd ever seen on him: a smile.

"At the end of the day, I want to get the guy just like you do," he said. "I know I'm an ass about it but I'm trying to find the best way to get there, just like you are."

"I know," Lily returned the smile. "I'm an arse about it, too."

"See? We don't hate each other. We're just similar."

"There's a thought," she snorted.

"Yeah," he chuckled before crying sounded down the hall. "Ah, shit. That's mine," he grimaced and got up. "You coming back to work anytime soon?"

"Could be a while, but I'll check in," Lily assured.

"Good. Hey. Really glad you're okay, boss," he added before ducking out.

The high from that conversation and the novels he'd gifted got Lily through the rest of the week. At long last, her final evaluation arrived in the form of the stubborn nurse.

Stryker spent the better part of five minutes squinting at Lily's monitors. Every thirty seconds, she scratched a single tally mark down on her clipboard. After she made another three marks, Lily broke the silence.

"Are you kidding me? Why is this taking so long?" Lily groaned. "Can I go home or not?"

"You can, but you'll need to be on bed rest for the next week to be safe," Stryker said. "After that, I'd like you to come back for a follow-up and a psych consult—."

"Wait, what? I do not need a psych consult!"

Stryker's eyebrows rose as she looked from the clipboard to Lily, who was sitting up on the edge of the bed. If the detective had been dressed in street clothes instead of still wearing the hospital gown, Stryker might not have known there was anything wrong with her.

"It's procedure, Lily," Stilinski reminded from the other side of the room, where he leaned against the wall beside the door. "The Chief isn't going to let you come back to work without the all clear."

"I don't need—." Lily cut herself off by clenching her jaw and then dropped her gaze to her lap. "I'm fine."

"Then proving it won't be a problem," Matt piped in. "Come on. Just say yes and we can get you home."

Lily glanced back up to Stryker, who sighed.

"I can't discharge you unless I know you'll come back, Lily. And I want you to be able to go home as much as you do."

Except Lily wasn't going home. She didn't know how she could ever go home again after what had happened there. The thought of going in to pack her things before they went to Matt's made her so sick, she hadn't even made it an option. Instead, she'd written out a list of her clothes and where the guys would be able to find them.

She nodded after a moment's hesitation and relented, "Fine. I'll come back in a week. Can I go now?"

"Yes, you can," Stryker smiled. "Go ahead and get changed. I'll bring the discharge papers in. Then you can leave."

Lily nodded. Both women ducked out of the main part of the room in opposite directions, Stryker to the hallway and Lily to the bathroom with clean clothes. After a few minutes, Stryker returned with the papers in hand, but Lily hadn't emerged again.

"Lily?" the nurse asked, unperturbed and not breaking her stride as she set the papers on the bedside tray table and walked over to the bathroom door. "I've got your papers if you're almost ready. Do you need any help?"

"No!" Then, in a quieter, calmer tone, she added: "No. I-I can do it…"

"I have no doubt you can," Stryker replied in a kind voice as she leaned against the doorjamb. "I just thought I could get you out of here a little faster, that's all. I can send the guys out to the waiting room, if you'd prefer."

The statement drifted into the abyss of unspoken and unanswered question. Lily didn't reply but after a few seconds, the door clicked and opened slightly.

"You can come in," she murmured.

Lily stepped behind the door to shield herself from the view of the guys, although she had yet to start undressing. She released the door once Stryker stepped far enough in, and it swung shut behind the nurse with a loud *fwack*. Lily flinched and blinked at it as if caught between dazed and on the verge of tears.

"Sorry," she whispered. "I-I can't…"

"You don't have to explain anything if you don't want to," Stryker said and stepped over to the pile of clothes to pull focus back to the task at hand. "Jeans first. That'll be the easiest."

Lily allowed Stryker to help her don the jeans without complaint. Once they were zipped and buttoned, the redhead relaxed enough to let Stryker remove the hospital gown. Dressing was a snap from there, even around the sling Lily's arm rested in. Once she was dressed, Stryker waited without complaint while her charge fiddled with the strap of her sling and made sure every button and zipper on her outfit was fastened. Then, she took a breath and let Stryker help her out of the bathroom.

"I'll walk you all out, if that's okay. Who wants the papers?"

"I'll take them," Matt said and looked them over.

Stilinski's concerned gaze lingered on Lily's face, which was slanted down toward the floor in a half-hearted attempt to hide her watering eyes.

"There are instructions for cleaning both wounds, and a diagram on how to put that sling on. She should really be wearing it for two to three weeks. She can take it off to shower, but that's it. That wound was pretty deep and we want to give it a chance to heal properly without risking the stitches opening."

"Got it. We'll make sure she keeps it on."

"Good. All other instructions for care are in those papers as well, but if you have any questions, call me or your primary doctor. Okay? You three are free to go," Stryker smiled.

"Thank you," Lily uttered, slouching as she walked out with the other two.

She didn't speak for the rest of the evening.

36.

BLOOD RELATIVE

"Detective Faye, could you describe for the jury what transpired on the evening of the fifteenth of April, beginning when you left your shift at the Sixth Precinct?"

Silence prickled through the courtroom as all eyes targeted the wilted flower on the stand, the flame diminished to a flickering ember. The detective the prosecutor referred to seemed to have vanished; in her place slumped the epitome of mistrust and resignation as she faced off with her would-be murderer. Paranoia clawed at her eyes, begging her to look at the man who tried to kill her, just to prove he wasn't going to lunge at her and try it all again.

But her green irises fixed on her attorney with undeterred resolve that even fear couldn't shatter. She would not look at Russell Jordan, because she knew what she would see. She knew, and it was terrifying.

If she looked, she would see a man putting on an act in front of his wife and eldest child. She would see a mouth stretched open in disbelief, a jaw slack with horror as she began to detail the heinous acts he stood accused of, the patch of gray hairs on his unkempt beard that sprouted due to the stress of his incarceration. She would see a broken man.

And she would know it was all a lie.

She had seen who he truly was. Looking at him now would only cause her to see that night over again in vivid detail, which was the last thing she needed while trying to explain its events. She would feel every stab of the rigid blade, every hit from his rough hands, and every inch of him as he pressed his full weight onto her in an effort to both arouse and subdue. She would hear every threat, every click of the handcuffs locking her into her fate, every blare from the sirens of an ambulance too far away to save her life.

She would look into his eyes in the courtroom and see them as she had on the night of his fourth attempted murder. In that moment, she would no longer see the warm eyes of a coworker telling her how to dry her rain-soaked shoes. She would not see the teary eyes of a man facing a life sentence. All she would see was a calm gaze devoid of emotion. She would see nothing but blackness in his eyes, like that of a shark stalking its next meal.

All she would see if she looked at him now was death.

So she stared down her own attorney with unrelenting determination as she talked the jury through her version of the events in a detached, monotonous tone. Her volume was drastically lower than the man's as she spoke, but it didn't matter. The participants in the courtroom entered into the same unspoken vow of silence and held a collective breath for the duration of her testimony, so she was well heard.

"Detective?" The attorney's voice dropped to hushed tones to perpetuate the solemn atmosphere when she finished her initial account. "You said you thought the assailant would try to catch you off guard at your home. Can you explain what led you to this conclusion?"

Lily reached for the water in front of her and took a sip to wash away the lump in her throat. She set the glass down with a louder thunk than anticipated and flinched at the noise. Her gaze returned to the lawyer.

"I knew it wouldn't take long. The killer had committed three murders prior and left the third victim with a message that singled me out as the next target. I had also received anonymous threats throughout the investigation, which increased in frequency and intensity as I fit the pieces together. After I solved the case, I waited while I tried to make sense of the evidence for the inevitable trial, and I worried when I left work that night that I had pressed my luck too far."

She said it all in an attempt at a professional tone, but it came off robotic and stiff. The feelings of unease she suffered on the night in question were ones she hadn't admitted to the Chief, or even to Matt and Stilinski. She knew appearing broken up over the attack several months after it meant Alcarez might give her lower profile cases in the future. With stakes that high, she had to prove she could discuss the assault without panicking.

"Officer Isaacs cleared the place so I thought I could make it until Officer Stilinski arrived, but as soon as I walked in, I could tell something was wrong. It just felt like…" She trailed off and closed her eyes before finishing, "…like I had run out of time."

Her attorney let the jury ruminate on that for a moment before he asked: "And could you identify your assailant in this courtroom? Point him out for the jury?"

Lily knew the importance of showing no hesitation, no matter how much the idea of looking toward Jordan made her want to throw up and burst into flame. Any pause would give his attorney fodder to question her recall abilities during the cross-examination. She pointed toward the ex-cop and spoke his name with an abundance of trembling. She looked past him and tried to ignore his silhouette in her peripheral.

"Thank you, Detective. Now I'd like to ask you a few questions about the homicide cases you were working on at the time of the assault. Take us back to the first case. Walk us through your understanding of the killer's actions."

Lily remained silent for a long moment. Between her hospital stay and the months it took to prepare for the court case, the facts almost felt muddled. It took some time to remember what evidence they'd filed with the jury and what she could speak to.

"I submitted a timeline," she said after a moment, though she looked toward the Chief on the other side of the room for confirmation. "Along with a file detailing Det—Mr. Jordan's whereabouts on the nights of the first and second murders."

"Please let the record show that the witness is referring to Exhibit D," her attorney said. "Go on."

Lily nodded and said, "Based on the compiled evidence, I have come to conclude that the killer stalked Ms. Anderson both at her school and her workplace leading up to the evening in question. That night, he made a sexual advance and followed her home when she rejected him. When he found an area in which she was isolated, he threatened her at knifepoint and forced himself on her. At some point in the early stages of the assault, she began to fight back. He slit her throat once and proceeded to stab her until she stopped fighting. Then he carried out the sexual assault, saw she was still alive, and sliced her throat for the second and third times. He assumed this would kill her and fled into the Montview apartment building across the street.

"That was when Kayla Simmons arrived on the scene, moments after the attack. According to her witness testimony, she heard Ms. Anderson's screams from around the corner but didn't want to investigate until she knew she wouldn't be in danger. She called the ambulance and tried to stop the bleeding from the wounds to Ms. Anderson's throat. Meanwhile, the killer cleaned up in Amy Mallory's residence, left his bloody clothes in the washer, and ducked out before anyone knew he was there."

"You don't mean to suggest he ran out in the nude?"

"No. He had clean clothes at the Mallory residence."

"And why would he have clothes there? Why would Amy Mallory let him in so late at night covered in blood?"

"She didn't let him in. Her son, Aiden did. Amy Mallory was still at work. Jordan had clothes there because he has been in a relationship with Amy for years, which continued even after he married."

The silence snapped as a wave of murmurs swept around the courtroom, but Lily and her attorney weren't finished.

"What makes you think they were having an affair?"

"Take a look at Aiden Mallory's birth certificate," Lily answered as her spine straightened, weight lifting off it with every piece of evidence she delivered. "Russell Jordan is his biological father."

37.

TRAUMA

Despite the judge's best efforts and threats to remove almost everyone from the courtroom, it took five minutes to silence the crowd. Everyone loved a good scandal.

Lily dared to glance in Jordan's direction while the rest of the courtroom howled like monkeys. It was worth seeing him out of the corner of her eye if she got to gauge his wife's reaction to the news of the affair; however, the seats containing Mrs. Jordan and their eldest daughter sat empty. Lily cleared her throat as she began to choke on pride.

"I believe Aiden's birth certificate has been entered into evidence," she added once the room quieted to murmurs again. "But Amy was livid when she found out Aiden had let him in covered in blood. They must have spent ages cleaning their apartment; when I conducted a second interview with Amy, the entire place smelled like bleach. At that point, they must have realized they were accomplices. They tried to cover for it by taking me out."

She indicated to her forehead, where a small sliver of a pale scar remained.

"They went on trial for assaulting a police officer shortly after Jordan's arrest."

Her attorney verified this and glanced back to his notes.

"Let's move on to the second homicide. Have you established the timeframe for that event?"

"Absolutely. I spoke to Ms. Simmons approximately three hours before her body was discovered, which narrows the timeframe significantly. Jordan wasn't on a shift that day—it was Friday, three days after Ms. Anderson's death—and he didn't have an alibi for that timeframe. I suspect he didn't think he needed one yet. Three days after the initial investigation, I had no reason to look at our own department for suspects. Day four changed that."

"What happened on day four? This was Saturday, correct?"

"Yes, sir," Lily confirmed. "On day four, I found the third threat telling me to halt the investigation. Unlike the first two, this wasn't email. It was a typed letter placed in an unmarked envelope in my personal inbox on my desk."

"And why did this lead you to suspect your coworkers?"

"The envelope didn't have stamps or post office markings. It was hand delivered, and the only people with access to my area are other officers. My name wasn't on it, either, so nobody else but the killer could have known to drop it at my desk."

"Was that when you began to suspect the defendant?"

"No, of course not. I didn't realize it was Jordan—."

"Objection!" Jordan's lawyer finally recovered a word, and the rest tumbled out naturally. "That's speculation. My client has not been convicted of anything!"

"Sustained, Davis," the judge granted, leaving Lily to correct.

"I didn't *suspect* Jordan until I reviewed the forensic analysis of the geographical locations from which the threats were emailed. I triangulated their positions based on the report and found Amy Mallory's apartment right in the middle. And then I read an article in the New York Post that contained background information on Jordan, and that's when it all clicked."

"What did the article contain that solidified your theory?"

"The subject of Jordan's doctoral dissertation."

"Which is of significance?"

"The utmost. His dissertation regards the Bystander Effect, which was a theory developed from the murder of a woman named Kitty Genovese in the middle of a heavily populated area. Ms. Anderson's injuries and the location almost perfectly mimic the same murder, nearly down to the number of stab wounds."

"And you had previously determined that the information from the first homicide was relevant to the other two?"

"One of the threats said I would be his fourth victim, so yes," Lily stated, her eyes narrowing. "We were able to determine that whoever killed Ms. Anderson was responsible for killing the sole witnesses to the crime preceding their own deaths."

She reached a shaky hand toward her water again. Her gaze swung to her boss as she raised the glass to her lips and drained it. She needed this to wrap up.

He sat forward and cleared his throat before reaching for his own glass. The attorney glanced back and met his gaze. After an imperceptible nod, he looked to the judge.

"No further questions, your Honor," he said and took his seat.

The judge sat back and glanced to Jordan's attorney. "The defense may cross-examine."

Jordan's attorney, Mr. Davis stepped forward with an eager half-smile, and Lily felt sick all over again. There would be little the man could do to sway the opinion of the jury that Jordan was guilty of committing this crime. The best defense now was to convince the jurors that Jordan had committed the assault but none of the other crimes, and the only way to do that would be to destroy Lily's credibility as both a detective and witness. The attorney wasted no time in using this tactic.

"Detective, I want to discuss the firearm in your possession at the time of the assault," he stated. "Was that your personal firearm?"

"No, sir. That was my service weapon."

"So you went home with your service weapon. What is the standard protocol for officers wishing to do that?"

"We have to obtain permission from the Chief and sign out the weapon and any ammo inside it," she said. "I was given permission to—."

"And did you—?" the attorney tried to cut her off.

"I wasn't finished," she spoke firmly over him, her eyes narrowing.

The man paused, his jaw slackening as he stared back at her. The outburst left him scrambling for a reaction long enough for Lily to explain herself. When the judge didn't interrupt to chide her for decorum, she continued.

"I had written and verbal permission from the Chief to carry it with me, fully loaded, at all times. This transpired after the threats became too numerous and graphic to ignore. On the day permission was granted, I signed out before serving a three-day leave of absence. We agreed that if this issue was not resolved by then, we would reevaluate whether or not I needed to continue carrying my service weapon while off duty." Her eyebrows rose as she looked to the attorney. "*Now* I am finished."

He shifted his weight from his front foot to the back as she spoke, and now clutched his notepad to his chest.

"All right. So you followed protocol on the weapon. Let's move on," he spoke, nearly without missing a beat. "So was it your intention before the assault to accuse Detective Jordan of any crimes?"

"Yes, sir."

"What brought you to the conclusion that Detective Jordan had anything to do with the murders you have accused him of committing?"

"There have been several incidents pointing toward him. I believe we've entered the case report containing my findings into as evidence, if you'd like me to read my summary from that?"

"I'd like to have you recount them in your own words. What made you suspect Detective Jordan of committing these murders?"

She would have much preferred to read her statement instead of recounting from memory as guided by a hostile attorney. Due to the sheer volume of evidence she'd finally connected back to Jordan and all the ties from him to the victims, she knew there were things she was going to leave out that had been crucial to solving the case and had led to his incarceration. It was a lot of information to recount.

"I recounted the timeline through the first murder in depth, but there is one connection between the defendant and Ms. Anderson that I'd like to clarify," Lily told him. "When I conducted my interview with the victim's father, Michael Anderson, he told me his daughter had several minor altercations with a student in her degree program. He identified this student as a woman with the first name Jordan. I thought finding her might be relevant, so I had an officer look up the roster for her classes and find a woman with the first name Jordan. Instead, he discovered that the only individual named Jordan who shared multiple classes with Ms. Anderson was Russell Jordan. I probed a bit into this finding and asked Mr. Anderson if it was possible his daughter had been referring to a man instead of a woman. He said it was. He always assumed Jordan was a female but confirmed that his daughter never referred to the individual by gender, only name. As we could find no evidence of a female named Jordan in more than one of Jessica's courses, we concluded that Jessica had previous altercations on the school's campus with Russell Jordan."

She finished speaking and shot a quick glance to the clock. It was three minutes past four o'clock. Her entire torso throbbed with a dull aching, but it was beginning to intensify. Sweat beaded her forehead as the urge to take a couple of the painkillers she'd weaned herself from began to overtake her. At the very least, she needed acetaminophen to get her through the remainder of the trial.

"Your Honor," Mr. Jefferson spoke up as he followed his client's gaze to the clock on the wall. "I'd like to request a brief recess at this point. My client has been on the stand for hours and it looks like she may need a painkiller."

"Objection," Mr. Davis glared behind him. "Your Honor, any medication may have side effects that prohibit Detective Faye from providing an accurate testimony."

"For God's sake, man. Have a heart," the judge said as he glanced to Lily. "Do you have prescribed medication?"

"I just need an Advil, your Honor. Nothing that will cloud my judgement or recall abilities."

"Then I am granting a fifteen minute recess. Court will resume at four eighteen exactly," the judge said and banged his gavel.

Lily held still for a few seconds before she pushed herself up and navigated off the witness stand. She allowed her attorney to lead her and the Chief to a side room, where she once again collapsed in a chair. She stiffened a little as Alcarez walked behind her and took a seat next to her, but she said nothing. Her discomfort with the proximity wasn't worth mentioning.

"Thank you," she said as Jefferson poured her a glass of water. "How much longer do I have to do this?"

"They'll conclude at five. I don't know how much more this guy can squeeze out of you," Jefferson said as he passed the glass to her, oblivious to her wince at the wording. "If you need to stop, you can. You know you only need to be up there as long as you want to be."

"Davis isn't going to stop. Now that he knows I'm slowing down, he's going to try to find ways to throw me off. The more desperate I am to leave, the easier it'll be for him to put pressure on me to say what he wants me to."

"But you're not going to do that. You're going to stay focused, maybe truncate your account of the second victim and her connections to Jordan. Mention it briefly but move onto the third victim as soon as you can. That's where you're going to win over the jury because that's when you knew your life was being threatened. Keep the focus there and remember to use those words. You had no doubt your life was being threatened and that you were the next target. And remember, you're the one in control here. Stay on message and leave when you want to leave."

Lily nodded and twisted the pill bottle open. The lid popped off abruptly and she lurched forward to catch it as it tried to topple out of her fingers. She caught the lid, but sent a jolt of pain through her abdomen again. It still twinged most days, but sitting in an uncomfortable chair to give testimony for hours aggravated the old wound more than usual. Her stomach had developed its own pulse. Something as simple as sitting forward too quickly under those circumstances proved to be nearly impossible.

"Are you okay, Faye?" the Chief asked, one hand hovering in front of her as if to provide a safety net for the slippery lid.

"I'm f-fine," she insisted and hung her head while she rode out the flow of pain that ebbed through her.

"This wouldn't be a bad side to show the jury, Faye," Jefferson prompted before she had fully recovered. "I know you're concerned about looking weak in front of the defense. That's always a concern for me as well, so I understand. But you're coming across a little robotic."

"What do you want me to do, cry?" she snapped. She knocked back the pills and chased them down with a few gulps of water before snarling at him, her eyes dancing with pain and fury. "I'm a detective, Jefferson. Speaking like this is my job. I'm practiced in court."

"It's not an issue of looking practiced or like you know everything. It's appealing to the jury. They're people. As bad as Jordan's crimes are, he still looks human because he's been sitting over there sniffling and acting scared."

"So what? They're going to deny the overwhelming evidence in front of them and let a triple homicide and sexual assault go just because he looks more sympathetic than I do?"

"They might, Faye. I know you've seen it happen before. All I'm saying is that's the angle we need to play. You don't need to cry but you need to convey the effects of what's happened. Not just to you, but to the victims' families, too. This isn't something you just bounce back from, and I know you haven't."

Lily didn't know that she ever could. How was she supposed to convey that to a jury of people who probably had little to no understanding of what she was going through? How was she supposed to tell them that her entire life had been uprooted when a trusted coworker attempted to assault and kill her? How could she explain that being in a room with primarily men, or that being alone in a room with two of them now, made her want to throw up? How was she supposed to describe the feeling of constantly drowning in air, or of being trapped despite a lack of physical restraints, or the paralyzing fear that gripped her every time she spotted handcuffs, or the dread filling her at the thought of returning to her home? How was she supposed to bring any of that to light when she could barely stand to admit it to herself?

"I just want to be done with this, Jefferson."

Truth be told, she needed to be with Matt and Stilinski again. Despite her general aversion to men, those two were her support system. It was driving her mad not to be able to see them for the duration of the trial, but that was the downside of their involvement as witnesses.

"And I want to get you there, okay? I'm going to try my best. I just need you to work with me."

She sat back in her hard, half-backed wooden chair and raised a hand to her face. She pinched the bridge of her nose, if only to mask her eyes while she closed them and attempted to massage away the tears gathering there. The last thing she needed to deal with was the stifling panic attack she could feel seizing up her lungs, which would force her heart to work itself into a frenzy until it gave out altogether. If anything, she needed to remain calm enough now so she could talk it out with her friends later.

"I'll do what I can, Jefferson," she relented through a shaky exhale. "The last thing I want to do is let him walk."

"We're not going to let that happen," the Chief insisted. "No matter what, you're going to be safe. We'll figure this out."

"We're not going to have to," her lawyer resolved. "I know this is a rough day but get through the rest of your testimony and I'll bring it home for us. I promise. They won't let him go now, anyway. He's a rapist and a murderer, for God's sake!" He didn't seem to notice Lily flinch at the words, so he pressed on. "Worst that happens, we can get a life sentence with parole."

Lily was flushing red now, gripping the glass so hard her fingers were turning white. She wondered how much force it would take to crack.

"I can't have him out on parole," Alcarez spoke up, eyeing his detective. "We can't let that happen, Jefferson. Do you know the statistics on how many criminals commit more crimes during their paroles?"

"Do you?" Jefferson asked snidely.

"I am the Chief of Police, Jefferson! Of course I do," he snarled. "And we are not going to give him that opportunity. Do you understand me? I am *not* letting that happen while my Head Detective is trying to recover from this!" he snapped and punctuated his point by slamming his fist on the table.

Lily sprang out of her seat as the phantom echoes of a gunshot rang through her mind. She walked to the corner of the room and braced herself against the wall with her right hand. Her head hung as she took in quick breaths and puffed them back out too loudly. She couldn't hear her breathing, though; the ringing in her ears and the torrent of past conversations drowned out all other sounds.

"I might have gone a little easier on you," the sickening voice that haunted her dreams nightly rose in the back of her mind again. *"Move...We don't have much time...This could have gone so differently, Faye..."*

Then, all she could hear was an endless cycle of various people asking if she was okay. Did she look okay to any of them? Why was that the go-to question everyone asked after a trauma?

"Faye? Hey, I'm sorry. I didn't mean to do that. I wasn't thinking," Alcarez said, too closely to her ear.

She spun back toward him and swung her hand through the air, but the Chief leaned out of the way so the attempted blow whiffed past his face. A primal fear fractured her face as she stared at him and he took a step back. She felt like a wild animal backed into a corner by a hunter.

He raised his hands and continued to step backwards until he was on the other side of the table.

"Faye, it's okay. We're here to help, remember? I'm sorry. I shouldn't have done that."

Jefferson watched in awe as the two interacted, his eyes wide with the wonderment of a child introduced to a new exhibit at the zoo. He sat back in his chair and crossed his arms as he watched Lily inch her way back toward the table. When she finally sank back into her chair, trembling, he pointed at her with a slick grin.

"That's the emotion we're looking for. Show that to the jury and you're golden."

Alcarez glared down at the lawyer and hissed, "You want this to be the last case you work on for the state, Jefferson? That's not emotion. That's *trauma*, and I'll be damned if you actually try to coach her to play that up while she's dealing with PTSD."

"The jurors need to know she's dealing with this at all! They're about emotion, and she doesn't look like she has any!"

"It's a coping mechanism, you idiot," the Chief seethed. "You are not going to exploit it. You are going to do your job and get this guy put away for life without parole. Got it?"

"Yes sir," Jefferson said and shrank back in his chair, cowed into backing down under threat of losing his income. "I'll make sure my closing statement puts him away."

Lily couldn't wait that long. She couldn't sit in anticipation for the verdict to be assured Jordan would be imprisoned for his crimes. She would have to buck up and find some way to cement his guilt in the minds of the jurors. If that meant showing emotion before she'd processed feeling it, so be it. She could deal with the fallout of her own emotional state after the sentence was handed down, which meant she had to pull it together now.

"I'll deal with it," she said in a feeble voice. She cleared her throat and inhaled slowly. "But he is fully responsible," she added in a low, dangerous voice. "Don't let him get away with anything less."

"I'll bring it home. Don't worry," he nodded before getting up. "Are you ready to go back in there?"

She responded by standing up, but paused before they walked back in to add, "For what it's worth, thank you."

The attorney gave a solemn nod. "It's my job," he said. "And I'm getting damn sick of these guys walking free."

"Me too," she whispered.

"Faye, I am sorry," Alcarez said, still looking like a clumsy child who had accidentally kicked a puppy.

"It isn't your fault," she shook her head. "It's something I have to learn to deal with."

She hoped it would get easier to handle even though it wouldn't go away completely, but for now? It was time to put all this behind her.

38.

WE WONDER WHY

"And what makes you think Detective Jordan had anything to do with the third victim?"

"This was the most obvious of all," Lily said as she rubbed at the corner of her eye. "At this point, I had already established that whoever was sending the threats to keep me off the case was the killer. Nobody else would have the motive for threatening me. Aside from the other evidence I've mentioned, this cemented the connection because the most obvious threat was actually written on the victim's body."

"That seems awfully paranoid, doesn't it, Detective?"

"It's not paranoid," she clipped as she zeroed in on him and glared. "Jordan wrote my name on the victim's corpse."

"Objection. That's speculation."

"That he did it?" she growled for clarification before the judge could respond.

"No, that it was my client."

"Fine. The killer wrote my name on the victim's corpse."

"Thank you. Let's move on to the other evidence at the crime scene. You allege that you found biological material on the victim?"

"We did, and we had it tested at the lab for a positive ID of both the victim and the killer," she confirmed. "We had hair from both individuals, fiber samples left behind on the victim's scarf, and skin cells left on the victim's jacket that turned out to be dandruff from Mr. Jordan."

"Speculative."

That was it. He had just figured out what it took to pull the hair trigger connected to her emotions.

"It's not speculative!" she burst and caused the jurors to jump, nearly in unison. "Dammit, it is *not* speculative! We received the DNA results from the lab, and they are Jordan's, beyond a reasonable scientific doubt!"

"Detective, watch your volume in my courtroom," the judge warned.

Lily clenched her fist and let her nails dig into the palm of her hand. Her eyes squeezed shut as she tried to withdraw into herself. It was a dangerous place to be right now but it was also the only hope she had of calming down enough to testify without destroying her credibility.

"I'm sorry," she whispered after a few seconds. "But we subject victims of sexual assault to this kind of relentless questioning and try to criminalize them when they run to the system for safety, and then we wonder why nobody ever presses charges against their assailants. I'm trained to be questioned, and even I can't do this anymore. I can't function like it's business as usual after what I've been through."

She lingered in her hunched position for a few seconds to rub at her face. When she looked up again, she could barely see the courtroom for how much her eyes were watering.

"How would any of you feel if you'd been forced to sit in the same room as a man who had tried to sexually assault and murder you?" she whispered in a shaking voice. "Would you make your own children endure the same thing I'm enduring right now? Mr. Davis, your Honor, jurors—with all due respect, I'm exhausted, I'm in pain, and I want to go home and put that horrible night behind me. So if you want to ask me about the rest of the connections, Mr. Davis, I would be happy to speak to them. Otherwise, I'd really like to call this off and let the jury decide on Jordan's fate. Because I've had enough."

The combination of her tears and her choked voice had the intended effect on Davis, and hopefully on the rest of the courtroom. Lily swore she saw a juror dab at his eyes with his sleeve.

Of course, she was more focused on Davis. This was their first face-off in which she'd been personally affected, and she had little doubt that he was ready to deal with the implications of that in the courtroom. His typical methods of trying to lead the questions in a different direction to leave room for reasonable doubt weren't going to work this time.

He fiddled with his tie clip and stared down at it while he reevaluated the situation. His weight shifted back and forth a few times before he looked up at her, his gaze sharp and piercing. One quick glance at her haggard and broken expression softened his own. His hands rose, unbuttoned his suit jacket, and settled on his hips. He began to pace again, prowling like a caged animal.

Lily took advantage of the silence. The longer it lasted, the more uncomfortable the rest of the room became and the more sympathetic the jurors would be to her plight. She set a hand over the scar on her stomach and grimaced. It wasn't truly necessary, but she needed to remind the jurors of the struggles of healing from assault.

"Yes, good point," Mr. Davis said at last. He cleared his throat and crossed his arms, his hands burrowing into his armpits and thumbs resting on his shoulders. "Well, then… Uh, the defense rests, your Honor."

"Thank you, Detective Faye. You're welcome to return for the sentencing, but you are adjourned," the judge said and waited for her to join the Chief and Jefferson. "We will reconvene for final statements and a verdict tomorrow morning at nine a.m. Court is adjourned."

As soon as she was able, Lily pushed her way out of the courtroom to find Matt and Stilinski waiting in the hall.

Matt was seated on the bench across the hallway, bent over with his elbows resting on his thighs. He held an empty styrofoam cup between his hands, the rim of which appeared to have been meticulously torn off. Stilinski was hunched as well, though he was pacing back and forth in front of the bench. He had crossed one arm over his chest and settled the other hand over his mouth, spindly fingers covering large lips. Both snapped to attention as she walked out, but Stilinski was the first to approach while Matt hung back.

"Hey! What happened in there? Are you okay?"

Lily looked straight between them and opened her mouth. Instead of speaking, she drew in a slow breath and lifted one shoulder in a shrug. Her part of this madness was over. The relief of being back with the two people who meant the most to her intermingled with her exhaustion and pushed her into a mindset of near nothingness. After the last few days, all she wanted to do was stop thinking, and she was finally with people she could trust to take care of her if she let that happen.

"Lil?" Matt frowned.

She turned her gaze to his face, which was wrinkled with worry. Then to Stilinski's and noted how similar the boys looked right now. Rather than mimic their concerned expressions, she shook her head.

"Let's get a drink."

39.

VERDICT

The second Lily stepped outside, dozens of reporters surged toward them. A cacophony of noise erupted as cameras clicked and flashed, and a multitude of journalists shouted all their questions for Lily at the same time. They crowded as close to her as they could; not for the first time, she was glad to have Matt and Stilinski flanking her to make sure nobody jostled or further injured her.

"Hey, back off!" Stilinski snapped and held his arms out to push through the crowd and create a path for Lily and Matt. "We're not commenting on the trial."

"Detective Faye!"

Amidst all the voices, that one made her pause. She knew that squawk anywhere. She stopped and glanced over to see Alyssa Spencer squeezing through the swarm toward her.

"You," she pointed out. "Call me next week. We'll talk. Until then, no comment," she announced before pushing her way through the crowd to get to Stilinski's squad car.

Stilinski held the door open so she could slip into the passenger seat before glancing to Matt.

"You okay with riding in the back? We can pick up your car later."

"Sure. I've never been in the back of one of these things," he said and frowned at Stilinski's skeptical snort. "What?"

"Nothing," the cop grinned and opened the back door for him.

"Convincing," the tech muttered as he ducked in. "You doing okay, Lil?"

Lily glared out the window at the reporters, trying to determine which she felt more: fury or revulsion.

"No," she admitted as they pulled away from the courthouse. "Give it time."

They gave her the night, which they finally agreed to spend at Matt's house. Lily refused to let Stilinski out of her sights; since she was staying with Matt, that was where Stilinski was staying, too.

That was what led Stilinski to creeping around an unfamiliar apartment the following morning. Somewhere after Lily's third cosmopolitan, he and Matt toted Lily back to the apartment and planted her in the living room. Matt offered the guest room to Stilinski, who now had the unfortunate task of trying to tiptoe around the cramped space without waking its other occupants.

As he stepped out of the bathroom and saw a flickering light down the hall, he realized his efforts were for nothing. He followed the light into the living room and found a hungover Lily staring at the television from the same chair she'd slumped into the night before. He noted the glass of water left for her was still full and she hadn't discarded the heavy blanket Stilinski draped over her before he went to bed. Based on her haggard appearance and the bags under her eyes, she hadn't slept.

"Hey..." Stilinski greeted, his volume only loud enough to announce himself.

He realized now why she had so strongly demanded to sleep in the chair; even drunk, she recognized the chair's back faced a wall and gave her a good vantage point of all the apartment's doors.

"Have you been up all night?" he asked.

Lily reached a hand out, but Stilinski wasn't sure what he was supposed to be handing her.

"Lily?"

"Here," Matt spoke up as he stepped out of the kitchen with two colorful, mismatched mugs in hand. "Careful. It's hot," he warned as he pressed the plain yellow mug into Lily's extended reach.

"Thanks," she murmured as she took on its weight and supported it with both hands.

She rested her lips on the edge of the mug and blew soft ripples into the beige liquid. Her eyes didn't move from the television or from the media ribbon scrolling across the bottom. As she took a sip of the steaming coffee, a reporter appeared and echoed the words displayed on the screen.

"Here, I'll get another one for me," Matt said and handed the second mug, which asked, "Have you hugged your forensic scientist today?" in cheery white letters, off to Stilinski.

"Thanks. Has she been up all—?"

"Shh!"

The two glanced over to Lily with arched brows, but she didn't notice. She reached for the remote and turned up the volume.

"We are moments away from a verdict regarding the State versus Russell Jordan in a triple homicide and attempted murder of a fellow officer. We've been told the trial reconvened this morning for closing arguments and the verdict. So far, the jury has been in deliberation for about twenty minutes, but it isn't expected to take long. This is, of course, coming off the heels of Detective Lily Faye's emotional and shocking testimony yesterday, which was met with considerable outrage on the detective's behalf. Many on the jury seemed sympathetic and awed by Faye's findings and personal run-in with Jordan."

"Oy. Get on with it already," Lily glared at the digitized woman.

"As for Detective Faye, media outlets have been largely unsuccessful in their attempts to make contact after she was spotted on her way out of the courthouse last night. Reports indicate the detective paused only to promise an exclusive interview to New York Post reporter, Alyssa Spencer. So far, there is no indication as to why Faye made this promise, but our reporters are working tirelessly to obtain a statement."

"Well, you're not getting one," Lily interjected again.

Unfazed and uninterested, the anchor continued with filler information for a few more minutes. Lily was finally spared the repetition of her own background and relationship with Jordan when the courthouse doors opened and the spokesman of the jury stepped over to a podium on the front steps. He unfolded a piece of paper and pressed it flat while reporters and cameramen swarmed around him. Lily tensed and leaned forward to hear, but she didn't need to strain. The apartment was otherwise silent.

"Good morning," the man spoke in the tremor of someone unaccustomed to the spotlight.

Sweat already prickled along his brow, and he licked his lips before he proceeded—a sign Lily automatically recognized as a mouth dried out from nerves.

"After a careful review of the evidence and testimonies provided, we the jury have reached a verdict. We hereby find Russell Jordan guilty on three counts of sexual assault, one count of second-degree murder, two counts of third degree murder, one count of attempted sexual assault, one count of attempted—."

The list of charges continued to roll, but Lily didn't care to hear the rest. She muted the television and dropped the remote as if it had sprouted fangs. She set her mug next to her forgotten water and slumped forward, one hand latching over her face as her entire body started to shake.

"Oh, shit," Matt murmured and crossed the room in three strides.

He knelt next to Lily's chair and set his hand on its arm, keeping his distance but staying close if she needed him.

"That's awesome, Lil. That's really good," he encouraged.

Lily nodded behind her hand and sucked in a quivering breath. She expelled it in a weak sob before inhaling again.

Stilinski gave her a minute before he knelt in front of her, making enough noise to alert her that he was there without startling her. He whispered her name and set a cautious hand on her knee, his touch light and unimposing.

"You were amazing, Detective," he encouraged alongside Matt's praises. "He's going away for life, probably without parole, because of you. Right?"

Another solid minute ticked by before she indicated she had heard either of them. She raised her head slightly and wiped her eyes. Her expression remained pinched and her chin wrinkled as she tried to collect herself, but she didn't hide from them again.

"I d-didn't think...it was going to end," she confessed in a strangled whimper.

"We know," Matt grimaced as he reached up to rub her arm.

"But it did," Stilinski smiled. "You're safe now, Lil. For good. He's never coming back."

40.

GETTING BACK

With only the sentencing to serve as the final reminder of the events Lily was trying to plant in the past, she took the next week to get back into a normal routine. She let Stilinski wrap up the case and write up its closing reports which connected the same dots the trial had. In the meantime, she finished a stint of well-deserved leave, forced herself into a sleep schedule that would coincide with her work schedule once she returned, and prepared for her psych evaluation. There was only one matter she needed to attend to in order to aid her own healing, and that meant following up on a promise.

"So, what's your play?" Alyssa asked as she slid into the seat across the table from Lily.

The detective looked up from a paper cup branded with a green sea creature and lifted an eyebrow. Despite her physical healing, she still sat in her chair with her spine too straight, as if worried that slouching even a little would cause the scar on her abdomen to tear open again. Even though her stature was tall, the detective's entire frame appeared to have collapsed in on herself like a star running out of nuclear fuel.

"I don't know what you mean," she uttered with a puzzled frown.

"Yes you do. What's your play? Asking me and only me to contact you, then agreeing to an exclusive interview? What do you gain from that?"

"I don't gain anything except a chance to tell my story to someone who will actually hear it and will publish it to people who will spread the word," Lily said. "The other journalists who were at the trial don't care about the person behind the headline. They just need to be the first one to write it out. I didn't want to talk to any of them."

"But you'll talk to me? I've been pestering you for weeks."

"You have been," Lily said with a slow nod. "And you're also the reason I thought to investigate Jordan in the first place. I owe you, like it or not. Let's just get through the interview and call it even."

"Fair enough," the woman nodded. "Do you mind if I record this?"

"Not at all," Lily said as she shifted against the back of her chair to take some of the weight off her tense abdomen and back muscles.

"Thanks. So, how are you feeling?" Alyssa inquired as she dug out an old fashioned tape recorder. "How's your arm?"

"Better, thanks. It's mostly a matter of building back muscle now."

"Good. I'm sure that's not an easy recovery process," she noted with what Lily could have sworn was a hint of sympathy. As soon as she clicked the record button, the tone evaporated: "So, Detective, what are your thoughts on the verdict?"

Lily took a sip of coffee before she answered, "I'm satisfied with it. It's hard to be happy in these cases even without the, ah, personal component..." She took another sip and cleared her throat before explaining, "Because you know how many people have already suffered. But I'm glad he got what was coming to him. The evidence against him was pretty overwhelming."

"So it seemed. Were there any points in the trial where you doubted he would serve three consecutive life sentences?"

"Honestly? I doubted they would even find him guilty," she said. "Look, the thing you have to understand about him is that he's a sympathetic kind of guy. He has an extremely unassuming personality. To his coworkers, he was a soft-spoken, well educated, hard working man. He looked to be a dutiful husband and father, too. Obviously, it came out during the investigation that the only truth in those assumptions is that he's well educated. But I was worried the jury wouldn't see it that way, even with the evidence."

"What makes you say that? Surely you have more faith in the jury than that."

"I do in most criminal cases. I count on the jury thinking of themselves as morally upstanding people and viewing the criminal in front of them as a monster who carried out actions no decent person could ever fathom. Criminals, especially in homicide cases like this, aren't seen as human. But he was. He made himself look like a victim, sitting there in handcuffs two rows ahead of his horrified wife and crying children while we described how he mutilated women for his own pleasure."

A young man in a visor and an apron glanced toward the women, then hastened to finish refilling the straws and the napkin dispenser. He scurried back behind the front counter, black apron flapping around his knees.

"You thought that tendency to view people as monsters would be suspended in this case?"

"I was almost sure of it."

"What made you think that way?"

Now there was a question to deal with before her psych eval. She took another drink to stall as she reasoned out her answer.

"Because I knew him," she said at last. "I've worked with him for almost seven years, and thought I knew all his quirks. I knew what he liked to do on the weekends. I knew he was so proud of having saved the money to go back to school. Hell, I was there when his acceptance letter came in. He read it out loud in the station. We had his favorite cake the next day to celebrate." She bit her lip and said, "And even after what he did to all those women, after what he tried to do to me, I still see him that way. I don't think he's a monster.

"It all feels like I had a terrible dream. The kind where you you're upset and off-put the entire day, but you try not to let it affect your relationship with the poor guy because he's so nice and he couldn't control what his dream self did. You see what I mean? So, I was worried, Alyssa, because if I still don't think poorly of him, how could I expect the jury to?"

Alyssa sat in silence. The tape recorder clicked. Both women swigged their coffees.

The reporter shifted before she asked, "So there was no point during the trial where you thought you'd won?"

"No, I don't think so. I was concerned about it up until I heard the verdict. Even after that, it was kind of hard to believe. You work so hard to bring justice to the victims and their families that it's always kind of shocking when you get the results you're looking for."

"Hopefully in a good way."

"Yeah, I suppose. It's more a sense of relief than anything. That's the downside with every homicide. Sure, you've pulled a murderer off the streets, but they've already killed. The best we can do is prevent it from happening a second time, or third, or fourth."

"The victims' families seem to be relieved as well. Your work made a big difference for them," Alyssa encouraged and even went so far as to offer a smile in truce.

"I haven't had a chance to speak to them since before the trial, but that's good to hear. I only wish I had been able to prevent most of the case earlier," Lily said.

She took a longer drink this time and let her gaze wander around the cafe.

"I'm sure there won't be another case of this caliber, but do you think you'll be able to use lessons learned from your mistakes in this case to improve your methods and the speed of solving the next homicide?"

"Hell yeah," she scoffed, though it was a humorless sound made at her own expense. "I might actually listen to you during the next investigation."

"I would appreciate it," Alyssa chuckled. "So, Detective. Where to next? What will you do now that life is returning to normal?"

It was Lily's turn to smile. Her definition of normal was anything but, which was exactly why she was excited to get back to it. It would help her focus on the present and not be consumed by the tragedies of the past. She needed to move away from the past.

"Well, right now, I'm going to the hospital for a follow-up so they can clear me to work full-time. After that, I'm going to do what I always do: protect the people of New York City the best I can."

"That's great to hear. All of us at the New York Post wish you well," Alyssa said and thanked her before she ended the recording. "And give me a call if you have any interesting stories you want me to cover."

Lily drained the rest of her coffee and promised she would. She bade the reporter a good day before walking out onto the cool New York streets. She turned toward the nearest subway station and grinned to herself as she walked down the dirty stairs into the overheated tunnel.

It was time to get back to work.

41.

FAYE AND STILINSKI

"Faye!"

Lily flinched at the shout and brought a hand to rest against her abdomen as the scar twinged at the sudden movement. Her eyes glided toward the wall hiding the Chief's door from view and narrowed.

"Why the yelling?" she grumbled. "Every time."

"Oh, come on, Detective," Stilinski laughed from the seat he had claimed at the vacant desk across from her. "You can handle it."

"I've only had two cups of coffee today," she huffed, as if her capabilities to deal with people were directly correlated to the amount of caffeine pumping through her system. "That is not enough to deal with this. He's gonna want to talk about how I'm *feeling*."

"So? You're feeling good enough to be back at work. Just tell him that," he pointed out. "C'mon," he added and walked halfway with her before branching off to his own desk. "You got this, Faye."

Her lips pursed and her eyes narrowed as she cast a sidelong glance at his retreating form. Still, she continued into the Chief's office and pushed the door shut behind her.

"You wanted to see me?"

Alcarez nodded and sat forward, hands folded in front of him on the desk.

"I wanted to see how you were doing today."

"Uh, fine, I guess. Wounds are all healed," she said, holding his gaze even as discomfort swelled into a lump in her throat.

"What about the rest of you?" he asked. His expression softened from irritation to concern as he clarified, "How about your mental health?"

Now, she averted her eyes to stare at the lip of his desk while she considered the questions and found she had no answer prepared. Compartmentalization was the key to her survival in this line of work even before the Jordan case, and the practice had become such an ingrained habit that it happened automatically in the face of her personal trauma. She hadn't allowed herself to come to terms with many aspects of the case yet, and so she hadn't spent much time thinking about whether or not she was mentally okay. As day-to-day life continued and she established a normal routine again, she assumed she was fine. In fact, the Chief was the first person to make her question her belief.

"I'm functioning," she said finally. "It's still not... easy to come back from something like that." She wet her lips as the words stuck under the lump, and then she forced them out. "Particularly when it comes from someone you've trusted to have your back."

"Faye, I'm not asking you to defend yourself," he pointed out with a gentleness in his voice that conveyed neither sympathy nor dissatisfaction. "I think you've been doing plenty of that. I just want to know that I'm going to do everything I can to help you process this."

"I appreciate that..." Her tongue flicked across her bottom lip again, and then her top row of teeth ground into it. "I guess... I just haven't really..." She struggled to put the words together in her head before they slipped out of her mouth. "...figured out what I need yet. There hasn't been a lot of time to think about it."

"There's never going to be time to think about it if you don't want to," he said. "But you know my door is open when you figure it out."

Lily noted the opportunity he was handing her, to close the conversation and walk out. Still, she didn't move. Her feet had turned to cement blocks, too heavy for her to drag out of his office. Her hands clasped together and twisted, as if there was something living under her skin she was trying to strangle. Then, indignation sparked through her and obliterated the tightness in her throat.

"Why don't I feel more bothered by this?" she asked and looked up at him. "Am I that incapable of emotion?"

His eyebrows rose at the question. He leaned against the back of his seat and the dull thud of his foot tapping against the floor beneath his desk sounded.

"No…" he answered after a moment. "Please know that I mean this to respect your point, Faye, but I've seen you on your worst days. You're not incapable of emotion. Hell, you probably have more of it than most of the people here. You just know how to direct it into something productive. I can't tell you you're not bothered by what happened, because I can see how you still are. That doesn't just go away, even if you don't let yourself recognize it for what it is."

"I suppose not," she answered, staring at the bulletin board hanging on the wall past his ear as she let his words register. "I…" She licked her lips and braced herself. "I think I've been trying to tamp it down until we wrapped the investigation. It might be good for me to take a couple vacation days," she said. "At the end of the week, once I finish wrapping up the paperwork. Just to get some space on my own terms for once."

He knew better than to argue when she admitted she wanted to take vacation days.

"You got it. Thursday and Friday?"

"Friday and Saturday, if that's okay. I already have Sunday off."

"Yep. I'll mark it down now. You just come back Monday ready to jump back in."

"Absolutely. Thanks, Chief." Her back straightened as if the conversation had been a barbell set on the back of her neck that someone relieved her of.

"You did a good job, Faye," Alcarez told her before she could walk out, then grinned. "And I'm glad to see your PR work got better when it counted."

"Spencer turned out to be more of an ally than I expected… although I still can't stand her," she snorted.

"You'll find plenty of reasons to butt heads with people no matter what the circumstances. But you know how to do it and get answers, so I'm not going to hold it against you."

"I don't butt heads with everyone," she defended on autopilot, and then winced. "Most people," she conceded. "At least Stilinski and I actually get along."

"I am impressed with that, I will say. Nobody else would have wrapped up these cases that quickly. Not bad work from either of you."

Lily had to agree. "You know, I'm going to need a new detective for the team," she pointed out. "Maybe a partner, even. Someone I can really trust."

Alcarez smiled and crossed his arms.

"We do have an opening now, don't we?" he asked. "I think it's high time you got a partner. You got anyone in mind?"

Lily smiled and glanced toward Stilinski's desk.

"Thought so. Good. We'll have a formal interview on Monday, then. You want to talk to him?"

"Yeah, I'll take care of it now. I'm heading out after that, though. Haven't had a decent night's sleep in weeks."

"All right." He waved her away. "Have a good evening, Faye. Good work."

Lily walked to the door and twisted the knob, shooting a small, grateful smile back toward her boss.

"Thanks, Chief."

She moved back to her area to collect her purse and jacket, then leaned over her computer. She navigated her mouse to hover over the envelope icon at the bottom of the screen, showing a notification for a new message. A bitter and quiet laugh sounded from somewhere in her stomach and she right clicked to exit the program without checking to see what the new message was. Then, she shut her computer down for the first time in a month and walked over to Stilinski's desk.

"Hey. You getting out of here anytime soon?" she asked.

"About to head out now," he confirmed as he logged off and swiveled toward her, his lanky legs catching him before he spun all the way around. "Got any crazy plans tonight?"

"Oh, yeah. I will be sleeping a full eight hours," she grinned. "Mental, yeah?"

"*Bloody* mental," he joked and reached out as if to nudge her, although he didn't quite connect. "Can I walk you out?"

"Sure. Are you coming over tonight or just heading home?"

He shrugged as he stood and collected his coat from its hook. "I don't have plans. I can hang out, if you and Matt don't mind."

"Not at all," she smiled. "I mean, I guess I'm speaking for him here, too, but that's his fault for letting me stay with him."

Stilinski laughed and walked out with her. "Exactly. He knew what he was getting into."

"Especially with me around. I'm a handful."

"Are you? Thanks for pointing that out, Sherlock. I *never* would have figured that one out on my own."

"Hey! No need to be a prat," she laughed, the sound bubbling out of her throat as she walked with him. "Speaking of Sherlock, though: I've been doing some thinking lately. How do you feel about detective work?"

ACKNOWLEDGEMENTS:

The first acknowledgement must always be to the one true Author and Creator, my savior Jesus Christ. Thank you for the talents and ideas you have allowed me to share.

To Mom, Pops, Em, Clint, and Jessie. Your support and encouragement mean the world to me.

To my friends. Your unbridled enthusiasm is shocking and humbling. I hope you're still enthusiastic now that you've read my first publication.

To everyone who contributed their talents to this novel: my editor, my cover artists, and my fellow indie authors.

To Audrey, Kelsey, and Ari. Thanks for putting up with my far-fetched plots for the past decade.

To Kelsey yet again, for inspiring most of the characters in this novel.

To all my Patrons. This truly would not have happened without your financial contributions.

And to you, my reader. Thank you.

ABOUT THE AUTHOR:

C.M. Lowe began writing when she was six years old and hasn't been able to kick the habit since. Her love for the mystery genre began at a young age, when her mother became a Private Investigator trained at the Police Academy.

By 27 years of age, C.M. Lowe received a Bachelor's of English and a Master's of Human Services Counseling, which lend themselves to creative writing and the human psyche, respectively. C.M. Lowe's favorite pastimes include solving the Hunt a Killer subscription boxes and police ride-alongs, both of which have provided inspiration for her upcoming works.

The Kitty Genovese Murders is her debut novel.

www.ingramcontent.com/pod-product-compliance
Lightning Source LLC
Chambersburg PA
CBHW070544120726
47909CB00007B/2229